The Big Gamble

Second Edition

The Big Gamble

Second Edition

Mike Faricy

Library of Congress Control Number: 2023918904
paperback ISBN: 978-1-962080-45-3
e-Book ISBN: 978-1-962080-46-0

MJF Publishing books may be purchased for education, Business, or promotional use. For information on bulk purchases, please contact the author directly at mikefaricyauthor@gmail.com

Published by

MJF Publishing
https://www.mikefaricybooks.com

Acknowledgments

I would like to thank the following people for their help and support:

Special thanks to my editors, Kitty, Donna and Rhonda for their hard work, cheerful patience and positive feedback.

I would like to thank Ann and Julie for their creative talent and not slitting their wrists or jumping off the high bridge when dealing with my Neanderthal computer capabilities.

Special thanks to Ann for her patience.

Last, I would like to thank family and friends for their encouragement and unqualified support. Special thanks to Maggie, Jed, Schatz, Pat, Av, Emily and Pat for not rolling their eyes, at least when I was there, and most of all, to my wife Teresa whose belief, support and inspiration has from day one, never waned.

Prologue
June 2018

The minister forced a smile and said, "Ladies and gentlemen, I would like to present, for the first time, Mr. and Mrs. Colton Ferral." There was a pause before a few hands slowly applauded. "You may kiss the bride."

Colton wrapped his arms around Maddie in a bear hug, plastered his mouth over her lips, and bent her backward. He held that position for an uncomfortably long time. There were a couple of gasps. Maddie finally beat her bouquet against his shoulder three or four times before he uprighted her. He ran the back of his hand over his mouth and grinned.

The minister leaned forward, said something to the couple, and they left the altar. As they headed out of the church, Colton gave the thumbs-up with both hands. Maddie had a look on her face suggesting, *'Someone do something, please.'*

I was seated in the back, watching more than a few heads shaking as the couple made their way down the aisle. The minister fled into a side room, and the congregation began to follow the wedding couple out of the sanctuary. Maddie's eyes flared for a half-second as she spotted me. Her new husband sneered, pulled her arm, and they disappeared out the door.

Her parents looked heartbroken. Both her sisters appeared to be in shock. Since I was seated in the back, I was one of the last people to exit.

Her parents were accepting congratulations, or maybe it was condolences, in the vestibule. Apparently, the groom's mother had already left. I waited as the line slowly moved forward. Finally, facing her folks, I said, "Hi, Mr. and Mrs. McGuire. I'm Dev Haskell. Congratulations on the wedding. Colton's a lucky guy. Maddie's a wonderful woman."

"Haskell? You went to high school with Madeline. I thought you were in the army?" her mother said.

"I was, but now I'm back in town."

Her father shook his head and said, "This guy makes even you look good."

"Terrence, now stop. That's enough. Nice to see you again. Thank you for coming, Mr. Hassle," her mother said and turned to the elderly couple behind me. I saw no point in correcting her on my name.

I'd been surprised to receive the wedding invitation, debated about attending, and in the end, skipped the reception and headed down to a new bar I recently discovered.

This year
One

It was cold outside. Morton and I hurried into The Spot. The temperature had dropped to around ten, and we were only halfway through the eight inches of snow forecast. I closed the door behind us and stomped my feet, knocking off the snow. Morton spotted my office mate, Louie Laufen, sitting on his usual stool at the end of the bar.

Louie gave Morton a nod and proceeded to open a bag of pork rinds. Morton took off, damn near pulling my arm out of the socket as he made his way toward Louie. His tail bounced off every other person standing at the bar.

"Well, Morton, thank you for helping Dev find his way across the street. How are you? Did you miss me over the last fifteen minutes?" Louie said, leaned over, and served up a handful of pork rinds. Morton had licked his hand clean in a second or two and was searching the floor for any errant crumbs.

"Usual, Dev?" Mike, the bartender, asked.

"Yeah, a Summit, and you better give Louie a refill, so I don't have to listen to him bitching."

"Still snowing outside?" Louie asked.

"Afraid so. Not looking forward to shoveling this stuff tomorrow morning. How'd your case go this afternoon?"

"About what I expected. License revoked, and my client will be spending weekends locked up. It was his second DUI, and they don't look kindly on that."

"Wasn't he going to agree to treatment?"

"Correct, he was. It seems he had a last-minute change of heart, even after I warned him. I get paid whether or not he follows my advice, but apparently, he knows the system better than I do. What were you working on?"

"Just verifying information on job applications for my insurance client. You know, where people worked and how long. I'm checking on arrest records, DUIs, the usual bit. It's boring work, but who cares? I wish I had a few thousand additional applications to verify."

"Things still slow?" Louie asked, just as Mike delivered the drinks.

I pulled out the last two bills in my wallet, a ten and a one, and gave them to Mike. "Keep the change, Mike."

"Gee, thanks," he said and gave me a look.

"You know, you and Morton are rattling around in that big old house. You ever think of doing an Airbnb or something?"

"Airbnb? No thanks. I don't want to be cooking meals for folks. Having to listen to someone complain that the sheets aren't starched, or the towels aren't soft."

"You might want to check it out, Dev. I don't think it's like that. From what I read, the vast majority of guests are pretty nice and not demanding. You could set out some fruit and cold cereal for breakfast, and that's all they expect. They aren't looking for some fancy. over the top place. That's why they aren't booking into a hotel. You could pick up maybe seventy-five bucks a day for pretty much doing nothing except changing sheets."

"You don't have to cook them dinner?"

"No, not at all, and with a restaurant right across the street and a half-dozen other places within walking distance, you'd be the perfect location. Think about it, historic neighborhood, close to downtown, fifteen minutes from the airport. You'd be a natural."

"Hmm-mmm, I might have to give it some thought."

Louie bought a round, gave Morton the rest of the pork rinds, and we were home an hour later. It was still snowing, and I was glad there wasn't much traffic. I grabbed some leftover pizza from the fridge, settled in front of the TV, and opened my mail. There were four envelopes. One was a schedule for the next six months of recycling pick up. The other three were bills, one of which I'd apparently missed last month. Now I had two monthly payments plus a past due charge. I could make the payment, but I'd be running on financial fumes for the next week or two.

Louie's Airbnb suggestion started bouncing around in my thick skull. After thirty minutes of failing to focus on the movie I'd chosen, I wandered upstairs and looked at my spare room. The double bed featured a pile of summer clothes I'd tossed there two months ago—same thing with the sandals and tennis shoes scattered on the floor. The chest of drawers was filled with clothes I hadn't worn in over three years. The top drawer held, among other things, four framed photos of women who had dumped me over the years.

The closet was no different. I couldn't even remember where or when I got the tux. There were four out-of-date sport coats and a half-dozen ties I figured were mine, although it had been so long since I'd worn them, I couldn't be sure. Two of the ties played a Christmas carol when squeezed. There was a small pile of lingerie on the closet shelf, all different sizes.

I began carrying everything downstairs and piling it by the front door. I'd donate it all to a facility tomorrow. I went online to the Airbnb site and registered.

The following morning, I was up early and ran the snowblower on the driveway and sidewalks. I loaded up the car with old clothes, left Morton in the kitchen. We'd gotten almost nine inches of snow overnight, and there was a snow emergency in effect. One of the benefits of living on a busy street is we're one of the first streets plowed.

I backed out of the garage, down the driveway, and headed to the donation site. All the clothes were clearly going to waste, collecting dust in my spare room. Hopefully, someone would get some value from them. I drove back home, grabbed Morton, and we headed down to the office.

Louie was at his picnic table desk tapping keys on his computer. "Sleeping in late?" he asked without looking up.

"Actually, no. Hard as it may be to believe, I took your advice from last night."

"You're running an ad on the Hot Hookups dating site?"

"No, I'm going to do Airbnb. I just took all the clothes out of my spare room and donated them this morning. There's a double bed in the room. I'll pick up a couple sets of sheets and some new pillows. I probably should get some bath towels too, come to think of it. Anyway, I'll be up and running in no time. Thanks for the idea."

"You're really going to do this?"

"Yeah, I checked it out online. Based on what I have to offer, you know, one room, I'm limited on what I can charge. But, with some coffee, fruit, and cereal in the morning, it's not like I'll have to be cooking breakfast, lunch, and dinner. This is going to be good. Thanks again for the tip."

"My pleasure. I didn't really think you'd want to do it. Good for you, Dev. It may be just the thing to get a somewhat even cash flow going in your life."

"We'll see. I'm looking forward to it. I've got a couple of things to line up, starting with I have to get a key for the lock to the room. The lock in the door is original, so it's a hundred and forty years old, but I got a pal in the lock biz. In fact, I should give him a call, now."

"Good luck."

I ended up leaving a message for Reggie, my locksmith pal. I fooled around in the office, made a couple of phone calls, and took Morton on a short walk. Reggie called me back just before 4:00.

"Yeah, Dev, returning your call. You locked out of the house again?"

"Surprisingly, no." I went on to explain what I needed.

"Shouldn't be a problem. This is the original door hardware, right?"

"Yeah, as far as I know. I'm thinking one of those skeleton keys."

"Yeah, probably. You home now?"

"No, but I can be there in about ten minutes."

"Take your time. I'll be there in a half-hour."

"Just pull into the driveway. I'll park in the garage," I said, and we disconnected.

TWO

Tue to his word, Reggie pulled into the driveway a half-hour later. He opened the rear of his white paneled van, grabbed two small boxes and a tool belt, and headed to the front porch. I was watching him and opened the door as he climbed up the steps.

"This snow could leave anytime, and it would be okay with me," Reggie said and stomped his feet on the porch before he stepped inside.

"With any luck, four more months, and most of it should be gone."

"Yeah, right," he laughed. "Want me to take my shoes off?"

"No, don't worry about it. Come on upstairs," I said, and we headed up to my spare room.

"So, you're going to be renting this out?"

"I'm gonna try Airbnb. Maybe have someone in here for one or two nights. Renting the room to someone for an extended period would be more of a pain for me."

"Well, you got a nice place, in a nice part of town, so you should do all right." He was down on his knees, shining a flashlight into the keyhole. He nodded as he examined the exposed lock mechanism. "Yeah, pretty standard cast iron horizontal rim lock. With any luck, I got just what you need," he said and opened one of the small boxes. It was full of brass skeleton keys. He inserted a key in the lock and turned it. A brass deadbolt suddenly appeared on the side of the door.

"Oh, man. That's great," I said.

"Yeah, chances are this hasn't been operated since the first world war. Let me just squirt some graphite in there to make sure it remains operational," he said, then produced a small tube and squirted some black powder into the lock.

"I'll leave this graphite with you. The key is fifteen bucks. I'd recommend you get three or four of them. They have a habit of disappearing."

"Better give me four," I said.

He smiled at that, pulled out three more keys from the box, and handed them to me. "Cash, check, or credit card, whatever is easiest for you."

"Credit card would probably be the best," I said, remembering my bank balance. "Can I talk you into a beer?"

He checked his watch, nodded, and said, "Yeah, I can do that."

We headed down to the kitchen. I handed him my credit card and grabbed two beers out of the refrigerator. He pushed some buttons on a white credit card machine not much bigger than my cellphone, and I inserted my card. A moment later, my paper receipt rolled out, sixty bucks for the keys and another sixty for the house call. A hundred and twenty bucks total. I couldn't rent the room without a key, so I chalked it up to the cost of doing business.

We stood in the kitchen sipping beers. Reggie told me he was making an Airbnb call at least once a week. Folks like myself just getting started or homes needing more keys or, in some cases, new locks.

He left after one beer. I put three keys in a kitchen cabinet and placed the fourth one in the lock on the spare room door. I climbed in my car and drove to a discount store where I picked up two pillows, two sets of sheets, and two prints on canvas, a sky with clouds and a stream in a forest. I was tempted to get the naked blonde woman sitting in a giant martini glass but, after some internal debate, decided that may not be the best idea.

Three

I was on my computer the next morning when the phone rang. The number came up as 'unknown.' "Dev Haskell," was how I answered, thinking if I said Haskell Investigations, it might scare a potential Airbnb customer away.

"Hey, Dev, it's Wink," the voice on the other end said.

Wink. Luther Winkler, an old high school pal. I'd been involved in his attempt to impersonate Bono a couple of years back. Pretty much a disastrous experience, but I still considered him a long-term pal. I hadn't talked to him in over a year.

"Hey Wink, how's it going? Before you answer, if this has anything to do with another Bono gig, count me out."

"Oh, man. Don't even bring it up. No, I just came across some bad news in the paper and wondered if you'd seen it."

"Bad News? What, is the IRS going to be investigating my taxes?"

"Stop it, something else I don't want to hear about. No, I was reading an article about a woman who was skating down on the river. She ended up falling through the ice."

"Eeew, she okay?"

"There's no sign of her. They figure the current probably moved her downstream somewhere. They're thinking it might not be until spring before they find the body."

"Oh, gee, that's too bad. What was she thinking? You know, even as kids, we knew it wasn't safe to skate on the river."

"Yeah, but that's not why I'm calling you."

"I'll check out the article and—"

"Dev, the woman who fell through the ice. It was your high school sweetheart, Madeline."

"You mean Maddie McGuire? The girl in our high school class. She married some thug with the last name of Ferral."

"Yeah, the girl that dumped you. She invited you to her wedding, didn't she?"

"Ahh, yeah, yeah, she did," I said, and suddenly, the image of her being dragged down the aisle and out of the church with a shocked look on her face flashed into my mind. "Tell me again. She was skating on the river?"

"Yeah, and apparently, she fell through the ice and got carried away. Probably couldn't get out from beneath the ice. I don't know how long she could stay there before she drowned."

"Not very long. What the hell was she thinking? She was a really good skater. I think she got a scholarship to the University of Wisconsin or somewhere for synchronized skating. I can't believe— You sure it was her, Wink?"

"That's what the article said. They referred to her as Madeline Ferral."

"Yeah, that was her husband's name."

"And that's the name of the woman in the article."

"Wink, thanks for the call. Let me check out that article, and I'll get back to you."

"Yeah, okay. Let me—"

I hung up on him and Googled Madeline Ferral. Halfway down the page, I found the link to the article and clicked on it. It was actually in yesterday's paper and wasn't much of an article, about a half-dozen sentences that basically told me what Wink had said. Her car had been spotted. There was a hole in the ice, and her purse and shoes were found on the shore. Based on the rough description, I had a general idea of where this happened.

I turned off my computer and kicked myself for not contacting Maddie over the last few years. How hard would it have been to see how she was doing and to wish her well? I called Wink back. We chatted for maybe ten minutes, exchanging a couple of stories, and then Wink had to ring off. I put Morton in the car, and we headed down to the office.

Louie wasn't in, but the coffee pot was on, and there was about a half-cup of coffee in the pot. I turned it off, dumped the coffee in the sink, and let the pot cool down before I refilled it.

I went online to check my Airbnb ad, but after twenty minutes of never finding it, I gave up.

I placed a call to my pal Aaron LaZelle. He headed up the homicide division in the St. Paul Police Department. I was ready to leave a message when he answered. "LaZelle."

"Hi Aaron, it's Dev."

"Hi Dev, I was going to give you a call. Did you read about Maddie McGuire?"

"Yeah, Wink called me, and I read the little article a couple of minutes ago. Are you guys investigating it?"

"There's nothing to investigate. She wasn't robbed. Her purse with her billfold and car keys and her car were still there. It looks like an unfortunate situation, but there's no indication of anything criminal."

"But even as kids, we knew not to skate on the river, and she was quite the skater. She got a college scholarship for skating."

"When was the last time you saw her?" Aaron asked, ignoring my last statement.

"I went to her wedding a few years ago. Never did talk to her. Maybe caught her eye on her way out of the church. The guy she married seemed like a jerk."

"Colton Ferral. He's been a person of interest in a few matters. As far as I know, that's it. I don't believe he's been charged in the past few years."

"What was he suspected of doing?"

"The usual, stolen good and drugs, he graduated up to more financial scams. His name came up a couple of times in the murder of some undesirables, but nothing ever stuck. And, I would have to add, he wasn't the sole suspect."

"He sounds like an up-and-coming Tubby Gustafson. Was Maddie still married to him?"

"I'm presuming they were still married, but I don't know that. Your assessment sounds correct. I'm sure Gustafson views him as potential competition."

"You think someone might have murdered her to send a message to her husband?"

"No, Dev. Absolutely not. There's nothing in any way, shape, or form to suggest anything other than a most unfortunate accident occurred."

"Did anyone on your team investigate the scene? It would seem to me—"

"Hello, is anyone listening? Let me state it again. Nothing indicated anything but an unfortunate accident. She was skating on the river, Dev. We've known since we were kids that it's not safe to do that. Unfortunately, Madeline seemed to forget that."

"Yeah, I guess you're right. Well, thanks for taking my call."

"I wish I had better news for you, Dev. Maybe look at it this way. If she had to die, isn't it better it was an unfortunate accident that happened while she was doing something she loved doing? As dark as it is, that seems a lot better option than having her throat slit or being shot or raped."

"Yeah, I guess you're right. I'm just kicking myself for never getting in touch with her after her wedding. Still have a soft spot for her in my heart, I guess."

"Probably a good idea you didn't get in touch. You know, the old boyfriend thing. No offense, but it works both ways. If she was interested, she could have gotten in touch with you."

"Yeah, you're right. Hey, Aaron, we need to get together for dinner sometime. If memory serves, it's your turn to buy, so I'm thinking of some really expensive place."

"Yeah, or we could just meet at McDonalds, since it's really your turn."

"That works, too."

"I'll give you a call when things loosen up. Thanks for calling, Dev," Aaron said and disconnected.

I thought about what he said. He was more or less right, except for one thing. Maddie had contacted me. She sent me a wedding invitation. But, other than watching her being dragged down the aisle on the way out the door, I never did anything.

Four

I slept off and on that night and was up just after 5:00 the following morning. I didn't learn anything new scanning the internet for two and a half hours. Morton eventually wandered into the kitchen. I gave him his morning head scratch and then let him out the backdoor. He stood on the back porch looking at all the snow then slowly made his way down the steps and maybe three feet into the yard where he did his business. I couldn't really blame him. Three minutes later, he was scratching at the backdoor.

I let him inside, and he promptly shook off all the snow onto the kitchen floor. When he was finished with his breakfast, we climbed in the car and took a roundabout way to the office.

I drove through downtown and across the Mississippi on the Wabasha bridge. I took a right at the second stoplight and followed the road upriver. In a couple of short blocks, I was past the St. Paul Yacht Club and in Cherokee Regional Park. The only tracks in the snow were from deer, fox, and the occasional coyote. After maybe a mile, I passed an area with tire tracks. The tracks led to the river no more than twenty yards from the road. I pulled over, climbed out, and walked toward the river.

The tracks were in the snow we'd gotten three nights ago. From what I could determine, maybe a half-dozen vehicles had been here. It was clear by the tracks that four different cars pulled off and stopped close to the river's edge. I took them for probably police cars. The heavier set of tracks, with duel rear wheels, had clearly backed into the area.

The tracks stopped at a point, and there was snow piled behind the end of the dual rear wheels. It was probably a tow truck that had loaded a vehicle, most likely Maddie's car, and hauled it out of the area. I made a mental note to check the impound lot.

I walked to the river's edge. The river was frozen, but the wind had blown most of the snow off the ice. I could see the area with thin ice where Maddie had fallen through. If she'd gone all the way under, the river current could have swept her downstream. Even if she'd only drifted a few feet, given the shock from the cold, the weight of soaked winter clothing, and the river current, it would be damn near impossible to find your way back to the hole in the ice. She could have hit her head on the edge of the ice and been unconscious. She certainly would have been in severe shock from the cold. It was a hell of a way to go, damn it.

There was nothing else to see. All the footprints pretty much trampled the snow. I couldn't see anything that looked like it might have come from a woman's dainty foot. I don't know what I had expected to find. A note in a bottle? A heart drawn in the snow with my name in the middle? To be honest, I hadn't thought about Maddie since her wedding, and I was pretty sure, other than inviting me to watch her get married, she'd never thought of me.

Life works in strange ways.

I walked back to my car, followed the park road through the park heading upriver and past the Pool and Yacht Club. I took the 35E bridge across the Mississippi and turned on the Randolph Street exit down to the office. Louie wasn't in, and amazingly, the empty coffee pot had been turned off. I made a fresh pot, worked at not thinking about Maddie McGuire, and got back to vetting employee applications for my insurance client.

Louie wandered in that afternoon. He gave me his usual wave as he set his briefcase on the picnic table then removed his coat. As he sat down, I got up, poured him a coffee, and set it in front of him. After a couple of sips, he'd recovered from the stair climb up to the office and said, "How's your day going?"

"Okay, I guess. Not much shaking. Just working these job applications."

He nodded, took a few more sips, and said, "You okay? You're sounding a little down."

"It's nothing," I said and went on to tell him about Maddie.

"Oh, she sounds like she was pretty nice."

"She was. Too bad I never really picked up on it. At least she had the good sense to ditch me."

"But she sent you an invitation to her wedding, and you went?"

"Yeah. Not sure why I went. Maybe just to see who was lucky enough to marry her. Turns out the guy's a real jerk. Aaron LaZelle described him as a competitor of Tubby Gustafson's. I guess I'll always wonder if maybe she didn't want my help to get out of that predicament, you know, marrying Colton Ferral, and I completely missed it."

"Dev, you didn't even have your P.I. license then, did you? Quit beating yourself up. You ever think maybe she just wanted you to know that she was marrying someone. The guy may be an awful person, but at the end of the day, she made the decision of her own free will."

"Yeah, I know. It just seems like such a waste of a really classy person. God, she didn't deserve the way she died, and she sure as hell didn't deserve to be married to that prick Colton Ferral."

"Yeah, okay. But she made the choice to marry the guy. She could have said no. And as far as not deserving to die that way, yeah, you're right. I don't want to push this, but did you ever think maybe she knew what she was doing?"

"What do you mean?"

"She's a big skater, right. But you said it yourself a few minutes ago. Growing up, we all knew you don't skate on the river. It was beaten into us. You don't walk on river ice. Yet, there she is, an adult. A smart, educated individual, and she's skating all by herself on the river. I mean this nicely, and I'm not condemning her. But do you think that maybe she was hoping that's what would happen? Maybe she was in a dark place, and that seemed to be the logical way out."

"You mean she committed suicide?"

Louie nodded and said, "Yeah, maybe. Every park in town has an ice rink or two. Yet she goes down on the river?"

I gave a long exhale and thought about that.

Louie waited a minute or two, then turned on his computer and started tapping keys.

Eventually, I said, "You know, I never thought about it that way, but maybe you're right. Maybe, for whatever reason, she found herself in a dark place, and, unfortunately, that seemed like the logical way out."

"We'll never know for sure. Maybe she left a note somewhere. Who knows? It's just another yank of the chain for every one of us to realize that we don't have anything to bitch about. No matter how bad we think things are, there's always someone who has it worse. All we have to do is look out the window, and we'll see them," Louie said.

I nodded and said, "Yeah, you're right. We both know good folks who are no longer with us. It's just that I keep thinking if only I'd checked in with her. Asked how she was doing, you know?"

"Yeah, and I'd say that's pretty normal. But the second half of that is if only she'd touched base with you. You would have offered support, comfort, whatever she needed. You would have, Dev. It's the type of person you are. But she didn't get in touch, and there's only so much you can do. Beating yourself up, now, when something happened through no fault of your own, doesn't help. Maybe look at all the clothes you donated the other day and know that there are folks out there who will consider themselves very lucky to have gotten them. You'll never know who they are. They'll never be able to thank you in person. But by donating, you helped them out in a big way. You did more for them than most people on any given day, and you're a good guy for doing it. Focus on that, rather than this unfortunate situation."

"Yeah, thanks, Louie. You're right, as always," I said and went back to going through the job applications.

Five

On Sunday, a brief obituary for Maddie appeared in the paper. It listed her date of birth and that she was survived by her husband, Colton Ferral, as well as her two sisters and her parents, just three short lines. A memorial service was scheduled for 10:00 the following morning at the same church she was married in.

I kicked myself for donating my half-dozen ties and out-of-date sport coats. I took out a pair of slacks, my cleanest shirt, a sweater, and an overcoat with a black velvet collar from the closet and laid them out on the bed in the guest room. I still hadn't had one call for an Airbnb rental.

I was up early Monday morning. I sent Louie an email telling him I probably wouldn't be in until sometime in the afternoon. I let Morton out and filled his food and water dishes. I'd shoveled an area in the backyard to serve as a latrine for him. It made the cleanup easier for me, and at least when he came back in, he wasn't shaking snow all over the kitchen floor.

I had a light breakfast, double-checked my emails for anything regarding Airbnb, and hit the shower. I pulled on the clothes I'd laid out, tossed a biscuit to Morton, and headed out the door. I was sitting in the church ten minutes before Maddie's memorial service began. I guessed the attendance at no more than half of what it had been for her wedding in the same church three years ago. But then again, this was a winter Monday morning, a workday, instead of a sunny June Saturday. That, plus all the years that had passed since our high school days, it actually was an okay turnout.

Maddie's two sisters, a blonde and a redhead, escorted their parents down the aisle. They settled into the first pew on the right side of the church. Maybe five minutes later, her husband, Colton Ferral, waddled past and sat in the first pew on the left side of the church. He looked to be a good hundred pounds heavier than what I remembered. No one sat with him in the pew.

The minister, different from the man who had officiated at the wedding, stepped onto the altar one minute after Ferral oozed into his seat.

The service was short and not very sweet. It lasted all of twenty-five minutes. Obviously, there was no casket, and so once the minister left the altar, Ferral stood and left without so much as a nod to Maddie's family.

A few people followed him out, presumably friends or family. I heard two guys mention a celebration at Ferral's as they gave one another a high five. Most of the congregation formed a line and began to offer condolences to Maddie's family, still seated in the front row. I made my way to the back of the line and inched forward. There was a lot of handshaking, hugs, and the occasional kiss exchanged.

It took almost longer than the service to make my way up to the front pew. Maddie's parents forced a smile, but their eyes were slightly swollen and red-rimmed from crying. I gave my condolences to them, and they nodded, not really registering what I'd said.

I introduced myself to her sisters, and they both flashed a smile.

One of them said, "Maddie mentioned you from time to time. You were a soldier, and now you're a detective, aren't you?"

It was my turn to nod and get misty-eyed as I said, "I'm a private investigator. Your sister was a wonderful woman. The world looks a little less bright with her passing."

"Would you happen to have a business card? My name's Amy, by the way," the redheaded sister said.

"And I'm Hannah," the blonde added.

Surprisingly, I did have a business card. I pulled out my wallet and handed it to Amy. "Thanks," she said.

"If there's anything I can do for you or your folks, please give me a call. Maddie was one of the reasons I made it through high school, only because I wanted to keep up with her. Fortunately for her, she had her sights set a lot higher than the likes of me."

"Yeah, well, too bad she ended up where she did," Amy said.

"Amy, we promised we weren't going to say anything. Let's just let it go," Hannah said and smiled. "It was nice to finally meet you, Dev. I can see why Maddie liked you."

Amy hit her on the shoulder.

"Nice to meet you two. I meant what I said. If I can be of any help, please let me know. Are you going back to the house?"

"The house? On Summit Ave? Ferral's dungeon? Maddie hated the place. Oh God, no."

"I heard there was something going on there. I thought it might be a luncheon or something."

"None of our family and no one we know would be caught dead there," Amy said.

"He didn't welcome us when Maddie was alive. We certainly wouldn't be welcome now," Hannah said.

"Okay, like I said, call me if I can be of any help."

They both smiled and nodded, then turned their attention to their parents, who were staring straight ahead, stone-faced except for the tears running down their cheeks. I took a side aisle out of the church. Other than Maddie's family, I was the last person to leave.

I climbed into my car and thought for a moment. Obviously, no love lost between Maddie's family and Colton Ferral. I thought about the two guys mentioning the 'celebration' at Ferral's house. Summit Avenue was a street full of mansions from a different time. The oldest mansion on the street was built by a guy named David Stuart back in 1858. He died shortly after moving in. For the next hundred years, mansions of every description were built along the four and a half-mile street.

I pulled onto the western end of Summit and drove for a little more than a mile before I came upon a line of expensive cars. Mercedes, Cadillacs, and a handful of Lexus were parked along the street. Two couples were laughing and joking as they made their way up the front sidewalk of a red-brick house. As they approached, the front door was suddenly opened by a smiling guy in a black tux. I guessed that was Ferral's place.

Six

I had to park at the far end of the block and walk back to the house. Ferral's place was a three-story red-brick structure with white trim and a curved front porch with large white pillars. I could see the guy in the tux through one of the leaded glass panels on either side of the oak front door. Just like the couple I'd seen, as I began to climb the three steps to the porch, the front door opened, and the smiling guy in the tux said, "Welcome, sir, please come in. Thank you for joining us. You can check your coat in the room just across the hall. Enjoy yourself."

I stepped over to a room with a sliding door maybe eight feet high. The door was partially pushed back into the wall, and a mahogany table blocked the entrance. The room had a fireplace, and the walls were lined with bookcases. Who knew Ferral could read?

A young woman, maybe nineteen or twenty, smiled. I took my coat off and handed it to her. She placed a wooden hanger in the coat and carried it over to a metal rack, one of a half-dozen in the room. She smiled again and handed me a round tag with the number 116 written on it.

"Enjoy," she said.

The entryway floor was oak with what looked like a walnut parquet pattern along the sides. A large room was on either side of the long entryway. Two large crystal chandeliers hung from the ceiling, and an elegant stairway at the end led up to the second floor. Four sexy-looking women were sitting on the steps sipping drinks and laughing.

The two rooms were full of people. Everyone was laughing and drinking from what looked like glasses of champagne. Fires were burning in the fireplaces of both rooms. I stepped into the room on the left. A couple of people glanced over at me, but no one looked familiar.

"Care for a drink, sir?" another tuxedoed man asked. He held a round silver tray with eight or nine frosted champagne glasses.

"Yeah, thanks. Don't mind if I do," I said and took a glass. I figured it would be bad form to grab two glasses.

A painting of naked women sunning themselves on lawn chairs hung above a sixteen-foot table pushed up against the far wall. Two stacks of china plates were at one end of the table, and all sorts of food trays were arranged along the table. At the far end of the table were two large baskets of what looked like bagels. A smiling guy all dressed in white and wearing a chef's hat stood just beyond the bagels, carving slices of meat from a roast and placing it on people's plates.

I continued sipping, all the while glancing around and looking for Ferral. I didn't see him. I did recognize three guys. One named Ricky and another I knew only as Snake. The third guy went by D.A. I'd found out later the letters stood for Death Angel. I decided the other room might be more pleasant and stepped across the entryway.

Once again, I was met by a smiling guy in a tuxedo with a silver tray of champagne glasses. I set my empty on the tray and grabbed a full glass. It was more of the same, lots of laughing and talking. There was another buffet table similar to the one in the first room, except the guy at the end in the chef's hat was carving slices of ham. A painting of a naked woman on a brass pole hung over the fireplace. The room was just as crowded as the other, with one exception.

There, standing in front of the fireplace, stood Colton Ferral. I guessed his weight as somewhere north of three hundred pounds. He had his arm wrapped around the waist of a blonde woman who looked exactly like the woman in the brass pole painting. If I had to hazard a guess, I'd say she'd been partying since last night.

She held two champagne glasses and alternated her sips from both glasses. With his free hand, Ferral was in the process of doing a fist bump with two guys dressed in black who looked like the kind you wouldn't want to cross.

A door suddenly opened, exposing a kitchen area as an older woman stepped into the crowd. She was dressed in a black dress with white lace around her neck and shoulders. She was large, and her hair was dyed black. The type of black dye job that even I could spot from thirty feet away. Her hair was parted in the middle with at least an inch of gray roots showing, giving her a serious skunky look. She made a beeline toward the guy in the chef outfit carving the ham.

The crowd made an immediate wide path as she stormed through. I couldn't hear the exact words, but I picked up on the aggressive tone. Both Ferral and the blonde suddenly stood a little straighter. The blonde attempted to hide both champagne glasses behind her back.

The chef nodded vigorously as she poked a fat finger into his chest. People drifted further away as she ranted on for another minute or two then stormed back into the kitchen. She shot a look at Ferral along her way.

"No, his mother, Mona, wicked witch of the west," I heard a woman behind me say.

"Congratulations, dude," a guy said to Ferral. I wasn't sure if he was referring to Maddie's death or some illegal business deal.

Ferral settled any confusion on my part when he responded with, "Thanks, man. It's about time. She was a real downer. I won't miss her."

"You better not," the brass pole blonde said, and everyone laughed.

I took that as my traveling music. It would be best if I left rather than offer an objection. I drained my glass and set it on an end table as I stepped out of the room. I was suddenly feeling hot and knew I'd better get out of there before I threw caution to the wind and gave Ferral an honest appraisal.

I handed the woman hanging up coats my tag with the number written on it. I waited until she returned with my coat before I tossed a dollar in her tip jar. She didn't seem impressed.

"Enjoy the rest of your day, sir."

"Yeah, thanks," I said and headed for the front door.

The guy in the tux flashed a quick smile and opened the door for me.

I stepped out into the fresh five-degree air and felt relieved. Thank God Maddie's family hadn't been here. As I drove home, I couldn't shake Ferral's comment about Maddie being a real downer and not missing her. Fortunately, I didn't turn around and head back.

I let Morton out into the backyard, changed clothes, ate a quick lunch, and drove down to the office. Morton settled onto his pillow and was asleep before I'd finished making coffee. Louie wandered in a half-hour later. He was carrying his briefcase and a white Styrofoam food container. He settled in behind his desk, red-faced and breathing heavily.

I headed over to the coffee pot, filled his mug, and set it on the picnic table. Louie didn't say anything until he'd taken a couple of sips and had a mouthful of a BBQ sandwich. "How was the service for Maddie?" he asked, spitting bits of BBQ onto his computer keyboard.

"About what I expected. It was in the same church where she was married. Her husband, Colton Ferral, didn't give so much as a nod to her folks. He walked in just before the service started and left as soon as it was over. I stopped at his house after the service, a mansion over on Summit. A house full of sleaze-balls, and Ferral was telling everyone he sure wasn't going to miss Maddie. I figured that was my traveling music."

"You're kidding?"

"I wish I was, Louie. Maddie's sisters told me the family wouldn't be welcome, not that they'd go anyway. I get the sense that things were not good for Maddie. I wish I'd known. I could have helped her."

"Yeah, that's what she needed," Louie said and took another bite of his BBQ sandwich. This time, instead of spitting bits onto his keyboard, a large piece of meat rolled over the back of his hand and down his white shirt, leaving a trail. "Damn it," he said, grabbing the piece of meat and cramming it into his mouth.

"You never know how people are going to end up. If she thought you could help, she probably would have contacted you. You just don't know what was going on. Maybe she liked the guy or the money."

"Her sisters seemed to indicate she wasn't happy. They said Ferral didn't want them in his house. Said they weren't welcome, not that they would have gone anyway."

"Doesn't sound good. No wonder she was skating alone at night on the river."

"Yeah, that part still doesn't make any sense to me."

I wasted time for the next couple of hours, then took Morton for a walk and met Louie at The Spot. There were maybe a half-dozen people at the bar. Louie was on his usual stool at the far end. As we stepped inside, Louie stood on the bar rail, stretched, and pulled a bag of pork rinds from the rack. That was all the incentive Morton needed as he attempted to pull my arm from the socket. He strained at his leash as we headed toward Louie.

"Looks like you're having trouble keeping up, Dev," one of the guys at the bar said, and three people laughed.

Louie bent over with a handful of pork rinds, which Morton devoured in about two seconds. Louie seemed oblivious to the BBQ stain that ran down the left side of his shirt. Once Morton finished, he sat and gave Louie a mournful look, begging for more.

"I'll catch you on the way out, Morton," Louie said.

"What'll it be, Dev?" Mike, the bartender, asked.

"I think just a Summit for me. Louie, you ready for another?"

"Yeah, I think I better," Louie said, glancing at his nearly full glass.

We chatted on about nothing. Louie told me about his latest Driving Under the Influence client. Some woman drinking vodka out of a kids plastic Tippy Cup with a pink top. Unfortunately, the empty vodka bottle she'd set underneath the seat slid out after she rear-ended a mail truck. Since it was her second offense, the court hearing hadn't gone well.

"She'll have plenty of time to consider her options. She's looking at least at six months if not a possible two years," Louie said.

Mike stopped back and asked if we wanted another.

"I better not, been a long day. We're going to head home in a minute," I said.

He looked at Louie.

"Yeah, why not," Louie said.

"Coming right up."

"You sure you don't want another?" Louie asked as Mike headed down the bar.

"No, thanks, I've still got Maddie and her funeral on my mind. Probably a good idea if I don't have another."

"Wish there was something I could do for you," Louie said.

"Yeah, so do I. Interesting, I haven't seen or even thought about her for a few years, and now I can't get her off my mind. I just wish she would have let me know things weren't going well."

Sounds like she might have been depressed, and her world just kept getting smaller. You recognize anyone else at the funeral?"

I shook my head. "Other than her family, no. I didn't see anyone from high school. I think it was mostly friends of her parents and her sisters. It's strange because she was Miss Popular in high school. I don't know. It's just sad and makes me think I don't have anything to bitch about."

"Not that it ever stops you," Louie said as Mike set a fresh drink down in front of him.

"Say, Dev, I forgot to mention. A woman stopped in this afternoon and asked about you," Mike said.

"Asked about me?"

"Yeah, wondered if you came in here."

"What'd she want?"

"Just wanted to know if you ever came in. I told her you did, told her where your office is. She didn't leave a name. You in any kind of trouble?"

"Just the usual," I said, shaking my head.

"She was a brunette, very nice looking. I was putting beer into the cooler, and when I stood up, she was gone. Someone you're dating?"

"No, I got dumped maybe a month ago. Haven't been with anyone since."

"I'll put out a warning that you're looking," he said just as someone at the other end of the bar called his name and held up an empty glass.

"I wonder who that was. What was the name of that nurse you were dating? She was a brunette, right?" Louie asked.

"You're thinking of Meghan. Yeah, she was nice. Took a job down in Texas or New Mexico. I can't remember which. Another one who told me to never, ever call her again."

Louie poured the rest of the pork rinds into his hand and leaned down. Morton devoured them even faster than the first batch.

"I'll see you in the morning," I said.

"I've got a sentencing hearing at 9:00. So I'll be in whenever that's over."

"Good luck," I said, and we headed out the door.

It had begun to snow, so I let Morton in the backseat and then brushed the snow off the windows and the hood of the car. I took the city streets home instead of the freeway just because it was beginning to get slippery. There was hardly any traffic on the street. Apparently, everyone was staying home tonight. I took a roundabout way, avoiding the usually busy streets. I thought a car had been following me for the last ten minutes, but as I made a right-hand turn onto my street, it kept going straight and disappeared.

I pulled into the garage, and we headed inside through the kitchen door. The snow had picked up, and if it kept up at this rate, I'd have to shovel again in the morning.

Seven

I woke a few minutes before my alarm went off. I climbed out of bed and looked out the window. A snow removal crew was plowing the restaurant parking lot across the street. Based on what I could see, it looked like eight or nine inches came in last night. I got dressed, put the coffee on, pulled on a pair of work boots, and grabbed the shovel next to my front door. I stepped out onto the front porch and stopped.

A set of footprints came from the street, up the entrance to my driveway, along the public sidewalk, and up the sidewalk to my front porch. Whoever it was had smaller feet, most likely a woman or maybe a high school kid. The footsteps headed to the front window. Apparently, someone peered into the house. Given the amount of snow we received, this had to have been maybe two or three hours ago. Who would look in my front picture window at three or four in the morning?

I shoveled the snow off the porch and steps. I walked back to the garage and got out the snowblower. In forty minutes, I had my place cleared off as well as the public sidewalk for my neighbors on either side. The snow next to the sidewalk was piled about three and a half feet high.

Once I finished, I grabbed a shower and was on my second coffee when Morton came into the kitchen. I gave him his head scratch and sent him outside. He stood on the back porch and looked over his shoulder at me, suggesting I was a lunatic for sending him out in the snow. He remained on the porch until the last minute when he bounded down the stairs, left his deposit in the area I'd shoveled off for him, and then hurried onto the back porch and scratched at the door.

Once we'd finished our breakfast, we headed down to the office. The main streets were already plowed, so it was a relatively easy drive. I was in before Louie and made the coffee. I heard the stairs creaking, suggesting someone was coming up to the second floor. A female voice said, "Here it is," and I figured it was someone heading to the hairdressers just opposite the office when there was a knock on the door. No one ever knocks on our office door.

Morton looked up but didn't bark.

"Come on in," I called and headed toward the door as it opened. Maddie's sisters, Amy and Hannah, stepped in. Morton hopped off his cushion and hurried over, no doubt looking for a head scratch, which he got.

"Hi ladies," I said and hoped I didn't have a surprised look on my face. "Hey, I just put some coffee on. You want some?"

Amy nodded, and Hannah said, "That sounds great. You want us to take our boots off?"

"Are you kiddin'? You're liable to catch something from the rug." I grabbed my mug from my desk, Louie's mug from the picnic table, and pulled a spare mug from the file cabinet. The mug from the file cabinet read, 'You'd look better naked.' I poured coffee into it, handed it to Amy, and said, "Don't read this."

She immediately read it out loud and then showed it to Hannah. Fortunately, they both laughed. Louie's mug appeared reasonably clean. I filled it and gave it to Hannah, then filled my mug and said, "Grab a seat, you two. To what do I owe the pleasure? And, before you say anything, I want to say it was nice to see you and your folks yesterday. I'm really sorry it was under those circumstances. I haven't stopped thinking about Maddie ever since I learned about her accident."

The girls looked at one another. Hannah nodded at Amy.

Amy set her mug down on my desk and said, "That's why we wanted to talk to you. Umm, we, Hannah and I, don't think it was an accident."

I took a deep breath as I leaned back in my chair and exhaled. After a long moment, I said, "Do you have any proof of that?"

"Maddie told us she was going to divorce that dreadful husband, Colton Ferral. She'd been talking about it almost since the day of their wedding, but this time, she sounded really serious. They'd been arguing for quite a while," Hannah said.

"Yeah, she's been unhappy since the day she married him," Amy said.

"She told our dad as they were waiting to walk down the aisle at the wedding that she didn't want to go through with it," Hannah said and took a long sip from Louie's mug.

"Dad told her she had to."

"So, if she wanted to get out of the marriage, why didn't she just leave? She was one of the strongest, most independent women I've ever met. At least the person I know wouldn't have put up with shit from Ferral."

"He threatened her," they said in unison.

"Wouldn't that just make her all the more determined to leave?"

They both shook their heads. "He threatened to go after our folks. Not directly. He just told Maddie bad things would happen to them if she left. She knew he wasn't kidding. He's the world's biggest creep," Amy said.

"He and his mother," Hannah added.

I saw no point in mentioning I'd been at Ferral's following Maddie's funeral. I hadn't seen or really even heard of Maddie for at least three years. "So bring me up to date. What did Maddie do? Where did she work? For that matter, what does Ferral do?"

They glanced at one another for a second, and Hannah said, "She was stuck in a horrible situation. From the day they were married, she had to do whatever Ferral told her to do. He told her she couldn't get a job, so she didn't."

"But didn't she go to college and get a degree in teaching or education?"

"Yeah. She even taught in the St. Paul system for three years. But once she married that jerk Ferral, he put a stop to that," Hannah said. "She volunteered at the school, and he stopped that. She volunteered at Meals on Wheels, a senior facility, helped kids with reading, all sorts of things. But as soon as fat ass Ferral found out about it, he put a stop to it."

I shook my head. "And you think Ferral murdered her?"

They both nodded.

"Other than being very unhappy and married to a complete creep. Do you have any evidence? And, I'm not criticizing, I'm just asking."

"She was looking for an apartment. She looked online, using my computer," Amy said.

"Mine too," Hannah said. "Fat ass Ferral checked her computer all the time, and she didn't want to take a chance. If he found out, there's no telling what he would do. She was really scared."

"That's why her drowning is so strange. She wouldn't go skating on the river. She knew that wasn't safe. And then to go down there at night, all alone? No way she would do that," Amy said.

"Besides, she had a skating rink right in her back-yard. She skated there every day. Her going down to the river makes no sense at all," Hannah said.

"We can pay you if that's what you're worried about," Amy said and then bit her lower lip.

"Yeah, we can't pay you very much, but if you wanted to—"

"First of all, you're not going to pay me. I'll do this for free. Second, I don't want you telling anyone. Did Maddie have bank accounts?"

Both girls nodded.

"Do you know if they were joint accounts with her husband?"

"Really weird, they were joint accounts with Ferral and his mother," Amy said.

Hannah nodded. "Yeah, almost from day one, it was suddenly like a three-way relationship. His witchy mother was involved in everything. For the last year or so, they had separate bedrooms, Maddie and Ferral."

"We used to tease her that Ferral was sleeping with his mother," Amy said. "But then it quickly became apparent Maddie was in an awful situation, and try as she might, she couldn't find a way out."

I shook my head and said, "God, if I'd known, I don't know. I'd like to think I could have helped. I, I'm just having a hard time getting my head around this whole mess."

They both nodded.

"Maddie lost virtually all of her friends. Ferral either forbid her to see them, or more often, they all hated him so much they just stayed away, and that played right into his hands. He's a real bastard," Hannah said.

"Okay, let me do some checking, and I'll be in touch." I slid a notepad and a pen across the desk. "Write down your phone numbers and email addresses in the event I need to talk with you." I pulled two business cards out of the desk drawer and passed them over.

"Oh, I already have one," Amy said.

"Good, now you've got two."

They gave me thank yous, hugs, and kisses on the cheek before they left. I watched out the window as they stepped out of the building. They chatted for a minute on the sidewalk, hugged, and then Amy walked up the street, and Hannah walked around the corner. I thought for a moment then picked up my phone.

Eight

I was just about to hang up before I got dumped into voicemail. My pal Aaron LaZelle suddenly picked up and said, "Yeah, Dev, what's up, and no, it's still your turn to buy dinner."

"Hi Aaron, I'm actually calling about a case, but if you had time to talk about it over dinner, that would be fine with me."

"Dinner? Are you thinking tonight?"

"I can fit that in, if you can make it."

"I can, but it's going to be a little late, maybe 7:30."

"Works for me. Tell you what, dress warm, and let's meet on the patio at the Handsome Hog at 7:30."

"Earth to Dev, it's winter in Minnesota. Last time I checked, it was minus two, and it's forecast to drop down to minus twenty tonight."

"We'll be out there for one drink. They've got space heaters, fire pits, and this really cool bar made out of ice that's about twenty feet long. I drove past it this morning. There were already people waiting to get in, buy a drink, and have their picture taken."

"Hmm-mmm, a bar made out of ice. Yeah, okay, I'll meet you for one out there, but then we're inside for dinner, and remember, you're buying."

"Relax, I heard you the first time. See you tonight," I said and disconnected. I glanced out the window and saw Louie's faded orange Ford Fiesta parked behind my car. A moment later, I heard the stairs begin to creak. I quickly grabbed Louie's coffee mug. It was only half-empty from Hannah drinking from it, so I topped it off and refilled my mug. I set the mug on Louie's picnic table desk and sat down in my chair. As always, he opened the door red-faced and breathing heavily after climbing the stairs. He gave me a slight wave, set his briefcase on his picnic table, and settled into his chair. Morton opened one eye and then snuggled deeper into his pillow and drifted back asleep.

Louie took a sip of coffee and made a face. He seemed to sniff his mug a couple of times and took another sip.

"Everything all right with the coffee?" I asked.

"Yeah, it just smells, I don't know, nice."

"Oh, probably because I washed your mug," I lied.

"No, it smells a lot nicer than dish soap."

"How'd your sentencing hearing go?"

"Mmm," he said, taking another sip and smiling. "Better than we had a right to expect. Six months in the workhouse. Mandatory attendance at AA meetings. Her license is suspended for a year and then subject to review. She could have been locked up for two years. In fact, I more or less told her that was going to be what she should expect, so given the result, she was more or less okay. Told me she should have tossed the bottle instead of putting it under the seat, so there's still a lot of work to do. We'll see how her mandatory meetings go. Anything happening on your end?"

I went on to tell him about Maddie's sisters coming in and that I was going to investigate her death.

"No body yet?"

"Probably won't show up until spring at the earliest, if they even find it. But I couldn't tell her sisters no. Based on the story they told me, I wish Maddie would have tried to get in touch."

"I wonder if she had an inkling along those lines, and that's why she sent you the wedding invitation."

"I guess I'll never know. I'm meeting Aaron LaZelle for dinner. Maybe he'll have some thoughts."

"You know much about this Ferral person?"

"I'll know a lot more by 7:30 tonight." I turned on my computer and Googled the BCA, Minnesota's Bureau of Criminal Apprehension. It turned out Colton Ferral was charged with a Gross Misdemeanor. After pleading no contest to an assault, he spent a year in jail, paid a three thousand dollar fine, followed by two years of probation. That was back in 2012, theoretically before Maddie knew him. There wasn't anything that suggested domestic assault. I went through another half-dozen sites and came up empty-handed.

Based on the three bad actors I recognized at Ferral's after Maddie's memorial service, he was either smarter than your average criminal or awfully lucky.

Louie headed over to The Spot a little before five. I walked Morton around a couple of blocks, and we headed home. I pulled on a heavy sweater and wool socks, slipped into my walking boots and heavy jacket, and walked down to the Handsome Hog patio a block from my house.

The patio was fairly comfortable, given the temperature. Four fire pits were throwing heat from burning logs, and the space heaters seemed to be doing their job. The place was crowded, with about a dozen people lined up at the bar.

The bar was easily twenty feet long and constructed with massive blocks of ice. Behind it was an ice shelf twenty feet long and six feet high. Bottles of alcohol and wine were lined up on the shelves. In the middle was a carved logo for Maker's Mark bourbon. No sooner had I stepped onto the patio than I heard my name called. I turned, and there was Aaron. He said something to the three guys he was talking to and headed over to me.

"You been here long?" I asked and glanced at the drink in his gloved hand.

"Maybe ten minutes. Hey, surprisingly, you were right. This is really cool."

"Yeah, I'm guessing it's in conjunction with the winter carnival. Doesn't that start this weekend?"

"It's been going on for a couple of days already, Dev. You going to get something from the bar?"

"Yeah, I suppose I should."

"I started a tab in your name."

"Gee, thanks."

Since Maker's Mark was no doubt contributing to the cost of the bar, I thought it only fitting I have a bourbon.

"What can I get you?" the bartender asked. She was dark-haired, with flashing brown eyes and sparkling white teeth. She wore black earmuffs, a black ski jacket, and what looked like black insulated overalls.

I ordered a bourbon, neat. At no surprise, the glass was chilled. "That'll be six dollars," she said.

"Apparently, I have a tab going. Dev Haskell is my name."

She smiled and said, "Oh, yeah. The Lieutenant. I'll put it on your tab. Nice to meet you, Mr. Haskell."

"Please, call me Dev. And your name?"

"Isabella," she said and smiled.

"Nice to meet you."

Aaron and I stood and chatted for fifteen minutes. About once a minute, Aaron was nodding or saying hello to someone. We finished our drinks. I paid the tab, left a nice tip with Isabella, and we headed inside to the restaurant. As nice as the patio had been, I have to say it was nice to enter a warm room.

We grabbed a table and ordered another drink, beer for me, a glass of wine for Aaron. We studied our menus.

Our server returned with our drinks, and we placed our orders. Once he left, Aaron raised his glass in a toast and said, "Here's to you buying dinner. So, I'm guessing there's something or someone you want information on. Otherwise, you would have put up a fuss about paying tonight. What's up?"

"What makes you think I'm looking for information?"

"Well, for starters, you mentioned on the phone you had a question about a case," he said and took a sip.

"Well, umm, no. I might have a minor interest in one or two items and thought as long as we were getting together, you may have some morsel of information."

"Yeah, crumbs for the crumb. What do you want to know?"

"Do you know anything about a guy named Colton Ferral?"

"Colton Ferral, let's see. Well, first off, it wouldn't hurt him to go on a diet and drop a couple hundred pounds."

"Agreed. Career wise?"

"Career? He's an up and comer. At one point, maybe ten or fifteen years ago, he was just another thug. He's still a thug, but he's upped his game. He controls some betting operations. He provides loans initially tied into the betting operations, but he's expanded that over the last few years. He charges an exorbitant amount of interest. He's smart enough to have a couple of levels between himself and the actual operation. He deals in drugs to an extent, but it's been really hard, in fact impossible, to pin anything on him. He has a legal team, the Gauner brothers. They're a so-called independent firm, although I believe Ferral and his operation are their sole client."

"I don't think I've ever heard of them."

Aaron shook his head. "They're a couple of pretty odd ducks. You wouldn't hear of them unless you were involved in some lawsuit with Ferral. He actually has been a student of his mother. She was, or rather still is, a force to be reckoned with. Desdemona Ferral, she goes by Mona, not a nice person. Hard to believe now if you saw her, but apparently, her career began on stage, in a strip club. I don't think they ever knew who the guy's father was. She eventually worked her way up in the biz and ran a 'dating service' on the side."

"Charming, I checked him out online. All I came up with was an assault that got him locked up for a year. That was almost ten years ago."

"Sounds about right. I don't know that I would ever refer to him as smart, but he knows the biz. So, why the interest in him?"

"You remember my high school romance with Maddie McGuire?"

Aaron smiled and said, "We all thought she was really patient, and no matter how hard she tried, she wasn't going to be able to fix you. We also thought you were one lucky guy. If you're wondering about the body, we probably won't find it until spring."

"Yeah, well, her sisters paid me a visit this morning." I went on to tell Aaron about Maddie's funeral and my stopping at Ferral's after the service. How I saw his mother there and him with a blonde, who seemed to match the woman in a painting over the fireplace.

Aaron shook his head and said, "Just another person you look at and think, 'What the hell are you doing?' Makes all of us examine ourselves and come to the conclusion we're not doing that bad."

"What do you know about her going through the ice?"

"I'm presuming you're asking if there was any foul play. At this stage, there's no indication of foul play. I can tell you this. The first call came from a park service employee who saw her car parked at about nine in the morning. He stopped just to check, didn't see anyone. I believe there were a purse and some boots on the shore, and he spotted the hole where she went through, although it was beginning to ice over. Oh, and they found a powder-blue mitten on the ice.

"We never received a report from anyone saying she was missing. But then, if she'd been skating the night before, say twelve hours earlier, even if someone phoned in a missing person report, it wouldn't have been filed until after twenty-four hours, at a minimum."

"You said a blue mitten was found?"

"Yeah, that, and well, the vehicle registration and her purse with her identification. No sign of anything other than falling through the ice. God, I can't believe I didn't initially pick up on who she was. I saw the report for all of a minute or two. It's been listed as an accident, not a homicide, so in short order, we weren't involved."

"Is the blue mitten still held as evidence?"

Aaron nodded and said, "As far as I know, yes. That, along with her purse, and I think there's a pair of shoes or boots still in custody. No one has claimed them. Her car would have been towed to the impound lot. I don't know if it's still there."

I made a mental note to call one of her sisters in the morning.

"Did you have much contact with her?" Aaron asked.

I shook my head. "No. None, in fact. She sent me an invitation to her wedding. To be honest, I don't know if it was a plea for help or if she was sticking it to me. Her sisters told me she had doubts about the marriage but went through with it anyway. The little I know suggests she'd been pretty unhappy right from the start."

"That could be just about anyone, Dev. Look at the list of women who've dumped you."

"Everyone makes a mistake," I said.

Nine

The following morning, Morton and I were down in the office before 9:00. I put the coffee on and called Amy and then Hannah McGuire. I ended up leaving voice messages for both of them.

"Hi, this is Dev Haskell. Everything's fine on this end. Give me a call when you have a moment. No rush, I just have a question. Thanks."

Amy called me back around 10:30. "Hi, Dev, sorry, I was in a meeting when you called. What did you find out?"

"Nothing, really. I just have a question. When Maddie's items were found, her purse and shoes—"

"They were boots, actually."

"Yeah, thanks. When that was found, did you or someone in the family get the call, or did that go to Colton Ferral?"

"He must have gotten that call. No one in the family was contacted. As a matter of fact, he had some sleazeball lawyer call my folks. My folks called Hannah and me."

"Did you call Ferral?"

"What would be the point? He wouldn't have answered our call. We received a text message, again from the lawyer's office, and they—"

"That's the Gauner law firm?"

"Yeah, how'd you know that?"

"I spoke with someone. Ferral, well, and whatever his business interests are, make up their total list of clients."

"Figures. Their text message, this was on Saturday, had a copy of the obituary that was going to appear in the paper the next day, Sunday. Not so much as a condolence or a suggestion to contact them, nothing. Oh, and they mentioned the memorial service would be on Monday at our folks' church. That was in the obituary too. We attempted to contact the attorneys, my folks, Hannah, and me, but we just got put on hold. Never heard a word from fat ass Ferral or his evil mother. Wouldn't you think they'd at least talk to my folks?"

"Yeah, that's pretty damn low. I spoke with a friend in the police department. He mentioned Maddie's purse and boots along with her car—"

"Yeah, she drove a black Range Rover, not that it was really hers. Creepy Ferral held onto the key, so if she ever wanted to go anywhere, she had to check with him and get the car key."

"You're kidding me?"

"No, I'm serious. Of course, Maddie drove to the dealership and got a couple of spare keys. She gave one to Hannah, just in case Ferral found the one she had. That's how controlling that fat creep is, or was."

"So, no one in your family received her purse or the car or anything?"

"No, and our mom called as recently as yesterday to see if she could get Maddie's clothes or some personal items, and she was just put on hold."

"She called Ferral?"

"Yes, and the lawyers. Same result at both places."

"My friend with the police said they also found a blue mitten on the ice. Does that ring any bell with you?"

"A blue mitten? Yeah, absolutely. If it's the one I'm thinking of, and I'm sure it is, our mom knitted mittens for us on Valentine's Day last year. Mine are pink, Hannah's matched her hair, and Maddie's were light blue. We teased her and called her Virgin Maddie. We didn't say that in front of Mom."

"So it seems to fit, then."

"They found it at the river?"

"Yeah, but just one."

"Well, I know she really liked them. We all did. So, it wouldn't be unusual for her to wear them. The unusual thing is that she would be down there in the first place. That's so not like her."

"Okay, Amy. Thanks for calling. I'm going to keep checking. I think I might pay a call to the law firm. Maybe I can get some personal items for your folks."

"Oh, that would be nice, Dev. Thank you. You can tell them to get screwed from me."

"I'll hold off on that, at least initially."

She laughed, said good-bye, and disconnected.

Hannah phoned maybe an hour later. I told her everything I told Amy. She pretty much responded the same way, except her language was a little more colorful.

I finished our conversation by saying, "I'll pay a visit to this law office and see if we can't get some of Maddie's items for your folks."

"Oh, that would be so great, Dev. Would it help if I went with you?"

"Thanks for the offer, Hannah. I think at this stage, based on past behavior from these people, our best shot might be me just acting as an unattached third party."

"Yeah, you're probably right. Good thing these creeps don't own a bar, or a restaurant, or a place where they have to deal with the public."

"Yeah, it sounds like they might have some issues."

"A lot of issues. Let me know if I can do anything. Thanks, Dev," she said and hung up.

Louie wandered in after the noon hour. I went online and got the address for the Gauner Law Firm. Not a simple task since they apparently didn't advertise. I ended up going through the Minnesota Bar Association records and found their address downtown on Fourth Street in the Northwestern Building.

"You going to be here for a while?" I asked Louie.

"I'm here until the beverage hour at The Spot," he said and looked up from his keyboard. "You want me to keep an eye on his Highness?"

"If you wouldn't mind. I'll take him for a quick walk and then head out."

"Happy to help," Louie said and returned to his keyboard.

As I grabbed the leash, Morton stood from his pillow, stretched, and strolled over to me. I clipped the leash onto his collar, pulled on my jacket and gloves, and we headed out the door.

It was a balmy minus two degrees with a forecast of possible snow coming in tonight. We walked for two blocks. It was cold enough that Morton wasn't all that interested in investigating trees, front gates, and fire hydrants. We were back in the office in fifteen minutes.

I unclipped the leash, tossed Morton a biscuit, and headed out the door. Morton finished the biscuit in two bites and settled back onto his pillow.

Ten

The eight-story brick Northwestern Building is located on the corner of 4th Street East and Wall Street. It's right across from the St. Paul Farmers Market. Built in 1916, it was originally a railroad office building. Now the eight stories are largely filled with entrepreneurs, artists, and small businesses. Not exactly where I expected to find the Gauner brothers' law firm, but apparently they were located on the eighth floor.

I walked into the white marble lobby and took the elevator up to the top floor. I'd expected some form of security in the lobby, but there wasn't any. The Gauner brothers' office was number 802. I stepped off the elevator and took a left down the hall. Number 802 was located at the far end.

All the offices had a frosted glass panel with the office number and the name of the firm, company, or individual. The Gauner Law Firm had a solid wooden door with the number 802 attached to the wall. The firm's name wasn't indicated anywhere.

I attempted to open the office door, but it was locked. I pressed a button on the intercom.

A green light flashed on, and a female voice said, "May I help you?"

"Good afternoon. My name is Detective Devlin Haskell. I'd like to speak with Mr. Gauner," I said, hoping I might get one of them. "This is concerning Colton and Desdemona Ferral."

"One moment, please."

It was a very long moment, nearly five minutes, before the voice said, "Mr. Hassle?"

"Yes, I'm still here."

The door buzzed, and I heard a lock snap. I turned the doorknob and opened the door. About five feet inside the office stood a rather large, muscular guy. He had a head of close-cropped hair, barely long enough to pinch, and no neck. Just massive shoulders and arms that appeared to be stuffed into his black sport coat. He wore an open-collar white shirt. His black sport coat exposed a leather strap that, more than likely, was a shoulder holster.

"Hi, I'm Dev Haskell. I'd like to talk to one of the Gauner brothers," I said.

"What's this about?"

"I'd like to take that up with them. It concerns Colton and Desdemona Ferral. A private matter."

That seemed to get him thinking for a moment. Eventually, he asked, "Are you carrying?"

"No, I'm not. Feel free to search me," I said and began to slip off my jacket.

"That won't be necessary," he said and produced a wand about twelve inches long with a handle. "If you would just hold your arms out."

I extended my arms, and he waved the wand over me twice. "If you would take a seat, the receptionist will contact Mr. Gauner." He gave the receptionist a nod and then stepped over alongside her desk. I settled into a black leather chair and watched as the receptionist typed something on her computer. She pushed a button on the keyboard and smiled.

"It should just be a minute," she said and flashed another fake smile.

It was more like ten minutes. The muscle-bound guy stood behind the receptionist, and I don't think he ever took his eyes off me. Something finally dinged on her computer screen, and she turned toward the muscular guy and nodded.

"Please follow me, sir," he said and started down a hall.

I was out of my chair and hurrying to catch up. I smiled at the receptionist and said, "Thank you," as I hurried past. We headed down a hallway and turned a corner. He opened a steel door and stepped into a large corner office. I followed him into the office. As I entered, he stepped back into the hallway and closed the door behind him.

All four walls in the office were bare. Two large, identical desks were arranged at a forty-five-degree angle in the center of the room. The desks were positioned on a raised area so that the Gauners could look down on whoever was seated in front of them.

The seating was the weird thing. God forbid they would have normal chairs. Instead, three plastic dinosaurs, blue, green, and pink, were positioned next to one another. They were turned around actually, facing the door, which I guess made sense since their raised neck and head served as the back of the seat.

A bald man with close-cropped gray hair along the side sat behind each desk. Both men were red-faced. One of them had a gray mustache, but other than that, they appeared to be identical. Each desk had a nameplate with 'GAUNER' in white letters on a black background held in a brass holder.

"Take a seat, Mr. Hassle," the guy without the mustache said and indicated the three plastic dinosaurs centered between the two raised desks. To say the entire office was strange didn't begin to describe the situation. "You had some information regarding our clients?"

"Possibly. I'm aware of the apparent passing of Colton Ferral's wife in a recent skating accident on the Mississippi River. Apparently, her family has attempted to contact the Ferrals, as well as your office, but has received no reply."

"We've not been contacted by the McGuire family."

"I believe that's because all calls they've made to your firm or the Ferrals have either been placed on hold or disconnected."

"And what, exactly, was the purpose of these calls? Were they attempting to accuse Mr. Ferral in regard to this unfortunate incident? Our understanding is they've not been welcoming in any way, shape, or form to either Colton or Desdemona Ferral."

"My understanding is that any contact Mr. Ferral's wife attempted to have with her family was at best discouraged, if not aggressively blocked, by Colton Ferral. I'm not suggesting he was in any way involved in this unfortunate incident. That said, it would appear the last thing Mr. Ferral or his mother would want is for this sort of information to be made public."

"Just what are you implying?"

"I'm not implying anything. I'm telling you the family has attempted to contact Ferral, and you, to get some personal items belonging to their daughter, Madeline. Their calls have gone unanswered. Their next option may be to contact the authorities or—"

"The police aren't going to get involved in this."

"You're right, but the news media will. The moment they learn that Colton Ferral's in-laws have been shut off following the tragic death of their daughter, you're talking about a front-page headline and the leading story on the 6:00 news."

"Believe me, the Ferrals won't be interested in dealing with reporters."

"Which will make the reporters dig that much deeper. I'm just trying to warn you. They get shut off much longer, they'll go to the news media. Do you really want the media taking an interest in your only client and, by extension, your practice?"

"Is that a threat?"

"A threat? God, no. I'm just trying to save you and the Ferrals a major headache. If you want to ignore me, go ahead," I said, standing up. "But don't say I didn't warn you." I pulled out my wallet and tossed a business card on each desk. "That's my office address." I gave them my home address as well and finished up with, "Thank you for your time. I hope you can convince the Ferrals to accept a phone call or drop off some items at my office or home. I'll go to their residence on Summit Avenue and pick up the items if that would be more convenient."

With that, I walked to the steel door and opened it. The muscular guy was standing there, blocking my exit. He looked over my shoulder toward the two wackos seated at their desks. The guy who had done all the talking nodded, and the muscular guy said, "Follow me."

He led me down the hall, past the receptionist desk, and opened the door to the hallway. I felt like I was escaping from an alternative universe. As soon as I stepped into the hall, the door closed behind me, and I heard the lock snap.

I took the elevator down to the main floor and walked out of the building. I walked in the opposite direction of my car just in case they had someone following me. I went around the block and then hurried into my car and drove back to the office.

I parked behind Louie's Ford Fiesta, crossed the street, and climbed the stairs to the office. Both Morton and Louie were sound asleep. I got onto my computer and did a search on the Gauner brothers. Nothing came up other than the name in German meant rogue or crook, which only seemed fitting. I debated calling Maddie's sisters and immediately decided against it.

I checked my Airbnb account, still no activity. Louie's computer gave off a beeping tone maybe twenty minutes later. He blinked his eyes open, stretched, and groaned. "Oh, I must have closed my eyes for a moment. When did you get back?"

"Just a minute ago," I lied.

"Everything go okay?"

"In a manner of speaking." I gave him the short version of my weirdo story.

"Hmm, interesting. You mind if I ask around, see if anyone has any information on those two?"

"Not a problem on my end. Obviously, they're keeping the ultimate low profile. I'd be interested in anything you found out."

"I'm in the courthouse tomorrow. I'll mention them to a couple of people."

Morton woke maybe ten minutes later. He stretched and then climbed off his pillow and stood at the door. I pulled my jacket on, and we headed out for a walk. We met Louie in The Spot but only stayed for one before we headed home. It was snowing again, and I brushed off the car. I pulled into the garage, and we headed into the house through the kitchen door.

I ate leftover pizza for dinner, watched a two-hour movie I didn't really enjoy, and we were in bed by 11:00.

Eleven

Morton woke me with a bark and a growl. I glanced at the clock on the nightstand. It was almost 4:30 in the morning. Past experience had taught me that if Morton was barking in the middle of the night, something was up.

I took my Glock out of the nightstand and pulled on my jeans. Morton remained on the bed staring at the bedroom door and growling. The hair was up on the back of his neck.

I slowly opened the door and peered into the hallway. I didn't see anything unusual. I stepped out and peeked around the corner. The staircase was empty. I looked over the banister and down to the first floor, but I didn't see anything. I remained still for a couple of minutes and never heard a sound. I hurried back into the bedroom, pulled on a sweater and socks, and slipped some shoes on. I chambered a round in the Glock and headed downstairs.

The front door was locked. I checked the front room, the den, and the dining room on the way to the kitchen.

Fortunately, they were all empty. I cautiously approached the kitchen. It turned out to be empty and the door was locked. I glanced out the window. It was still snowing. I'd be shoveling in the morning, and I was glad I'd parked in the garage when I came home.

God only knew what Morton had been barking at. I went back through the house, rechecking the rooms, this time turning on the lights. Thankfully, I didn't find anything or anyone. I headed up the stairs, then stopped halfway up, turned around, and walked to the front door. Just like before, it was locked. I pulled the white lace curtain aside and glanced out at a beaten trail made up of dozens of footprints in the snow leading up and onto my front porch.

I looked left and right. No one seemed to be on the porch. I saw what looked like recent tire tracks, maybe a quarter of the way up the driveway, but whatever vehicle had been there was gone. I opened the door and stepped onto the porch. The footprints led to the window, and I slowly turned my head, following them for a couple of feet. I suddenly stopped and stared at the pile of boxes and clothes.

I stopped counting the boxes at twenty and looked at the stacks of blouses, slacks, and skirts. What the hell? Did someone dump all this stuff and run off? And then it dawned on me. Maddie McGuire. The Gauners must have gotten in touch with Colton Ferral, and this was all Maddie's stuff. I shoved the Glock in my belt, scooped up an armload of clothes on hangers, and carried them inside. I made five trips carrying clothes inside and laying them on the couch. Then I began hauling boxes. All sorts of things were packed in the boxes: more clothes, shoes, boots, china, books. It was like a moving day. The bad news was everything had been deposited onto my front porch. It took over a half-hour to haul all the boxes inside.

Once I finally finished, I locked the front door, put the coffee on, and rearranged the boxes so I could get through the entryway. I fried up a couple of pork chops and a red pepper for breakfast. After I had finished eating, I sent a text message to Louie telling him Morton and I would be late coming in. I checked my Airbnb site, nothing. I went onto YouTube and caught some news stories, then went upstairs and grabbed a shower. I was back downstairs finishing the last of my coffee when I heard Morton coming down the stairs. He stopped in the entryway, and I hurried out to see what he was up to.

Morton was investigating. He was in the process of sniffing all the boxes, moving from one stack to another, then back again. He wandered over to all the clothes I'd spread out on the couch. He spent a couple of minutes sniffing them and then moved back to the boxes. After his third time through the routine, I coaxed him into the kitchen with a biscuit and let him out the kitchen door. Once again, he gave me a disdainful look over his shoulder and then waited until the last minute before he headed off the back porch. He was back scratching on the door sixty seconds later.

It was after eight in the morning, and I called Hannah McGuire. She picked up on the second ring and said, "Dev, is everything all right?"

"Yeah, in a manner of speaking." I went on to tell her about my visit to the Gauner office yesterday and the early morning surprise left on my front porch.

"Are you sure it's Maddie's stuff?"

"Yeah, I'm sure. Well, I mean, pretty sure. I don't know anyone who would leave all this stuff on my porch. I've had things left here before. But it was always my stuff, and then whoever left it would leave a phone message that said to never, ever call them again."

There was a long pause, and then Hannah said, "That really happened?"

"Just a couple, maybe three or four times. But more to the point. I'm pretty sure this is Maddie's stuff, and it's not just clothes. There's china and crystal glasses. I don't know what else. I just wanted to get everything inside."

"Oh. My. God. I guess this is good news, sort of. Umm, I'll call Amy and tell her. We're both going to have to go to work. Would it be okay if we stopped by tonight?"

"Tonight, yeah, I guess so. I mean, I don't have anything planned. Listen, if it works, why don't you two plan on coming over for dinner. Does 6:00 sound okay?"

"It will as long as you let us bring dinner."

"You don't have to do that. I can—"

"We're bringing dinner, Dev. We'll see you at 6:00."

"Okay, see you then, and you're going to call Amy, right?"

"Yeah, as soon as we hang up. Oh, I know this is a pain, but thank you for doing this and talking to those lawyers. I think I'm going to hold off calling my folks until we're able to sort through all that stuff tonight."

"Yeah, sure. Look, I'll see you tonight," I said and hung up. I pulled on my jacket and grabbed the shovel. I cleared the steps and the porch, then got the snowblower out and did my driveway and the sidewalks.

Morton and I were down in the office before 11:00. Louie drifted in after lunch.

I poured him a coffee and waited until he'd recovered from climbing the stairs. "Got your text message," he said. "Didn't know if you'd make it in. Everything okay?"

"It just gets stranger and stranger, Louie." I went on to tell him about the early morning delivery.

"Yeah, you're right. That's pretty strange. As a side note, I did talk to someone who was in law school with the Gauners. He said they're identical twins. One is named Reginald. He has a serious speech impediment and rarely speaks. Archie is the guy that usually does all the talking. Reginald is the brains. At least, that was the way it worked in law school. They'd be at least in their mid-sixties now. It sounded like they were a strange pair forty years ago, and nothing's really changed. As far as my guy knew, they were sharing an apartment back then. He lost track of them after law school."

"That general description fits the two guys I saw. They had this muscle-bound enforcer character. He took me into their office, and when I opened the door to leave, he was right there, blocking the doorway until the one who did all the talking—"

"Archie," Louie said.

"Yeah, okay. Until Archie gave him the nod, and he escorted me out of the office."

"You think it was Ferral who dropped all that stuff on your porch?"

"I'm thinking he had someone do it. Given the physical shape the guy's in, he would have died of a heart attack before he finished unloading half the boxes. But from what Maddie's sisters told me about his tight control, I'm sure none of that stuff left his mansion without his okay. He probably sat in a chair next to the front door and pointed at stuff, directing what could go and what stayed. It'll be interesting to see what the sisters say. Hopefully, there's some personal stuff their mom would like."

"Maybe they should send Ferral a thank you note," Louie said and laughed.

"To paraphrase a woman at Ferral's house after the memorial service, I think the further we can stay away from that nutcase and his wicked witch mother, the better it'll be for everyone."

Twelve

my and Hannah arrived promptly at 6:30, a half-hour late, not that I really cared. I opened the front door to let them in. They took one look at all the boxes and clothes, handed me two pizza boxes and a bag with two bottles of wine, and went to work. I carried the pizza boxes and the wine into the kitchen. By the time I returned, they were holding outfits up in front of one another and reciting which function Maddie had worn them to.

"Oh, this was little Laurie's christening," Amy said.

"Remember this? She told us Ferral spilled a glass of red wine down the back. Look, you can still see the stain," Hannah said.

"Say, I wonder if we could maybe let the fashion comments go for the time being and start working our way through these boxes?" I said.

They both made a face. Amy stuck her tongue out. But they put the outfits down and looked at the stack of boxes.

"How about this, Dev? You'll carry the boxes into the dining room. We'll empty the contents onto the dining room table. If there's anything that we think our folks might like, we can set it aside. Some boxes are going to take extra time, and others we can glance at and set aside. Does that sound like a plan?"

I nodded, and we each picked up a box and carried it into the dining room.

"Oh, will you look at this, remember?" Amy said, opening her box and pulling out a doll.

"Her American Girl doll, oh, how cute. We all got one for Christmas," Hannah said.

I smiled, nodded, and said, "I'll go dish up the pizza."

When I returned with three pizza plates, the doll was seated in the center of the dining room table. Amy had taken a pair of red stiletto heels from a box and was trying them on. Hannah was rifling through a stack of notebooks with a disgusted look on her face.

"Can I talk you into a glass of wine?"

"Yes," Amy said and proceeded to walk into the front room wearing the stiletto heels.

"Wine would help," Hannah said without looking up.

I walked out to the entryway, grabbed two more boxes, and carried them into the dining room. Hannah had just finished placing the notebooks back in the box. I carried that box out to the entryway and began a pile of boxes already examined. I walked into the kitchen, filled two glasses with wine, and took them into the dining room. Amy was walking into the front room again, this time wearing a pair of black pumps.

I set the wine glasses on the table and said, "We've got an awful lot of boxes to go through, Amy."

She gave me a disgusted look, walked back to the dining room table, slipped off the pumps, and opened another box. I wandered out to the entryway and grabbed two more boxes.

Between the two of them, they worked their way through the first bottle of wine and the cheese and sausage pizza over the course of an hour. They'd gotten religion now and were opening boxes and rifling through the contents like they were on a mission.

I'd just opened the second bottle of wine and filled their glasses when Hannah said, "Oh, look at this, Amy. Maddie's Valentine's Day mitten." She held up a powder-blue mitten. It looked like one of the mittens my grandmother made for us when we were kids. We must have had two dozen pairs. During the winter, we always wore a pair with another two or three pairs resting on top of a radiator drying.

"Is there another mitten to match that one?" I asked.

"That's what I'm looking for now," Hannah said, pulling gloves, scarves, and knitted hats from the box.

"My cop pal told me they found a powder-blue mitten on the ice at the river."

"That doesn't make any sense unless there's another pair in here. Maddie wouldn't wear just one mitten or a mixed pair for that matter."

She went through the pile of items she'd just pulled from the box. Then went through the pile one more time, unfolding the scarves, turning the hats inside out just to be sure.

"No, it's all by itself. The other one isn't here."

"Maybe it ended up in another box. Keep an eye out for it," I said. Hannah returned everything except the blue mitten to the box and slid the box across the table to me. I carried it out to the entryway and carried two more boxes in.

There was everything from undergarments to books, makeup, shampoos, creams, brushes, combs, hair dryers. There was a jewelry box, but a quick look suggested anything of value, like diamonds, gold, or jewels, had already been removed.

By 10:30, they were two-thirds of the way through all the boxes. Amy suddenly sat in a dining room chair and said, "I'm sorry, but I need a break."

Hannah sat down and took hold of her wine glass with both hands. "I'm beat, Dev. I'm afraid we're going to have to leave this for another time."

The boxes that had been examined now made up the larger of the two piles in the entryway. But there were still nine boxes they hadn't gone through, not to mention the five armloads of garments on hangers that I'd piled on the couch in the front room.

"I think it would be a good idea if we knocked off for tonight. There's still a lot more to go through, although you've both done a hell of a job. None of this is going anywhere, so don't feel any pressure. Any idea when you want to get back at this?"

They looked at one another and together said, "Tomorrow night."

"You sure? There's no pressure."

"If you don't have anything scheduled for tomorrow night, hopefully, I'd like to finish up," Hannah said.

"If I have anything scheduled, I'll move it," I said, knowing I didn't have anything lined up for the rest of the week.

"You sure?" Amy asked.

"Absolutely. One thing. Well, actually two. First, I'm getting dinner tomorrow night, no discussion. Second, is there anything you want to take to your folks?"

"There's a number of things," Hannah said. "Our grandma's china. That crystal carafe."

"Don't forget the American Doll," Amy said and nodded at the doll seated in the center of the dining room table.

"Hopefully, we'll find the silver service and the place settings in one of those remaining boxes," Hannah said. "But if it's okay, I'd like to take everything going to our folks over all at once. They'll be happy to get it, but it's going to be a real heartbreak for them at the same time. I don't want to make that any harder than it has to be."

Amy nodded. "Does that sound okay? Will it work for you, Dev?"

"Not a problem, I mean it. In fact, I'll get some more boxes tomorrow, and we can repack the things going to your folks, so it doesn't look like it was just tossed in a box. The way some of these boxes were packed, it looks like they just shoved it off a shelf and into a box. We're lucky there's only been a few things broken," I said.

"Yeah. I'm curious to see if they bothered to send Maddie's laptop over," Hannah said.

"I didn't even think of that," Amy said and took a hearty sip of wine.

"It might be a good idea for both of you to come up with a list of things you would expect or hope to see. You know, like that doll and Maddie's laptop."

"The string of pearls we each got when we graduated from college," Hannah said.

"We're on for tomorrow night then?" I asked.

Both women nodded. We chatted about Maddie for the next half-hour, and I walked them out to their cars. Thankfully, they were both parked in front of my place, and their cars started. I hurried back inside and locked the front door behind me.

Morton was stretched out on the couch in the front room, lying on top of five armloads of silk dresses, designer blouses, and God only knew what else. Without a doubt, the most expensive bed he would ever sleep on.

I woke him up and let him outside, not that he wanted to go. He was back at the door in sixty seconds.

I let him inside, and he made his way upstairs. I put the wine glasses in the dishwasher and moved the various items set aside on the dining room table over to the sideboard. I got the coffee ready for the morning, checked the door locks once more, and headed up to bed. Morton was already asleep when I climbed into bed. I was out in about two minutes and slept until my alarm woke me the following morning.

Thirteen

Morton managed to pull the pillow over his head as the alarm went off. I laid in bed for a couple of minutes then hit the shower, dressed, and went downstairs. I turned on the coffee and fired up my laptop. I clicked on the Airbnb site, and surprise, surprise, someone actually sent a message, asking about availability.

I sent an immediate reply telling them that, yes, the room was available. Then I waited and waited some more. After ten minutes, I poured myself a coffee and cooked up some bacon, scrambled eggs, and toast. I checked my laptop a half-dozen times while cooking, but there was never a reply.

Morton wandered down maybe an hour later. He did his usual stretch just inside the kitchen and then wandered over to get his head scratched. I let him outside, filled his food and water dishes, checked my laptop again, and let him back in.

After checking Airbnb multiple times, I grabbed the powder-blue mitten from the sideboard in the dining room, and we headed down to the office. Louie was in, and what looked like a fresh pot of coffee was going. I poured myself a mug, topped up Louie's, and turned on my laptop. No Airbnb response.

I chatted with Louie for a couple of minutes and then called Aaron LaZelle, expecting to leave a message. He answered on the third ring, "I can't do dinner tonight."

"Not a problem. I happen to be booked for the evening."

"Seriously, there's a woman in town that hasn't been warned about you?"

"As a matter of fact, there are two, sisters, and they're coming over tonight." I went on to tell him about my meeting with the Gauner brothers, the mound of boxes and clothes left on my porch, and Maddie's sisters examining items last night. "Actually, that's why I'm calling you. One of the things they came across was a hand-knit, powder-blue mitten. Both girls identified it as one of the Valentine's Day mittens their mother had knitted for them last year. They each got a pair, a different color for each girl. Maddie's pair was powder-blue."

"Okay, so that would seem to be one more confirmation that, unfortunately, it was Maddie McGuire who went through the ice," Aaron said.

"Well, yeah, maybe. Except this is what her sisters told me. They said Maddie wouldn't have worn just the one mitten. She would have worn a matched pair, certainly a different pair, if she could only find the one blue mitten. You think you could check and see if Maddie's personal items were returned to Ferral? If they were, well, then that would explain the one mitten, but if they weren't… I don't know. Doesn't it sound strange she'd just wear one mitten?"

There was a long pause on the other end of the line before Aaron said, "Give me some time, and I'll make the call. You going to be in the office this morning?"

"Yeah, as a matter of fact, I brought the mitten they found last night. What if I run it over to you for a comparison?"

"Hold on, Dev. First, let me see if those personal items have been claimed. I'll get back to you."

"Okay, I'll be here," I said, but Aaron had already hung up.

He called back not ten minutes later. "Aaron?"

"Yeah, Dev, two calls were made to the Ferral residence. No answer. All those items, the boots, the purse, and the mitten, are still here. I checked, and the vehicle, a 2020 black Range Rover, was recovered from the impound last Monday. It was paid for by Colton Ferral."

"You got a time on Monday when he was down there to get it?"

"Yeah, they open up at 8:00, and his form is stamped at 8:47 Monday morning."

"So he's down there to get the car, and the memorial service for his wife is at 10:00 that same morning?"

"Yeah, more than a little bit odd, but nothing illegal about it."

"I'd like to head down there and compare the two mittens. Can you arrange that with someone so I can—"

"I'll go you one better. Stop in and see me, and we'll both go down there. This sounds like it might be heading toward a homicide investigation."

"I'm leaving now," I said.

"What's up?" Louie asked as I shoved the phone in my pocket.

"Something's not quite making sense on Maddie's deal. I'll know more when I get back. You going to be here for a while?"

"All day unless someone calls. Don't worry about it. Get this mitten sorted out. We'll be fine."

"Thanks," I said as I grabbed my jacket and headed out the door.

Fortunately, the mitten was just where I left it, on the passenger seat of the car. I waited for a bus to pass then pulled a U-turn on the street and headed to the police station. I parked across the street in the gravel visitors parking lot. With the temperatures hovering in the negative numbers, there were plenty of parking places. I hurried into the station and didn't recognize the sergeant at the desk. I told him I had an appointment with Lieutenant Aaron LaZelle in homicide.

He nodded, looked at a note next to his phone, and said, "You're Devlin Haskell?"

"Yes," I said.

"Have a seat while I call up there." I walked over to a row of orange plastic chairs. By the time I sat down, he was hanging up the phone. "Mr. Haskell, the Lieutenant is on his way down. If you'll step over here, I'll give you a visitors pass."

I hurried back to the desk, and he handed me a white plastic visitor's pass with a clip. I attached it to my jacket and went back and sat down. Aaron appeared about five minutes later. He opened a security door and called, "Dev."

I hurried over and followed him down a hallway. We took an elevator down two floors and stepped out. The evidence room was right in front of us. Aaron held the ID hanging around his neck in front of the keypad, and the door buzzed. He pushed it open, and we stepped into the room.

There was a long counter in front of us with racks of shelving behind it. All sorts of boxes were lined along the shelves. I began counting the lines of shelves and stopped at twenty, just as an officer appeared from one of the aisles carrying a box. "Oh, hey L.T., perfect timing. I've got it right here."

He set the box down and slid a form across the counter to Aaron. Aaron signed the form and said, "Thanks, Paulie. Any place special you want us?"

"No, help yourself," Paulie said and nodded at a series of a dozen cubicles against a far wall. Only one of them was occupied. We walked over and sat down at the cubicle three spaces away from the guy reading what looked like some sort of note. He was wearing latex gloves.

It dawned on me I hadn't brought any gloves, but fortunately, there was a box of them lying on the desktop.

The guy reading the note set it down, glanced over, and said, "How's it going, L.T.?"

Aaron looked over and said, "Hi, Donnie. You learning anything?"

"Nothing new. Our boy was one unhappy individual."

Aaron shook his head and said, "Some poor kid blew his brains out." He handed me a pair of latex gloves, slipped a pair over his hands, and opened the box in front of us. He took out a paper form listing the contents then proceeded to pull the items out one by one. A black leather purse, a billfold, a pair of black boots with fur around the top. A bag that held miscellaneous items from the purse: a nail file, various makeups and creams, credit cards, a small notebook with a pen, two tampons, a hairbrush, and a comb, dental floss, an open package of mints, Kleenex, sunglasses, hair bands, bobby pins, and a phone charger. Last, but not least, he pulled out a powder-blue mitten.

I pulled the mitten Hannah found last night from my jacket pocket and placed it next to the one from the evidence box. We both looked at them for a long moment.

"They look the same. I'd say it's a safe guess they're a pair," I said.

Aaron nodded and said, "Let me grab a form, and we'll submit it for examination." He pushed his chair back and walked over to the counter. Paulie handed him a form and an evidence bag.

Aaron wrote some information across the top of the bag, placed the mitten I'd brought into the bag, sealed it, and set it off to the side. "You see anything that catches your interest?" he asked.

I looked at all the items from the purse. "I'd like to take a look at that notebook and her billfold."

He pulled the two items from the bag and set them in front of me. I picked up the pocket notebook. Three things were written on the front page, 'eggs, sugar, flour.' The rest of the notebook was empty.

Her billfold held twenty-one dollars cash and the usual pictures, a business card from a doctor, her driver's license, and Blue Cross insurance card. Nothing appeared unusual.

"Does it seem strange her cellphone isn't in here?" I asked.

Aaron seemed to think for a second or two and then shook his head. "It wouldn't be unusual for a phone to be in someone's pants or jacket pocket."

Aaron returned the items to the box, placed the sheet with the list of items on top of everything, and closed the box. He put the evidence bag with the blue mitten on top of the box and took them back to the counter. He had a brief conversation with Paulie, and we left.

"It's going to take a couple of days to compare those mittens," Aaron said as we stepped out of the elevator on the first floor. "You know, you said her mother knit those mittens?"

"Yeah, for Valentine's Day last year. Three pairs, one for each of the girls. Each pair was a different color."

"It would help if she had the yarn she used, and we could compare those mittens to the ball of yarn."

"I'll call the girls and see if they can get it. If there's some of that yarn left, I should be able to have it to you by tomorrow."

"Keep me posted," Aaron said, and we shook hands.

Fourteen

I phoned Amy and Hannah when I got back to the office and ended up leaving a message for both of them. "Hi, it's Dev. Planning to see you tonight at 6:00. Call me when you get this. I'd like you to pick something up from your mom before you come over."

Louie must have gotten a call because he was out of the office. I clipped the leash on Morton's collar, and we headed out the door. We crossed the street and walked two blocks up to Rooster's BBQ deli. I ordered the pulled pork shoulder BBQ sandwich and fries. The high for the day was forecast for -5F, so Morton didn't waste a lot of time checking out every tree and fence gate. It only took five minutes to make it up to Rooster's and another five to make it back.

I tossed Morton a biscuit when we got back to the office. He grabbed it and settled onto his pillow. I poured myself a coffee, opened the Styrofoam container with my BBQ pork sandwich, and my phone rang.

Amy was returning my call. "Hi, Amy. Thanks for calling back."

"Sorry I couldn't take your call, Dev. You need something from my mom?"

"Yeah." I went on to explain my meeting with Aaron, and his request for the ball of yarn Maddie's mittens came from.

"So what does that mean? They think someone stole her mittens?"

"No, they're just trying to verify that the mitten found at the scene did, in fact, belong to Maddie."

"But we both told you mom knitted those for Maddie as a Valentine's Day gift."

God save me. "Yes, and the police would like to document that by examining and testing the yarn. So, if you or Hannah could see if your mom has any of it left and bring it with you tonight, I'll take it down to the police tomorrow morning."

"Yeah, I guess I can do that," she said, making it sound like it was going to be a problem.

"Great, or have Hannah get it, just so they can examine the mittens. Okay?"

"Yeah, I guess. See you tonight," she said and disconnected.

I took a deep breath and focused on my BBQ pork shoulder and fries. Louie arrived maybe a half-hour later. As per usual, the staircase creaked and groaned under his weight. He opened the door red-faced, took two steps into the office, stopped, and said, "BBQ pork shoulder from Roosters?"

I'd finished my sandwich fifteen minutes earlier, and the Styrofoam tray was in the wastebasket.

"Yeah, Louie. Gee," I lied, "I would have saved you some if I knew you were going to be back so soon."

"Oh, a client was arrested early this morning after running a light and getting pulled over." He seemed to think for a moment and said, "I'll be back in just a moment." He set his briefcase on his picnic table and hurried out the door.

I watched out the window as he waddled across the street, climbed into his car, and drove up the street. He was back ten minutes later with a bag from Rooster's. He set the bag on his picnic table and then rubbed his hands together as he walked around the table, took off his coat, and settled into his chair. He opened the bag and pulled out a white Styrofoam carton. He opened the carton revealing a BBQ pork shoulder sandwich and fries. I was about to say something when my phone rang. Hannah.

"Hi Hannah, thanks for calling me back."

"I just got off the phone with Amy. She'll stop at Mom's on the way over to your house and see if she has any of that yarn left."

"That'll be great. Hopefully, she'll have some, and it will match up with both mittens."

"And then what?" Hannah said.

"Well, it presents the question of why a mitten was found at the river, but the other one was apparently still at home. You two said last night it didn't make any sense that Maddie would have worn just the one mitten. I happen to agree with you. We'll see if anything happens from there."

"Okay," she said. "You sure you don't want us to bring dinner tonight?"

"Very sure. Thanks for offering, but I've got it covered."

"What are you making?"

"It's a surprise, Hannah. I promise you'll like it."

"I'm sure we will," she said. We chatted for another minute, and then she had to go.

"They're coming over again tonight?" Louie asked through a mouth full of BBQ pork shoulder.

"Yeah, hopefully, we'll get through most, if not all, of Maddie's items. There's an awful lot of stuff, and it's got to be emotionally hard on both of them, but they'll get the job done. They'll be going through stacks and stacks of clothes tonight. Designer dresses and blouses and stuff. I just hope they don't start trying stuff on and then want to get a mirror to see how they look." That got me thinking, and I began to come up with a plan.

Fifteen

Morton and I headed home a little before 5:00. I stopped at Solo Vino, the wine shop just up the street from me. I picked up two bottles of wine. We headed into the kitchen, and I let Morton out the backdoor. I set the wine in the refrigerator and called La Grolla, the Italian restaurant just across the street. I placed three orders for Pollo Champagne, pan-seared chicken breasts with shallots, sun-dried tomato, and Champagne cream sauce. I hurried across the street and picked up the order a little before 6:00.

Back in my kitchen, I phoned Amy to remind her to check with her mom on the ball of yarn.

"Relax, Mr. Hyper. We're on our way there now. Hannah's with me."

Perfect. "Okay, so you'll be here around 6:30?" I asked, not mentioning they'd be a half-hour late.

"Yeah, that's about right."

"Good, I'm cooking our dinner now, so don't waste time."

"What are you making?"

"Dinner," I said.

"Should be interesting," she said, sounding like she meant anything but.

I lined a large pan with tin foil. Each order had two small chicken breasts, and I lined them up in the pan. I covered the pan with tin foil and placed it in the oven. I'd gotten two orders of bruschetta and arranged that on a platter and set it on the counter. I set out silverware and wine glasses, let Morton back inside, and waited.

Five minutes before they were due to show up, I turned on the oven and then placed a saucepan and a frying pan in the dish rack so it looked like I'd washed the pans after cooking the meal. I took the trash bag out to the bin so there wouldn't be any hint of ordering from the restaurant. At 6:40, Amy pulled in front and parked.

I met them at the front door as they were climbing the steps to the porch.

"Oh, perfect timing, ladies. I was just about to open the wine. I thought we'd have dinner and then get started on the rest of the boxes. Does that sound okay?"

"What did you make for dinner, peanut butter sandwiches or hotdogs?" Amy asked as they stepped inside and laughed.

Morton greeted them by knocking his head against their knees and accepting a head scratch.

"Yeah, right. No hotdogs. I wanted to keep it simple, so a little bruschetta and then some chicken breasts with a cream sauce."

"You made that?" Hannah asked, not sounding too convinced.

"Yeah, I placed it in the oven to keep it warm. Come on back," I said.

"Oh, before I forget," Amy said. She reached into her purse and pulled out a plastic bag with a small ball of powder-blue yarn. "A gift from our mom."

"Oh, thanks. I'll take this down to the police tomorrow morning. How about some dinner?" I said and walked back toward the kitchen.

They both stared at the bruschetta platter on the kitchen counter. The room had the slight smell of the chicken and Champagne sauce. As I opened the refrigerator for one of the bottles of wine, I caught them looking at the pans in the sink.

"I guess I didn't know you could cook, Dev," Amy said.

"Oh, yeah. My mom was a great cook and a great teacher. I think she wanted to be sure I didn't show up for meals every night."

We ate some bruschetta and sipped wine for maybe ten minutes before I dished up the chicken breasts.

"Mmm-mmm, really good," they said almost in unison after the first bite.

"Just a little chicken recipe my mom liked to do," I lied.

We finished dinner, I refilled their wine glasses, and we moved into the dining room. I already had two boxes on the table. They each took a sip of wine, and I headed back to the kitchen to load the dishwasher. Of course, the girls only ate one chicken breast, but that was okay. I set the two leftover breasts back in the pan and placed the pan in the fridge. Once that was done, I walked back to the entryway and grabbed two more boxes. Things went a good deal faster than the night before, partly because most of the boxes contained odds and ends. Three of them held books. Both women seemed much more focused tonight.

"Okay," Hannah said after about an hour and a half. "Ready to start on the clothes?"

"Finally," Amy said.

I looked at the two of them and said, "No."

"What do you mean, no?" Amy asked.

"Look, I know what's going to happen. Those are all lovely items, designer dresses, blouses, scarves, slacks, really nice stuff. Rather than have me stand around and watch, wouldn't it make more sense for you to haul all those items to one of your places? That way, you can stand around in your underwear and try everything on. You can look at yourselves in the mirror, decide who is going to get the particular item. You can drink plenty of wine, take whatever you want, and I won't be in the way."

They both nodded and smiled. "That sounds like a great idea."

"Good, so you're finished going through the boxes. Now, feel free to leave everything here. You can come back another day to get the things for your mom. In the meantime, you can decide on what you want to do with the rest of this. Again, no pressure."

"Oh, Dev, you are so sweet," Hannah said and gave me a big kiss on the cheek.

Amy did the same thing and squeezed my hand.

"Okay. So what do you say to one more glass of wine? After that, we'll load the clothes in the car, and you can get out of here."

They both nodded, and we headed into the kitchen. Over the glass of wine, we all told Maddie stories. Being their older sister, and me a high school boyfriend, they laughed about the flat tire at the prom. I told them about the cracked windshield one night when I went to hit a mosquito. I told them how I pretended to try out for the senior class play so I could meet Maddie. We had a lot of laughs, and then we loaded up Amy's car. The clothes, piled in the backseat of her Hyundai Tucson, went up almost to the ceiling of the car, blocking any hope of looking out the rear window.

"You sure you don't want to leave any of these here? You can come back tomorrow and get them," I said.

Both women shook their heads.

"No," Amy said. "I'm only ten minutes away."

"You sure?"

"Yes," they said in unison. I got a kiss and another hug from both of them. I told them no rush on everything in the boxes stacked up in my entryway and the dining room. I stood in the driveway and waved as they pulled away from the curb and drove off. By the time they'd reached the end of the block, I'd hurried back inside to the warmth of my house.

Morton had already reclaimed the couch in the front room. He was stretched out on the couch and opened one eye to check who had just walked in the door. As soon as he saw it was me, he went back to sleep. I headed into the kitchen, washed the wine glasses, and ate the rest of the bruschetta. I went onto YouTube and checked a number of news sites. The normal bit of craziness was going on in Washington, and the gunpoint carjackings and robberies continued in town. I checked the door locks and turned off the kitchen lights as I made my way toward the stairs. I double-checked the front door locks, left the porch light on, and headed up to bed.

Morton was already asleep on my bed. I brushed my teeth and was heading back into my bedroom when the doorbell rang. I glanced at the digital clock, 11:20. The doorbell rang again. I took my Glock out of the nightstand and headed downstairs. I was almost at the door when the doorbell rang once more. I pulled the curtain aside and looked out at a woman standing on my porch. Her back was to me, and I couldn't recognize who it was. She was a brunette with hair just below her shoulders. She wore a nice jacket, fancy slacks, and leather boots with heels. Obviously, she didn't appear to be homeless. I looked left and right and didn't see anyone else on the porch. Maybe it was whoever sent the Airbnb message?

I moved the Glock to my left-hand, keeping it at the ready but out of sight. I opened the door and asked, "Can I help you?"

Sixteen

I just stood and stared. "Yeah, Dev, can you let me in, please? I'm freezing my ass off out here."

I continued to stare.

"Did you hear what I just said? It's freezing out here. Can I come in, please?"

"Oh, yeah, sorry, Maddie. I just— What the hell are you doing here? You're supposed to be dead. I mean—"

"Sorry to disappoint you," she said as I moved back, and she stepped inside, pulling a black suitcase behind her. "Oh, God, I'm so cold."

"What are you doing? Where have you been? Everyone thinks you're dead. Your sisters were just here. They've been going through all your stuff. You have to call your folks right now. They're broken-hearted. What the hell happened?"

"Just calm down, will you? God, you got something warm I can eat? I've been sitting in that rental car for the past two hours waiting for my sisters to leave. I see they didn't have any trouble grabbing all my clothes." She shuddered and blew on her hands to warm them.

"Okay, look, come on into the front room. I'll get a fire going, and while you warm up, I'll get some chicken I made tonight."

"Sounds good. Chicken that you made? You sure it's not from that restaurant across the street. I think I saw you carrying a pretty big bag out of there earlier tonight."

"You want something to eat, or do you want to give me a hard time?"

"Okay, okay, just saying."

"Hey, Maddie—" I said and wrapped my arms around her, then all of a sudden, we were both crying. Eventually, we pulled apart, and I said, "Let's get that fire going, and you can tell me what's going on. It's just great to have you back. Really great."

I pulled a chair in front of the fireplace and started a fire. Maddie kept her jacket on, and Morton sat in front of her with his head on her lap. I microwaved the two chicken breasts and brought them out to her along with a glass of wine. The fire must have done the trick because now her jacket was unzipped. She inhaled the chicken in about three minutes and handed the clean plate back to me.

"Can I get you something else?"

"Thanks, but I'm fine."

"You want to tell me what's going on?"

"It's kind of a long story."

"Well, I'm not going anywhere. Just in case you didn't hear me before, it's really great to see you. I want to know what's going on, but I'm thrilled to see you. That doesn't even describe it. I'm just—"

She reached over and squeezed my hand.

"Be right back," I said and hurried out to the kitchen with her plate. I pulled a bottle of wine off the rack, grabbed a glass for me, and hurried out to the front room. Along the way, I bit my tongue just to make sure I wasn't dreaming.

I pulled a chair up alongside Maddie and unscrewed the cap on the wine bottle. I filled both our glasses, and we sat and watched the fire, not speaking. I was afraid to ask a question, afraid I might upset her. Eventually, I tossed another log on the fire.

She looked over, took a sip of wine, and smiled. "Where to begin?" she said and slowly shook her head. "Well, the marriage was a disaster from about the time I walked into the church. All the signs were there, but I kept thinking I could fix things. I never realized the control Colton's mother had or how much of an absolute idiot Colton was. All that, plus, I had no idea what the family business was. I thought he was running an advertising firm, if you can believe it." She shook her head.

"I thought he was so successful. It just never occurred to me that everyone who crossed him ended up dead. It wasn't until I found myself on that list, his mother's death list, that I finally caught on." She turned and looked at me. "I'm really scared, Dev, and I don't know where to turn."

"You'll be safe here. I won't let anyone hurt you."

She smiled and shook her head. "That's very sweet of you to say. But it isn't just me I'm worried about. It's my mom and dad and my sisters. It wouldn't bother Colton one bit to kill any of us. That's why I wanted to make it look like I was dead. If they thought for a minute I was alive, my family wouldn't see another sunrise. I'm not kidding, Dev. You can't let anyone know I'm here, especially my family."

"I have a pal. In fact, you might remember him from high school, Aaron LaZelle."

She seemed to think for a moment before she asked, "Wasn't he an honor student?"

"Yeah, he was and student of the month a couple of times. He was captain of the hockey team, on the debate team for three years. The complete opposite of me."

"Yeah, but you were fun."

I didn't pursue that line of discussion. "Anyway, Aaron's on the police force. He heads up the homicide department. We can talk to him and—"

"Dev, no offense, but you're not listening. If the Ferrals even get a hint I'm alive, my family is dead. I can't go to the police. I have to figure something else out."

"Okay, so forget that for a minute. Here's what I want you to focus on. You can stay here as long as you like. I've got plenty of room. I'd love it if you'd share my bed, but no pressure. If you would feel more comfortable in another room, choose whatever one you'd like. I've got Morton. He's usually the only other one here. If you're really going to keep a low profile—"

"Absolutely. They get the slightest hint I'm still alive, and they'll deal with it in their own incredibly awful way. They're horrible people, Dev. Absolutely horrible."

"Okay, you don't need to convince me. Let me ask you some questions, just to make sure you're covered. Do you have a gun?"

"No, I've wouldn't know the first thing about a gun."

"Well, we're going to change that, starting tomorrow."

"But I don't want to—"

"If the Ferrals are as bad as you suggest, and I have no doubt they are, you need to be protected twenty-four-seven. I can teach you how to use a gun safely. You're not going to be wearing it on your hip or twirling it on your finger."

"Okay, I guess."

"Good. Now, where's your cellphone?"

She smiled and said, "I'm ahead of you on that. I tossed it into the river. I picked up a cheap phone a month ago. Just in case you're worried, I did plan this out before I staged my accident on the river."

"Credit cards?"

"I left them in my purse. I got two new ones back in August. I've charged a hundred dollars on the cards every month for the past five months and always paid the bill in full before it was due—same thing for my driver's license. I told them I lost mine and got a new one. I left all of that stuff in my purse on the shore so it would re-inforce the fact that I must have fallen through the ice."

"Where have you been for the past week?"

"I was in a hotel here for a few days and then rented a car with one of my new credit cards and drove to Wisconsin. I was about to lose my mind after staying in hotel rooms for the last seven days. But I wanted to be sure no one saw me. I just came back to town tonight."

"Good idea. You mind if I make a suggestion?"

"Okay," she said, drawing the word out.

"Either cut and dye your hair or get a wig."

"Here, hold this," she said and handed me her wine glass. She walked out to the entryway and wheeled in her suitcase. She laid it on the floor, unzipped it, and pulled out two wigs. One was blonde, and the other was red.

"I've got a checkbook for my new bank account, a thousand dollars in cash, and this," she said, holding up stapled together sheets of paper.

"What's all that?"

"My insurance policy. A list of people the Ferrals have murdered or are thinking of murdering, bank account numbers, passwords, two safe house addresses. I've got the addresses of his betting parlors. I think he currently has three of them, plus the names and addresses of a number of people selling drugs around town. I'm sure it's not all of them, but arresting these people and getting them off the street would certainly help clean up the city, at least for a little while."

"So why not turn that over to the police?"

"Because, Dev, as big an idiot as Colton is, the second this list of people and places started to go down, my family would be a target, and they would never see another sunrise."

She drained her glass of wine and said, "I'm really beat. Would you mind if I went to bed? I haven't slept very well for the past month. I had a three and a half-hour drive back to town this afternoon, and I'm really dragging."

"Yeah, sure, that would be okay. Zip that suitcase closed, and I'll take it upstairs for you."

She tossed the wigs and her list into her suitcase and zipped it closed. I picked up the suitcase before she could and headed for the staircase.

"What's with all the boxes?" she asked as we headed up the stairs.

"I'll tell you later. Like I said before, no pressure if you don't want to share a bed, but this is the guest room." I opened the door at the top of the stairs and turned on the light. There was a single bed, a chest of drawers, and a desk.

"This next room," I said as I walked down the hall, reached in, and turned on the light, "is my room." Morton was stretched out on the bed. He adjusted his shoulders a bit when the light came on but never opened his eyes.

"Looks like the spot in your bed is already taken."

"I could move him. It would only take a second."

"That's sweet, Dev. But all I want to do is sleep. Okay?"

"Yeah, okay. Just remember you're always welcome. This next room is my Airbnb room," I said and flipped on the light switch. The double bed with the new sheets was against the far wall. An upholstered bench was up against the foot of the bed. There was a chest of drawers with a mirror above it, a rocking chair with a cushion, and a full-length mirror was attached to the closet door.

"Oh, this looks great. Would it be all right with you if I took this room?"

"Yeah, I guess. Sure I couldn't talk you into—"

"Dev. I already told you."

"Hey, I was just going to ask if you wanted another glass of wine."

"Yeah, sure you were. If I recall, you used to be pretty good at giving me too much to drink and then—"

"I never heard a complaint."

"It never crossed my mind," she said and smiled. "Back up for a second. You said you rent this out for Airbnb?"

"That's the plan, but I just started, and I haven't had anyone use it. Go ahead and settle in. If someone wants to rent it for the night, I still have the spare room."

"Oh, it looks lovely. I think I'll be asleep before my head hits the pillow."

"I'll lay out some towels for you in the bathroom. I'm up around 6:30. Morton usually sleeps for another hour. If it's okay, I'm going to tell my office mate I'll be late coming in tomorrow morning, and we'll just deal with any questions you might have. Anything else you need?"

She shook her head.

"Do you drink coffee?"

"Yes, black."

"Perfect. I'll have it going when you get up, and I'll give you a tour of the kitchen."

"I'll look forward to that," she said and smiled.

I closed the door behind me and headed down the hall. I heard the door open after I took four steps down the hall.

"Oh, Dev. I just wanted to thank you for doing this. Otherwise, I— Well, just thanks. Really, thank you."

"Maddie, I'm just glad you're here, safe and sound. And I plan on keeping you that way."

She nodded, smiled, and closed the door. A moment later, I heard the lock click into place.

I set two clean white towels out in the bathroom and placed a spare roll of toilet paper on the vanity. I went downstairs, checked the locks, and glanced out the front window. A blue Nissan Altima was parked across the street in front of the restaurant. I guessed that was probably what Maddie was driving.

I left my Glock on top of the nightstand and climbed into bed. I heard Maddie close the bathroom door a moment later and I was sound asleep before she opened it.

Seventeen

I woke a couple of minutes before my alarm went off. I turned it off, laid in bed for another five minutes, and then headed into the bathroom. Morton was curled up in the hall, sleeping in front of the door to Maddie's room.

I shaved, showered, dressed, and headed down to the kitchen. I added three more cups to the coffee maker and turned it on. I sent Louie an email telling him I would be late coming in. I took the ball of yarn the girls dropped off last night and set it by the front door, so I wouldn't forget to deliver it to Aaron.

I read my emails, checked Airbnb twice, had another cup of coffee, and ate two pieces of toast with raspberry jam. Morton eventually wandered into the kitchen. I heard the bathroom door close upstairs. Maddie strolled into the kitchen forty minutes later. Morton met her as she entered the kitchen. She was wearing blue jeans and a gray sweater.

"Oh, Morton, I almost tripped over you in the middle of the night."

"Yeah, at some point, he left my bed and curled up in front of your door. No doubt offering protection."

"Oh, that's so sweet."

I pulled a mug from the cabinet and filled it with coffee. "You did tell me you like it black, didn't you?"

"Yeah, thanks, this is perfect," she said and took a sip. She held the mug out to examine. It was white with black letters that read, 'Nina's Coffee Cafe.' "Isn't this the coffee shop just down on the corner?" she asked.

"Yeah, I've got six of them, nice mugs, just the right size."

"Did you buy them, or did you steal them?"

"Why would I steal them?"

"Oh, God. That's what you did. You stole them. Didn't you?"

"Well, now wait, I wasn't really stealing them. I just kind of borrowed them."

"God, some things never change."

"Hey, is that blue car parked across the street what you're driving?"

"Yeah, it's a rental."

"I'm thinking you can park it in my garage, just to keep it out of sight. I usually park in the driveway, anyway. No big deal."

"Oh, thanks. Actually, I was going to return it. I just needed to get out of state for a few days. It's costing me a hundred and forty bucks a day, and I don't want to pay that."

"Where did you rent it?"

"Out at the airport."

"We can return it today if you want."

"That would be great," she said and sipped her coffee.

"You sleep okay?"

"I was out in about five seconds. I still don't feel completely caught up, but last night was the best sleep I've had in probably a month. I'm not kidding."

"Good, that suggests you're losing some of that stress."

"Yeah, thanks again for letting me stay here."

"Don't mention it. What do you fancy for breakfast?"

"What do you have?"

"Well, I can do oatmeal or scramble some eggs. There's toast and raspberry jam. I could make you French toast."

"How would it be if I made the French toast?"

"I can do it," I said.

"I'm sure you can, but I feel like I should start earning my stay, so let me cook breakfast. Then, what I'd like to do is see what you have on hand and make a grocery list."

"Works for me, but let's get that car returned first, so you don't get charged for another day. I'll drop you back here, and then I at least have to make an appearance in the office. Are you going to be okay here alone?"

"Oh, yeah, don't worry about that."

"Which brings up one other thing. Did you look in my front window a few days ago? It was snowing or had just snowed. I can't remember which."

"Yeah, but how did you know that? That's when I went out of town. It was maybe 4:00 in the morning when I looked in your front window."

"Yeah, I saw your footprints in the snow. Good, as long as that was you, no problem. Let me give you a quick tour of the kitchen, and you can make that French toast."

The tour took all of one minute. Maddie was making French toast, and I was sitting back sipping coffee and still biting my tongue to make sure I wasn't dreaming. We were discussing high school and where people ended up. It became obvious rather quickly that as out of touch as I was, Maddie was even worse.

She had information on two women who had been friends, although she hadn't heard from either of them in the past three years. I even brought her up to date on one of the women, now with two children and living down in Kansas City.

I filled her in on the little I knew about people, and by that time, we had finished the French toast. Maddie ran upstairs to the bathroom, and I cleaned up the kitchen. I followed her out to the airport, waited while she returned her car, and we drove home. I let her into the house and got her settled. We chatted for a minute, and she asked me about the ball of powder-blue yarn I'd slipped into my pocket, thinking she hadn't seen it.

I told her about taking the ball of yarn down to Aaron so they could run tests on it.

She told me she purposely left the mitten on the ice and agreed it was a good idea to take the yarn to the police, if for no other reason than possibly to apply pressure on the Ferrals.

I left Morton with her, got a quick kiss on the cheek, and headed out the door.

I pulled into the parking lot across the street from the police station and phoned Aaron. I ended up leaving a message.

"Yeah, Aaron, it's Dev. I'm leaving the ball of yarn with the sergeant at the front desk. Please call me just so I know you got it. Thanks." I ran the plastic bag with the ball of yarn into the station. I explained to the desk sergeant it was for Aaron LaZelle in homicide and left my card. Then I ran back to my car, literally, since the temperature was -11F.

Eighteen

Louie was in the office when I arrived. The coffee was on, and amazingly, there was enough to fill my mug. "You want me to make another pot?" I asked as I emptied the pot.

"None for me. I'm out of here in about fifteen minutes. Won't be back until late this afternoon. Where's Morton? Is everything okay?"

"Yeah, he's fine. I'm going to be doing all sorts of running around today, and I didn't want you stuck watching him."

Louie chuckled at that. "It's not like I have to do anything. He seems content to curl up on his pillow. I toss him a biscuit occasionally, and we get along fine."

As soon as Louie left, I phoned Ray Garcia. He owns Ray's Sporting Goods. More to the point, he has a gun range.

"Hi, Dev, long time no hear. How are things going?"

"No complaints from me, Ray. Hey, I wanted to bring a friend to your range today. You got any openings?"

"Shouldn't be a problem but let me check." I heard a keyboard clicking, and a moment later, Ray said, "We've got openings all afternoon and evening. We're open until 8:00."

"Can you schedule us for 1:00?"

More keyboard clicking, and he said, "You're good to go at 1:00. We'll see you then."

"Good. She's going to be firing a SigP365. Can you have a box of ammo waiting for us?"

"Consider it done," he said.

I hung up, checked my Airbnb site. Once again, no one had shown any interest. I phoned my pal at the insurance company to see if he had any more job applications that needed reviewing and left a message. I stared out the window for a long while, wondering how I could help Maddie. I pulled the box with the SigP365 from the back of my desk drawer, locked it in the trunk of my car, and headed back home just before 11:30.

Maddie was in the entryway, going through boxes of her belongings. Morton was stretched out on the floor next to her. He jumped up and demanded a head scratch as I stepped inside.

"See anything you like?" I asked as I quickly closed the door behind me.

Maddie literally jumped and let out a little scream. "Oh, Dev, you scared me. Did the Ferrals send all of this over?"

"I think so, along with all those clothes your sisters left with last night. I guess I failed to mention how it arrived." I went on to tell her the story. "Did you see the things in the dining room your sisters set aside for your folks?"

"Yeah, I already went through that. I'd forgotten about most of it."

"I'm just curious, did you have a lot of jewelry? We didn't really find anything. The girls mentioned a pearl necklace you each got when you graduated from high school or college."

"It was college. I didn't see it in the dining room. Did one of them take it?"

"No, it never arrived. There's a jewelry box somewhere in one of these boxes, but nothing of real value was in it."

She frowned and shook her head. "That figures, not surprising. Along with the pearls, I had diamond earrings, four pairs. Two diamond rings that belonged to my grandmother, my mom's mom. There should have been a diamond bracelet and two diamond pendants."

"Sorry, but none of those items were sent over, and your sisters went through everything. It took them two nights."

"Unfortunately, not at all surprising. God, I could kill Colton."

"Well, speaking of that. I have us scheduled for an hour on the shooting range, starting at 1:00 this afternoon. How about we grab some lunch before we go."

"A shooting range. You mean shooting with a gun?"

"Yeah, that's usually what we do there. I've got a nice little gun. It's compact, not too heavy, and this is the perfect way to learn how to use it. You have to keep yourself safe, Maddie."

"Yeah, I know, but a gun?"

"What do you think some thug Colton sends is going to do? Ask you nicely if you would mind getting into the car? At least with a gun, you can shoot it, and he'll probably think twice about getting any closer. Let's not worry about that aspect, and we can grab some lunch before we go."

She began to toss the items on the floor back into the box. I went into the kitchen and cooked up two grilled cheese sandwiches. Over lunch, Maddie described the items she'd seen in some of the boxes and how she'd acquired them. We finished up with a little dish of ice cream. Maddie put on her blonde wig, and we headed over to Ray's shooting range.

There were six other cars in the lot next to the range entrance. One of them, a dark green SUV, I recognized as Ray's. We climbed out of my car. I popped the trunk open and grabbed the box with the SigP365.

"If anyone asks, tell them my name is Karen," Maddie said.

"Got it," I said, and we hurried inside.

The actual range was behind a counter where Ray happened to be standing. We could see the range through the thick glass walls. There appeared to be three people firing, all guys, all wearing ear protection. When they fired, all we could hear was a muffled sound.

"Hi, Dev, good to see you," Ray said and held out his hand.

We shook hands, and Ray smiled at Maddie and said, "Hi, I'm Ray. We should talk. I've known this guy for years."

"Hi, I'm Karen," Maddie said. "We could trade stories."

"Dev tells me you're going to be shooting today. Is this your first time?"

Maddie nodded.

"Let me suggest something. Dev, nothing against you, but I've got a woman on staff, Luciana. She helps a lot of our female customers, especially first-timers." He looked at Maddie. "I can send her over if you'd feel more comfortable working with her."

Maddie turned to me and said, "Would you mind?"

"No, not at all. Great idea, Ray. Yeah, let's do it."

He picked up the phone and punched in three numbers, waited a moment, and said, "Hi Luci, I've got a woman back here, and it's her first time. Would you have time? Great, yeah, thank you. She'll be here in just a moment," he said.

A minute or two later, a dark-haired woman entered through a side door. I guessed she was in her late twenties, maybe thirty. She was Maddie's height, with dark brown eyes. She wore a black t-shirt with red letters that said Ray's Sporting Goods and had a butterfly tattoo on her forearm.

Introductions were made all around, and then Luciana grabbed two sets of ear protection and handed one to Maddie. She took the box with the SigP365 from me, picked up a stack of targets, a box of ammunition, and led the way onto the range.

Ray watched them walk through the door and then said, "I hope you don't mind Dev. But I've been doing this for a lot of years, and I picked up on her nervousness immediately. Most guys have been shooting since they were kids but not the women. Luci is really good. By the end of this, your girl will be a lot more comfortable and safer."

"No, I appreciate it, Ray. That was a good idea."

We watched for a couple of minutes, and Ray went off to do other things. Luciana spent the first ten minutes explaining things to Maddie. It looked like everything from safety to shooting stance. All the while, the pistol remained in the box. Eventually, she hooked up a target and cranked it maybe twenty feet downrange. She did more explaining as she had Maddie load the ten-round magazine. Finally, Maddie assumed the position and fired once.

As soon as she fired, she looked over at Luciana with wide eyes. Luciana smiled and nodded. I took a chair and paged through a couple of magazines. Occasionally, I stood just to check on Maddie, but she seemed to be doing just fine.

At one point, Ray wandered back and asked, "How's it going?"

"Seems to be going pretty well. Your Luciana knows exactly what she's doing. Maddie, or umm, I mean Karen looks like she's getting the hang of things." Ray gave me a thumbs-up and disappeared again.

The girls stepped out of the range almost an hour and a half later. Maddie was all smiles and carried a stack of targets.

"How'd you do?" I asked.

"Go ahead, show him," Luciana said.

Maddie spread the targets out along the counter, one after another, and grinned.

"This was the first one, five rounds," Luciana said. There was one bullet hole off to the right of the target. Apparently, the other four shots had missed completely.

"We worked on trigger squeeze and sight alignment, and Karen made really great progress. Look at this one compared to the first target," she said and took the target at the far end and laid it next to the first one.

There were five bullet holes in the target. Two of them were even in the black circle, both in the area marked seven. The bullseye was marked 10, but it showed definite progress.

Ray came back, and we settled up. I gave Luciana a nice tip and left with the pistol, ten rounds of ammunition, and the final target. Maddie was all smiles.

"So, what did you think?" I asked.

"A lot better and a lot more interesting than I expected," she said. "I was used to TV where they just pull the trigger a bunch of times."

"Yeah, that's not how it works."

"You're telling me. Thanks for doing this, Dev. I hope I never have to use the gun, but I wouldn't mind going back there sometime to shoot some more."

I took that last comment as a mark of success.

Nineteen

On the way back to my house, Maddie informed me that from now on if we were out and about, she would introduce herself as Karen. Once in the house, she handed me a grocery list she'd written, and I headed down to the office. Louie wasn't in. I drummed my fingers on the desk for five minutes and then drove over to the grocery store and picked up the items on Maddie's list. I dropped the groceries off at home and headed back to the office. I phoned Aaron LaZelle and disconnected before I had to leave a message.

I checked Airbnb, and surprisingly, there was a message. A couple named Hoover wanted to rent the room. I quickly responded to their inquiry, telling them the room was available and sending them the per-night cost. I didn't expect to hear back. Their response came through almost immediately. They wanted the room and paid for three nights in advance. They told me they were coming to town in two days.

I viewed this as a double win. I had my first Airbnb customers and, since they were going to take the room, maybe that would serve as an incentive for Maddie to join me in my room.

Louie never did return to the office, so I hurried home just after 5:00. I parked in the driveway and hurried into the house. As soon as I opened the door, I smelled something delicious cooking.

Morton was in his bed in the kitchen, gnawing a bone. He looked up from the bone just long enough to recognize me and then returned to his project at hand.

"Hi, Dev, hope you don't mind, but I decided to cook dinner."

Mind? Hardly. Be my guest. It smells delicious. What are you making?"

"Nothing fancy. We'll be eating pork chops with roast peppers and potatoes. I baked some brownies for dessert and made a little guacamole for beforehand. Can I pour you a glass of wine?"

"Are you going to have one?"

"I will if you will."

"Yeah, I'd love some."

"Good. Why don't you settle onto one of those kitchen stools, and I'll get the wine?"

I did just that, and a moment later, we were clinking glasses.

"You do anything this afternoon? I mean, other than making this delicious smelling dinner?"

"Yeah, I took a nap, slept for a good hour, then went through some more of those boxes. Probably a third of that stuff out there, I keep asking myself, 'What in the world was I thinking hanging on to all of it?' How did your day go?" I apparently debated a little too long because she finally said, "Okay. Something happened. What is it?"

"I got my first Airbnb client. A couple, they're arriving from Chicago in two days."

"Oh, congratulations, Dev. That's really good news. I suppose that means I should find a new location?"

"The only place you have to move is either into the spare room or in with me. No pressure, whatever you decide will be fine."

"Well, if you don't mind, I think, for the time being, I'll maybe take the spare room. I can move things in there tonight."

"They aren't coming in until the day after tomorrow. Take your time. You can settle into the spare room tomorrow."

We had dinner along with another glass of wine. After I cleaned up the kitchen, I hurried out to my car, grabbed the SigP365 pistol from the trunk, and took it into Maddie. "Put this someplace where you can get to it if you need to," I said and handed the box to her. I half-expected her to put up an argument, but instead, she smiled, gave me a kiss, and went upstairs.

She came down a half-hour later with an armload of sheets and pillowcases. "I figured if I have to move out of that room, I should do it now, and I can wash all these linens."

"Oh, that's really nice of you, Maddie, but I can wash those."

"No, it's the least I can do. I already moved into the spare room. Okay?"

"Yeah, not a problem," I said. "You know, I have another key for that Airbnb bedroom. I bet it will work in the lock to the spare room. That way, you can lock yourself in at night."

She smiled and said, "That would probably be a good idea."

I went upstairs to my bedroom, took one of the skeleton keys from my drawer, and tried it in the spare room lock. It worked just like the Airbnb lock. I squirted some of the graphite powder Reggie left with me into the lock. I turned the key back and forth to lubricate the mechanism and left the key in the lock.

Maddie was already running the sheets in the washer. I went into the den and turned on the TV. I was halfway through a movie of no redeeming value when she wandered into the den, yawned, gave me a peck on the cheek, and went upstairs to bed.

After the movie, I let Morton out, checked the locks, and we headed up to bed. I kept my fingers crossed on the outside chance Maddie might be asleep in my bed, but no such luck. I noticed that the key was out of the lock, suggesting she'd locked the door from inside the room. Morton took up his position curled up on the floor in front of the spare room door. I climbed into bed and slept soundly until my alarm went off.

Twenty

The following morning I was up, showered, shaved, and downstairs on my second cup of coffee when I heard Maddie close the bathroom door upstairs. She appeared forty minutes later wearing blue jeans and a white blouse. She insisted on making breakfast and got no complaint from me. We chatted over scrambled eggs and toast.

I got a smile instead of a kiss as Morton and I headed out the door. Louie wasn't in, so I put the coffee on and proceeded to burn my index finger, grabbing the pot incorrectly. I managed to spill my second cup of coffee on my jeans. I was beginning to wonder if maybe I should just head home since luck didn't seem to be running my way.

I heard the stairs begin to creak and groan as Louie made his way up to the office. The door opened, only it wasn't red-faced Louie. Instead, red-faced Fat Freddy Zimmerman and local crime lord Tubby Gustafson made their way into the office. Fat Freddy pulled back the chair in front of my desk. Tubby collapsed in the chair, and Fat Freddy settled into the chair next to him. Neither one of them spoke for a long minute as they caught their breath.

Morton recognized them and tried to settle deeper into his pillow. He turned his head toward the wall and placed a paw over his eyes.

Tubby coughed, cleared his throat, and said, "Haskell, against my better judgment, I'm in need of your assistance."

Yeah, my luck was definitely headed in the wrong direction.

"Only too happy to help, sir," I lied. "What may I do for you?"

Tubby closed his eyes and shook his head for a moment. "Two of my employees have been robbed. I want you to find out who is responsible for doing this."

"Me? What did the police tell you? Are they involved, sir? I'm sure—"

"You see, Frederick. This is why there is never any improvement. This is why it's such an agonizing process to attempt to deal with the inept. Haskell, the last people I want looking into my business operations are the police. I'm sure they'd be only too happy to become involved, and no doubt I'd find everything shut down in a matter of minutes."

"I see, sir, I think. Might this have something to do with one of your illegal gambling sites?"

"An incredibly poor choice of words, Haskell. I'm merely allowing individuals to place a wager in the hopes of making a profit. Is that any different than the day-to-day running of a business?" Tubby glared, and I had the distinct feeling he wasn't searching for an answer.

"Could you tell me what happened?"

Tubby turned to Fat Freddy and indicated me with a wave of his head. Fat Freddy cleared his throat and said, "In both instances, someone was transporting profits to our holding center when they were attacked and robbed."

"Attacked and robbed of your funds?"

"No Haskell, they only took the money they had in their wallets," Tubby growled. "Of course they ran off with my funds, close to twelve grand over the course of just two nights, damn it. Whoever did this knew when and where we were moving these funds. They shot both my couriers. Now, I want to know who did this. I want to find out how they got the information. And I want to find out who is in charge of this operation. This isn't just some fool in the right place at the wrong time. These robberies were planned by someone who knew what was involved and knew that they would be stealing from me."

Tubby's face was now beet-red, and his eyes bulged from their sockets. "I will expect you to find out who is responsible, or else."

"Do you have any ideas as to who it might have been, sir?"

Tubby shook his head. "Haskell, if I knew who did this, I wouldn't be wasting my time in this God-forsaken little hell-hole of yours. Fredrick, give him the list."

Fat Freddy pulled an envelope from his pocket and tossed it across my desk. I opened the envelope and pulled out a sheet of paper.

Tubby cleared his throat and said, "There are two addresses, two names, and a phone number after each name. Those are the names of my employees and their phone numbers. The addresses refer to the facilities where they were robbed. Find out who in the hell is responsible, Haskell."

"I'll contact you once I've learned—"

"You'll contact me the moment you can tell me who was involved, and I'll expect that information sooner rather than later. Do I make myself clear?"

"Yes, sir, it's just that I—"

"Silencio, Haskell. Against my better judgment, I've given you a golden opportunity to redeem yourself and finally demonstrate that you do, indeed, have some modicum of value. Despite the fact I've set my sights extremely low, I can only pray you're up to the task. As an incentive, let me warn you, do not disappoint." Tubby snapped his fingers. Fat Freddy jumped to his feet and pulled Tubby's chair back as he stood.

Tubby looked at me for a moment, shook his head, and groaned. "God, give me the strength," he said as they walked out of the office. I heard the stairs groan and creak as they climbed down to the first floor. A moment later, they appeared out on the sidewalk and waddled across the street.

Tubby was still mumbling, and Fat Freddy hurried past him. He opened the rear door on their black Cadillac Escalade. As Tubby slid across the seat, the car rocked back and forth. He settled in on the passenger side. Fat Freddy climbed in behind the wheel, said something to Tubby in the back, and then gave me the finger as he pulled away from the curb and drove up the street.

I sat at my desk, reading the sheet of paper a half-dozen times, wondering what I had done to make the Gods of Fortune hate me so much.

Twenty-one

I Googled both names on Tubby's list, Ollie Woods and Jake Butler. I'd never heard of either one of them. Ollie Woods had an Instagram account. There were a half-dozen photos of him in various bars. A polite description might use the word heavyset. I thought he just looked fat.

His dark hair appeared to be curly, trimmed on the sides, and longer on top. He was clean-shaven, and he had a tattoo on the left side of his neck. The tattoo might have been a bat, but I couldn't be sure. I found an assault conviction from 2018. He'd served twelve months in the St. Cloud reformatory and was released in the summer of 2019.

From the photo I found on Jake Butler's Facebook site, I guessed he was at least ten years older than Ollie Woods. He was lean in the photo. His face appeared lined, and he conveyed a sense of permanent unpleasantness. My initial reaction suggested he wasn't the sort of guy you'd give a hard time to.

Butler had been arrested more than a few times. Two driving under the influence charges, violation of a restraining order, felony theft, and drug possession. He sounded charming.

I phoned Ollie Woods first. He answered with, "Yeah?" I could hear music playing in the background and maybe someone talking. Of course, he could have just been parked in front of a TV.

"I'd like to speak with Ollie Woods, please."

"Who are you?"

"My name is Dev Haskell. I'm—"

"Whatever you're selling, I ain't interested. So you can kiss my—"

"Mr. Gustafson asked me to call you."

"Gustafson, he's got an open slot for me? Look, let him know I had nothing to do with—"

"I'm wondering if we could meet. I'd like to talk with you."

"Umm, yeah, I guess we could. Don't take this personal or anything, but I'd prefer if we met in someplace that's public."

"Yeah, I'm fine with that. In fact, that's probably better than you having to drive to my office."

"You got that part right. Since I can't drive right now. Still recovering from that bastard shooting me last month."

I guessed that was a result of the robbery. "You tell me when and where, and I'll meet you there."

"You know Tin Cups?" Woods said.

"Tin Cups? Out on Rice street?"

"Yeah, I'm here just about every day. Wanted to get a good seat for tonight, karaoke night."

Karaoke night? I checked the time on my phone. It was coming up to 11:00 in the morning. "Tell you what, Ollie. How about I show up in a half-hour, and I'll buy you lunch?"

"Yeah, that'll be great. I'll see you then, and please tell Mr. Gustafson I'm ready to go back to work for him."

"Yeah, I'll be sure to pass that on," I said and hung up. Poor Ollie sounded desperate. I took Morton for a quick walk around the block. I left a note for Louie, tossed Morton a biscuit, and drove over to Tin Cups. It's a neighborhood bar and restaurant that's been in operation for decades. I'd been in the place a half-dozen times. The neighborhood, like much of the city, had fallen on some hard times. There was a gunfight in the parking lot maybe two years ago. Over thirty shots were fired. Fortunately, no one was hurt, which might say something about the shooters.

I pulled into the lot, looked around the parking lot before I stepped out, and hurried inside. The place wasn't quite half-full, but then it was a weekday. I spotted Ollie almost immediately. Given his size, he was hard to miss. He was seated in a booth, literally taking up the entire side of the booth. He wore a white sport shirt with a gray Tin Cups logo over the left breast. The logo was basically a tin cup set at a forty-five-degree angle like it was ready to pour. The words 'Tin Cups' were written in white across the gray cup.

"Ollie Woods?" I asked.

He looked up at me, took a sip from his beer, and said, "You the guy that called me?"

"Yeah, Dev Haskell. Mr. Gustafson sent me."

He smiled at that last line and said, "Grab a seat."

I slid into the booth and looked at the incredibly large individual across from me. I had guessed his weight at maybe three hundred pounds based on the Instagram photo. Now that I saw him in person, I increased that estimate to four hundred pounds. The neck tattoo was indeed a bat but a bat with crossed eyes. I wondered if that was intentional or a mistake but decided not to ask.

"So, Ollie, Mr. Gustafson wants to know how you're doing. How's the recovery coming?"

"It's coming. Fortunately, that prick that shot me didn't hit anything vital. Still, it ain't a hell of a lot of fun getting shot in the ass."

'Impossible target to miss,' I thought and, for just a brief second, I had a picture of Maddie's perfect target in my mind.

"You were working over on Payne Avenue, weren't you?"

Ollie nodded, shaking his three chins. "Yeah, I worked there every night. Once we closed, I'd lock up and run the receipts over to the Midway district. You know, the office over there."

I nodded, pretending to know where he meant.

"I never had a problem before. It was just like any other night, the usual bunch of players. No surprises, everyone betting. Things had pretty much shut down by about 2:00 in the morning. No one was playing blackjack or throwing dice. Six guys were left playing Texas Hold'em. They were regulars, played for maybe another hour, and were out of there by three. The dealer left maybe twenty minutes after that. I made sure everything was put away. I checked the security cameras to see if anyone was around outside."

"No sign of anyone?"

"Nothing. Just like every other night, I placed all the cash in the bank bag. My car was in the attached garage. The door was down and locked, like always. I unlocked my car, hit the button to raise the garage door, and all of a sudden, some bastard is behind me wearing one of them black balaclava things. He presses a gun against the back of my head and tells me to drop the bag and walk to the front of the car."

"And that's when he shoots you?"

"No, I already told this shit to Tub—er, Mr. Gus-tafson. I told the guy he'd better get out of there before he finds himself in real trouble. He takes a couple steps back. I thought maybe he was gonna leave when, all of a sudden, boom! The bastard shoots me in the ass. Hurt like a son-of-a-bitch, let me tell you."

"If the door was locked, how did he get in there?"

"That's the big question. Well, that and who the hell was he? Other than catching the balaclava out of the corner of my eye, I never really saw him. I couldn't tell you what he was wearing or how tall he was. It all happened so damn fast, and once he shot me, I was completely focused on that."

"Describe this place to me. It's over on Payne Avenue?"

"Yeah. The building is about a hundred years old. It's brick. Five stories. It was built as some kind of factory. I think they made windows and doors or something. We're located in the back of the building on the ground floor. We've got a separate entrance, a guard at the door, and no access to the rest of the building."

"What about the garage?"

"It's just one stall. Like I told you, there's a door from the gambling room that's always locked. I got the key for that, and then there's the garage door, and that's always locked. I got the only garage door opener, and it's in my car. My car is always locked."

"Did he go out the garage door?"

"No, he went back into the gambling room."

"Get you guys something for lunch, Ollie?" an attractive server suddenly said. She had an empty tray under her arm and held an order pad with a pen. She cracked a wad of pink gum about every other second.

"Give me my usual, Ginger."

"What about you?" she said. She blew a small pink bubble that popped, and she went back to cracking the gum.

"You got just a cheeseburger and some fries?"

She nodded, cracked her gum, and said, "Anything from the bar?"

I shook my head, and she headed over to the bar. Her figure looked just as inviting from the rear.

"I'm thinking of asking her out," Ollie said as she strutted away. "She told me she likes to gamble. I even invited her to the club, but she never showed. She goes to someplace that's really a dive. I heard she lets you score on the first night. Just waiting till I'm all healed up and then who knows…"

Four-hundred-pound Ollie rolling over on little Ginger. I was sure she'd be thrilled. "You think this guy could have been a customer? Maybe he hid somewhere like a restroom, a kitchen, or someplace until everyone left."

"I didn't see anything like that. There's just one bathroom. It's small with nowhere to hide. A couple of the guys playing cards used it as they left. There's no kitchen. The bar is actually just a dining room table, and I get all the drinks. Not like you could hide underneath the table."

"Anyone in there that was a first-timer?"

He shook his head, and I focused in on his chins, shaking from side to side. "No, and even if they were, anyone in there is vetted by Mr. Gustafson. You can't just show up with a bunch of pals. The business is gambling. Blackjack, Texas Hold'em, and we got a craps table. That's it."

Ginger arrived carrying her tray. "Cheeseburger and fries for you, darling," she said, setting the plate in front of me. "And two Minnie Tinnies for you, Ollie," she said, setting two platters down in front of Ollie. Each platter held five moderate-sized hamburgers surrounding a pile of French fries. "I'll be back with your beer in just a second, Ollie. You sure I can't get you anything, honey?"

"Maybe just a water," I said.

For the next half-hour, Ollie described the various clients to me through a mouthful of food. He ordered another beer and an ice cream sunday for dessert. I came away with the idea that the only involvement he played in the robbery was that of the victim.

I paid the forty dollar tab, gave Ginger a tip, and hoped she survived a night out with Ollie Woods. As I climbed out of the booth, Ollie groaned, grunted his way out of the booth, and headed to the restroom. I noticed he had been sitting on the largest foam donut cushion I'd ever seen. It was purple, had to be three feet across, and looked like it was squished and was never going to recover.

Twenty-two

I placed a call to Jake Butler and got dumped into his voicemail. "Yeah, Jake, I'm calling on behalf of Mr. Gustafson. My name is Dev Haskell. Mr. Gustafson asked me to talk with you. I'm wondering if we could meet sometime tomorrow, maybe for lunch. I'll buy. Give me a call back as soon as you can. Thank you."

Hopefully, by offering to buy lunch, he got the idea we could meet in a public place, and he'd be safe. Tubby had earned the reputation as someone you never wanted to cross, so I was sure this guy would be returning my call.

I headed back to the office. Louie was working away on his computer when I walked in. "How's it going?" he said without looking up.

"Okay, I guess. How about you?"

"Fine if you don't go into detail," he said, and so I didn't.

I emptied the pot into my coffee mug, turned off the burner, and then settled in at my desk. I made some quick notes on my meeting with Ollie Woods and phoned Tubby Gustafson.

"Mr. Gustafson's office," a guy answered, not Tubby.

"Yeah, this is Dev Haskell. I'm working on an investigation for Mr. Gustafson. I'd like to talk to him, please."

"And what is this regarding?"

I actually pulled the phone from my ear and looked at it for a moment. "I'd like to talk to him about the investigation he has me doing."

"One moment, I'll see if he's available."

It was three or four minutes before Tubby finally came on the line. I had no doubt he was involved in something important like getting his back massaged by the two Asian women who had the misfortune of that daily task.

"What did you learn, Haskell?" Tubby growled.

"I interviewed Ollie Woods this morning, sir. He described the circumstances of the robbery, such as they were. I would actually like to get into the area and look around. The way he described the place, it sounded next to impossible for anyone to sneak in or hide somewhere. That said, this guy apparently appeared out of nowhere in a locked garage, took the evening's proceeds, and shot Mr. Woods."

"So, you've gotten a taste of what we're up against?"

"Yes, sir."

"When were you planning to go over there?"

"I could go anytime this afternoon or this evening. The afternoon would be better. I'd like to look around, and I wouldn't want to disturb any of your clients this evening."

"I can have someone meet you there in thirty minutes."

"I'll be there. Thank…" Tubby had already hung up.

"Your close personal friend Tubby Gustafson?" Louie said and stopped typing for a moment.

"Yeah, someone knocked off a couple of his gambling clubs, and he wants me to find out who it was."

"Good luck with that."

"Yeah, you aren't kidding. I gotta go meet someone at this place in a bit. I'll drop Morton off at home."

"He can stay here if you want. I'm around for the rest of the afternoon."

"Oh, thanks, but I have no idea how long this is going to take, so I'll drop him off at home."

I clipped the leash onto Morton's collar, and we headed out the door. I hurried home and pulled into the driveway. As we stepped inside the house, I called, "Maddie?"

"Back here in the kitchen, Dev."

We walked back, and she was at the stove frying something.

"Everything okay?" she asked.

"Yeah, I've got to run and look at a building, and then I'll be back. The Airbnb couple is coming in later this afternoon."

"Anything I should tell them if you're not here?"

"Only that I'll be back shortly. They can settle in upstairs and grab dinner at one of the restaurants on the street. Maybe toss a couple of towels on the bed. I'll probably be back before they arrive. I better run. Any problems, Morton will sort them out for you."

"Don't be late for dinner," she said and smiled.

I hopped back in the car and drove over to the Payne Avenue building. As I drove to the rear of the building, the place was just as Ollie had described, a five-story brick building that was originally built as a factory. There wasn't a parking lot, just an alley, so I pulled alongside the back of the building.

Once I parked, I waited another half-hour for some idiot to show up. Since the temperature was hovering around zero degrees, I had to keep my car running. I was about to call Tubby when the guy finally pulled up. I recognized him as one of Tubby's crew but couldn't recall his name.

He pulled in behind me and gave a wave. I turned my car off and followed him up to the steel door. I noted there were four cameras around the back of the building. One just above the door, another maybe ten feet above that, and two more on either end of the building aimed at the narrow alley along the back.

"Hi, hope you didn't have to wait long. It was a bitch getting the keys and the code," he said.

"Not a problem," I said.

The steel door was three feet above the alley with no steps leading up to it. He reached up over his head, slipped the key in the lock, and unlocked the door. As soon as he pushed the steel door open, an alarm began to sound. We climbed inside. He read from a slip of paper and punched in a six-digit code. A moment later, the alarm stopped. There was another steel door, and he inserted a key in the lock and pushed that door open.

We stepped into one large room that was pretty much the way Ollie had described it. Nice enough, but nothing fancy. There was a craps table off to the right and a blackjack table off to the left. Straight ahead and further back was a large round table with eight chairs positioned around it. I figured that would be for the Texas Hold'em game. I noticed there weren't any chips, cards, or dice on the tables.

Right next to the door was a Formica counter with a computer and four black and white TV screens displaying the images from the cameras mounted on the outside of the building. At the end of the counter were stacks of blue covered books. I walked over and opened one of the books. It was a church hymnal.

"What's with this?" I asked.

The guy smiled. "If there's ever a raid, everyone is here for choir practice."

Vintage Tubby Gustafson.

Just like Ollie had described, there was a table up against the wall with liquor bottles and glasses. A small refrigerator, maybe three feet high, was positioned at one end of the table.

Back by the Texas Hold'em table, there were two doors. I walked over and opened a door. It was the bathroom. A toilet, sink, and a mirror on the wall, certainly no place to hide. I went to turn the knob on the other door, but it was locked.

"Is this the garage?"

"I guess. I've only been here once before, just dropping some stuff off." He moved his keyring and grabbed a key with a red plastic keycap. "This should open it," he said, not sounding all that sure as he inserted the key in the doorknob.

I heard the lock click, and he pulled the door open. We had to take three steps down to enter the garage. As we entered, the light came on, apparently activated by a motion detector. The garage was just large enough for one car, but that was it. Not so much as a broom or a snow shovel leaned against the walls. I walked down to the garage door. It was locked on either side with a deadbolt system that could be opened by hand or electronically. I remembered that Ollie had said he unlocked the door from inside his car.

"Not much to see," the guy said. "Whoever heads up security gets to park in here."

"There's more than one security guy?"

"There's four at this location. One watches the cameras, and two drive the van and then the head guy. He gets drinks for everybody here and makes sure everyone behaves themselves"

"That's what Ollie Woods was doing, right?"

He nodded. "I think that's the guy's name. He's a big fat guy."

"Yeah. Hey, back up for a minute. You said two guys drive the van? What's that?"

"The van? Oh, see, none of the customers actually know where this place is. They park in a ramp downtown. We know who they are, and they have to request a ride. So, we know when they'll be at the ramp. The van picks them up and drives them over here."

"Can't they see where they're being taken?

"The van's paneled, and the front seats are sectioned off so they can't see out the windshield. When they want to leave, the van gives them a ride back to the parking ramp. When they arrive or leave, the van backs up to the door, and they step into the van so they never really see the exterior of the building."

"And, no offense, but people put up with that?"

"Actually, it gives them a sense that they are in a very unique place. Obviously, the guys that come here, in fact the guys that go to all of our clubs, are serious gamblers. They're not going to waste their time at the Minnesota casinos. That's for the tourists. Same thing with going out to Vegas, although I know a number of our clients do go out there for the occasional gambling tournament."

"But they're loaded into the back of a paneled van?"

"Well, there are comfortable seats and an attractive hostess serving drinks. Anything else you want to take a look at?"

"No, I think that pretty well does it."

He climbed the steps back into the main room. As I followed him, it suddenly dawned on me that the garage was heated. I stepped back and looked for the heating vent. It was up in the ceiling, about two feet by three feet in size.

"Does Mr. Gustafson own the entire building?" I asked as he closed the door to the garage and locked it.

He nodded and said, "Yeah, I think he owns all the buildings where our facilities are located. That eliminates all sorts of potential problems for us."

"I'm sure it does. Well, thanks for your time," I said and held out my hand.

He squeezed it in a vice-like grip.

"Are you going to report back to Mr. Gustafson?" I asked.

"Of course, he always insists," he said and gave me a cold smile.

"Well, tell him this was very informative, and I'll call him in the morning."

"I don't know how well you know him," the guy said as we walked through the first steel door, and he closed it behind us. He placed his key in the door and locked it. "Just a little advice. Don't screw with Gustafson on this. He's pretty pissed off."

"Every time he has to deal with me, he seems to be pissed off," I said.

He smiled at that and then unlocked the exterior door. "Go ahead and take off. I've got to input the code and then lock the door. You got any questions, Mr. Gustafson's who you should talk to." With that, he pulled the exterior door open, and I jumped down three feet to the alley. I was in my car driving down the alley when he jumped out the door, pulled it closed, and then locked it. He stood and watched me until I turned at the corner and disappeared.

I drove home and pulled in front of the house, parking on the street. I figured I'd leave the driveway for my Airbnb guests, and if they wanted, they could pull into the garage.

As I walked up the sidewalk and onto the porch, Morton watched me out the front window. He hopped off the couch as I reached for the front door and met me just inside.

"I'm back, Maddie," I called.

"In the kitchen," she replied.

Morton and I walked back to the kitchen. The closer we got, the better it smelled. Maddie was seated at the counter watching the news on TV.

"Did our guests show up?" I asked.

"Not yet. I placed two towels and washcloths on the bed. And I turned the covers back, you know, like they do in hotels."

"Oh, yeah, good idea. Thanks, I never would have thought of that. Say, what do you have going for dinner? It smells delicious."

The doorbell suddenly rang. Morton barked, and I said, "I bet that's our guests."

Twenty-three

I closed the kitchen door behind me so Morton wouldn't follow and hurried out to the front door. Sure enough, the guy at the door had a suitcase behind him. Their car, a black Toyota, was parked in the driveway, and the trunk was raised. I presumed the guy's wife or girlfriend was getting something out of the trunk.

"Hi," the guy said and smiled. "We rented your room for three nights."

"Nice to meet you. Dev Haskell is my name. Please come in and get out of the cold. Can I help bring something in from your car?"

"No, he can get it. Nice place you have here. Real nice."

The 'he can get it' wasn't lost on me. I figured they must be a gay couple, not that I cared. "Yeah, thanks. It's an older part of town, old for this part of the country. You're from Chicago?"

He nodded.

"The forecast is for cold weather, at least the rest of the week. They're talking well below zero. If you want, you can park in the garage. If nothing else, it'll save you the hassle of scraping the windows off in the morning."

"Oh, thanks, yeah, much appreciated," he said as his partner stepped onto the porch.

I opened the door and said, "Hey, get in here and out of the cold."

He smiled and stepped in, pulling a suitcase and what looked like a sleeping bag piled on top. He looked similar to his partner, about the same size and maybe a little older. He held out his hand. "Ethan Hoover," he said, and we shook hands.

"Dev Haskell," I said and turned to the first guy.

He grinned, held out his hand, and we shook as he said, "Wilmer Hoover, Dev. Nice to meet you. We're so glad you had a room available."

"Speaking of which, let me show you the room." As we climbed the stairs, I mentioned the bathroom. I mentioned that Maddie would be in the spare room, although I referred to her as Karen.

"Here's your room," I said, turning the skeleton key and unlocking the door. The bed covers were pulled back just as Maddie had described. The white towels and washcloths were stacked on the corner of the bed.

"The closet is empty. Feel free to hang clothes and jackets in there. I'll leave the garage door opener and keys to the front door on the end table next to the front door. If you like, I'd be happy to build a fire for you down in the front room."

"Thanks," Ethan said, "but it's been a long drive, and we have a number of appointments over the next three days we have to prepare for. We're ministers, and we'll be spreading the Lord's word."

"Please put me on your prayer list," I said.

"We noticed there is a restaurant across the street. Is it any good?"

"It's very good, Italian food. There's a chicken place a block to the right as you step out the door and another restaurant across the street from that. To the left, as you step out the door, in the next block there's a great burger place. There's a Sushi restaurant across the street and three more restaurants almost right next to those two. You guys drink coffee?"

They both nodded.

"I'll have it on tomorrow morning, about 6:30, along with some fruit and breakfast cereals. Karen and I will adjust to your bathroom times, so go ahead and shower whenever you want."

"Thanks, Dev. We're looking forward to our stay. Would you mind putting that garage door opener by the front door? I'll pull the car into the garage in just a moment," Ethan said.

"I'll do it right now," I said. I noticed that their jackets were still buttoned up, and I hoped the temperature I had the house set at, sixty-nine degrees, was comfortable enough for them. I was going to mention it and then decided against it. "I'll leave you to it. Just give a yell if you have any questions," I said. I closed the door behind me and headed down to the kitchen.

"How'd it go?" Maddie said as I stepped back into the kitchen.

"They seem like nice enough guys. Apparently, they're ministers up here from Chicago to spread the word. I'm going to grab the garage door opener from my car so they can park in the garage. Oh, and I referred to you as Karen, okay?"

"Yeah, that's perfect. Thanks for doing that."

"How was Morton?"

"He seemed fine. When you left, he stood by the door for a few minutes but then settled down."

I reached into the cookie jar and grabbed a biscuit. "Good boy, Morton," I said and tossed the biscuit to him. I hurried out to my car and grabbed the garage door opener. I left it on the small table next to the front door, along with a set of keys to the front door.

Maddie had cooked up a delicious chili for dinner. I had two helpings, and we just chatted and enjoyed each other's company. No mention was made of Colton Ferral or his mother, and Maddie seemed the most relaxed I'd seen her since the other night when she knocked on my door.

We sat in the den and watched three episodes of some romantic series Maddie enjoyed. We heard the ministers leave and then come back maybe an hour later, probably after dinner. At ten, we headed up to bed. Maddie went into the spare room and locked the door. I stretched out in my bed, hoping she might tiptoe in, no luck.

Twenty-four

I was up early the next morning. I shaved, took about a three-minute shower, and got dressed. Morton was curled up in front of Maddie's room and didn't so much as open an eye as I walked past. I turned on the coffee, set out three unopened boxes of cereal, arranged coffee mugs, cereal bowls, and filled a salad bowl with a half-dozen oranges.

I checked the Airbnb site for my next customer, nothing. I'd made twelve cups of coffee and was on my third when Morton wandered into the kitchen. Not a sound from Maddie or the ministers. I let Morton out and filled his food and water dishes.

Just as I let him back in, I heard someone upstairs in the shower. Maddie came into the kitchen a short time later. I poured a coffee for her and said, "Anything from our guests?"

She shook her head and said, "No, I haven't heard a sound."

"The power of silent prayer," I said. We ate a couple of pieces of toast. I made oatmeal for both of us. We each ate an orange, and finally, I said, "I'm going to have to go to work. They seem like nice guys, but I'm going to leave Morton here with you just in case."

"Morton? What do you expect him to do?"

"Actually, nothing. But I don't want you alone."

"Oh, that's sweet, Dev. We'll be fine. If this damn temperature ever gets above zero, I'll take him for a walk."

"Well, then you're safe for the better part of the next week. We're in the deep freeze at least that long if not longer."

I diddled around for a minute or two, hoping for a kiss, and finally went down to the office. Louie wasn't in, although a full pot of coffee was on, so he must have already been here. I filled a mug, and no sooner did I sit down than my phone rang.

"Haskell Investigations," was how I answered.

"Yeah, I need to talk to Dev Haskell," a guy said.

"You got him."

"This is Jake Butler. I got a call from you yester-day."

Tubby's other guy who was robbed. "Oh, yeah. Thanks for returning my call, Jake. Mr Gustafson asked me—"

"First of all, I doubt he asked. He probably yelled at you. I've told him every way I can think of that I was shot in the knee. There wasn't a damn thing I could do. What's he want now?"

I understood where he was coming from with regard to Tubby. "What he wants is for me to find out who did this. I'd like to talk to you and hear your side of the story. I spoke with Ollie Woods yesterday and—"

"Yeah, I know. I phoned him last night. He said you were okay."

"High praise," I said.

Butler didn't seem to get the joke. "I'm still recovering from the gunshot. Bastard shot me in the knee. I had surgery two weeks ago. I was hoping I could get a knee replacement, but the damage to nerves and shit is so extensive I am just plain screwed. Damn thing still hurts like a bitch. You want to come over to my place to see me this morning, that'll be fine. I don't want to go anywhere, and I got a physical therapist coming here to torture me this afternoon."

"Yeah, I can do that. What's your address?" He gave me his address, and I told him I'd be over in the next half-hour.

I was somewhat familiar with the neighborhood. I knew a kid who lived there thirty years ago. It was originally a baby boomer neighborhood. All the houses were built in the early 1950s and immediately filled with young families. My pal's family was actually the second wave of folks arriving during the 80s and 90s. I guessed Butler's neighborhood was on the third or fourth wave by now.

His house was a gray rambler with white trim in desperate need of a paint job. At least the sidewalk was shoveled. I parked in front, climbed over a snowbank onto the sidewalk and rang the doorbell.

A big guy answered the door a minute later. If he was having knee problems, he certainly didn't show it. He was muscular, three or four inches taller than me, and apparently had never learned to smile.

"Yeah," he growled as a greeting.

"I'm here to see Jake Butler. He's expecting me."

"Name?"

"Haskell, Dev Haskell."

He nodded, unhooked the storm door, and stepped back so I could enter.

He closed the door once I stepped in and said, "Stick your arms out so I can pat you down."

I figured it would be the wise move not to object. I held my arms out, and he patted me down. Not what I would call gentle, but then again, if I thought Tubby was mad at me, I'd probably have someone doing the same thing.

"Okay, he's in that room," he said and indicated a door just off the kitchen with a flick of his finger.

I walked into the room. Jake Butler was sitting in a stretched-out brown leather recliner. His left leg was wrapped in gauze with a small pillow positioned on either side of his knee. "Haskell?" he said as he picked up a remote and turned off the TV.

"Yeah, nice to meet you, Jake. How's the knee?"

He shook his head. "Like I told you on the phone, it hurts like a bitch." He reached over for the crystal glass on the side table, a dark brown liquid with ice cubes. I figured it wasn't iced tea, and it was only 10:25 in the morning.

He set the glass down and looked at me. "So what did you want to know, besides the fact I'm basically screwed for life?"

Twenty-five

Butler went on to tell me about getting shot. Just like Ollie Woods' shooting, someone suddenly appeared from behind. The difference here was that the shooter didn't say anything. The first clue Butler had someone was behind him was getting shot in the knee. The shot was close range. Butler said his trousers had powder burns from a small-caliber weapon.

"All I know is I got shot in the back of my leg. The shot blew my kneecap out, and I was on the ground screaming in pain. I can tell you, without a doubt, it was the worst pain I've ever felt. I can't describe the shooter. It could have been a midget or a guy in a wheelchair. I have no idea. All I know is that was the most God-awful thing I've ever had done to me. Whoever it was, they disappeared with the bag of money I was carrying."

"Can you describe the bag to me?"

"Yeah, it's just a standard bag. The kind a bank uses for its night deposits. There's a zipper across the top with a little lock on it. The thing was brown leather. After Ollie Woods was shot a couple nights before, we added a tracking device to the bag. Not that it did any good. It was found about a block away in a parking lot. That suggests to me someone probably knew it was there before they even opened the bag."

"Did you hear a car drive away, footsteps running off, or—"

"Were you paying any attention to what I just told you? I was on the ground bleeding all over the place, screaming my ass off. Did I hear a car? You gotta be kidding! Christ, they could have honked the damn horn, and I wouldn't have heard it. It could have been one person or five guys. I got no idea." He reached over and took another sip of his drink. "The son-of-a-bitch took off in my car. They found it a couple hours later. It was only a block away sitting in a parking lot next to the tracking device."

"They have security cameras watching the exterior and the underground parking area?" I was thinking of the large heat vent in the ceiling of the attached garage where Ollie Woods was shot.

"Yeah, three cameras just covering the underground parking area and four more on the exterior of the building. Whoever did it has to show up on the security tapes, but no one has said anything to me about it."

"I haven't been to this place yet. I'll call Mr. Gustafson and check it out later today or tomorrow. What can you tell me about the actual club?"

"Well, Gustafson owns the entire building, all three stories. First floor is shops. Second and third floors are rentals units. He has a close relationship with the tenants."

"I'm not following," I said.

"Everyone there is pretty much employed by him in some way. No one living there would be stupid enough to do this. The club is actually in the basement. It used to be a Chinese restaurant, I think. That was years ago before Gustafson took it over."

"What about the customers?"

"You mean the club members? First of all, they pay a membership fee. They're vetted by Gustafson's staff of accountants. They have to make an appointment to attend. They can't just show up. Even if they wanted to show up, they wouldn't know where the place is."

"They get transported in a paneled van?"

"That's the place Ollie Woods works in. This club is a little more upscale. The members arrive in a limo. The windows have shades that are drawn so they can't see out of the limo. They're picked up at a specific time and at a specific location. There's a hostess providing drinks and, umm, maybe some additional service in the limo, depending. The club is for the heavy hitters. These guys are paying twenty grand just to become a club member and then an annual fee after that. They can't see out of the limo. It drives into the private underground parking area, pulls in front of the door, and then they get out."

"And this used to be a restaurant?"

"Yeah, but in those days, it had an outside door. You'd just walk down some stairs and into the place. This was in the years before handicap access became a big deal."

"So it's a very private experience?"

"Yeah, open three nights a week, Thursday through Saturday nights. Gustafson had the place soundproofed. I think you could shoot a cannon off down there, and no one in the apartments above would ever hear it."

"You serve food or anything?"

"Nope," he said and took another sip from his drink. "It's strictly business. Cameras are watching the exterior of the place twenty-four hours a day, seven days a week. There are four security guys, including me. Two or three hostesses serve the drinks depending on the number of reservations for any particular night."

"Business is good?"

"Business is always very good. There's usually a waiting list to get in on any given night. Members have to walk through a metal detector to enter. No one ever got out of hand. If anyone misbehaves, they would have been removed immediately. If that happened twice, they'd be out for good, no ifs, ands, or buts. The business is gambling. Gustafson is making a ton of money there, and God help anyone who messes with it. If he ever finds out who's involved in this, it ain't going to be pretty."

"Where exactly were you when you were shot?"

"I'd just left the club. Locked it up and was going to my car in the underground parking. In fact, I'd just opened the driver's door when I was shot."

"So they were in the underground parking area?"

"Yeah."

"And from what you're saying, the members have no idea where this place is, let alone how to get into it."

"That's right, they wouldn't have a clue. It's part of the hype about the place. You know, that it's so special and restrictive. Average folks aren't going to know about it, let alone ever get inside. I ain't naming names, but we got politicians and big ass heavy hitters in the business world. Some sports figures and an occasional movie star show up from time to time. You'd be amazed who's a member."

"And you've never had any problems before this?" I asked and nodded toward his extended leg resting in the recliner.

"Hell no. Gustafson runs a tight ship. My guess? It almost can't be one of the members. It has to be someone on the staff. All I can say is, I pity the bastard when Gustafson gets ahold of him. And, eventually, he will."

"Anything else you can think of?" I asked.

Butler shook his head and drained his glass. "You ever find out who did this, if there's anything left of them when Gustafson is finished, I'd love to deal with them."

"I'll be sure to keep that in mind, Jake. Hope your recovery continues," I said and extended my hand.

"Recovery? Are you kidding? I just got royally screwed," he said. He ignored my hand, picked up his empty glass, and stared at it for a moment.

"I'll let myself out," I said and walked out of the room. The big guy who let me in was seated at the kitchen counter watching some cooking show. It looked like he was taking notes.

"Thanks, I'm finished," I said.

He slid off his stool and hurried to the front door. He unlocked the doorknob, removed the security chain, and released the door lock latch. He opened the door, un-hooked the storm door, and stepped back so I could get out.

He didn't bother to say goodbye or wish me well. I headed to my car.

Twenty-six

I chatted with Louie for a minute when I got back to the office and then phoned Tubby Gustafson. The same voice as yesterday answered, "Mr. Gustafson's office."

"This is Dev Haskell. I'd like to speak with Mr. Gustafson."

"Is there something I could help you with?"

"Mr. Gustafson told me he'd kill anyone I talked to. Do you really think you can help me?"

"One moment, please," he said and quickly put me on hold.

Louie looked over at me, and I just shook my head.

"What do you have for me?" Tubby growled by way of a greeting.

"I just finished meeting with Jake Butler, sir. He didn't have much information. The night of the robbery, his attention was pretty much directed at what was left of his knee after he'd been shot."

"I suppose this means you want to examine the club."

"Exactly, sir. Both Butler and Woods seemed to think there had to be someone on the inside involved. Based on their descriptions of your security setup, I would almost have to agree."

There was a long pause before Tubby said, "I'll have someone call you later this afternoon." He hung up before I could respond.

I set my phone down, and Louie said, "Sounds like it was a charming conversation."

"Two of his employees were shot, and the evening proceeds from two of his joints were stolen. I've talked to both victims now, and the setup they describe, all the security, the procedures they have to follow, it's really amazing. They've both suggested it was probably someone on the inside who did this. What kind of nutcase would think it was a good idea to cross Tubby Gustafson?"

"I didn't hear anything on the news about this," Louie said.

"It wasn't on the news. Cops weren't involved. All I can say is, someone out there is living very close to the edge. I can't seem—" My phone rang, an unidentified caller.

"Haskell investigations."

"Dev Haskell?"

"Yeah."

"We met yesterday. I gave you that deluxe tour."

"Yeah, thanks again. I'm sorry, but I forgot your name."

"No, you didn't. I never told you. I just got a call from Mr. Gustafson. I'm supposed to show you around the club this afternoon. You've got the address?"

"Yeah, he gave me both addresses the other day when he came to my office. He and Fat Fred, err umm, I mean Freddy Zimmerman."

"That's okay, I get it. I'll meet you at the club at 1:00. There's a parking lot on the east side of the building. Pull in there, and I'll pick you up."

"I'll be sitting in my car. I'm driving a—"

"You're driving a black, Crown Victoria Police Interceptor, license number…" he repeated my license number. "I'll find you. Just don't keep me waiting," he said and hung up before I could tell him not to keep me waiting.

My phone showed the time as 11:30. "Louie, you interested in grabbing some lunch?"

"What are you thinking?"

"I'm thinking it's freezing cold out, so I'll run up to Rooster's and get two pulled pork BBQ sandwiches. You can pay for the sandwiches and stay nice and warm here."

Louie seemed to think about that for half a second before he pulled out his wallet and gave me twenty-five bucks. "That'll cover the food and a tip."

"You stay comfortable. Maybe put a fresh pot of coffee on while I'm gone. I'll be back in ten minutes." I pulled on my jacket and hurried up the street to Rooster's. Thankfully, I beat the noon-hour line. I was back in the office fifteen minutes later. I set a Styrofoam tray on Louie's desk and the other tray on mine. Then set about making a fresh pot of coffee since Louie had neglected his duty.

We ate and chatted. Louie inhaled his sandwich and fries in about four minutes. I ate at a more refined pace. I drove over to the building that housed Tubby's private club and parked on the east side of the building.

Just like Jake Butler had described, the place was a three-story building with shops on the first floor, a laundromat, an insurance office, a second-hand clothes store, and a bookstore. The second and third floors had the look of apartments; a large picture window, two bedroom windows with a smaller frosted glass window that was obviously the bathroom, sat between the bedroom windows. Looking at the building, I figured there were probably twelve units on each floor for a total of twenty-four apartments.

One o'clock came and went. The temperature was somewhere in the minus range, so even though I was parked in the sun, once I turned my car off, it started getting pretty damn cold after about four or five minutes. I let my car run until it warmed up then turned it off three separate times before a gray SUV pulled behind me and honked. I turned the car off for the fourth time, climbed out, locked it, and got into the SUV.

"We'll pull into the underground parking just like the limo does. The only difference is you can see where we're going," the guy said. No 'hello,' no 'sorry I'm twenty minutes late,' no 'nice to see you again.'

I didn't really care. His car was nice and warm. We drove out of the parking lot and down the alley. He pushed a button on a garage door opener attached to the sun visor on the driver's side. The gray garage door, the same color as the stucco, began to rise. I noticed that along with two security cameras and a spotlight over the garage door, there were two more security cameras at either end of the building.

We drove down a ramp into an area that was large enough to make a U-turn easily. "The limo your club members arrive in, how big is it?" I asked.

"It comfortably holds twelve passengers, including the hostess. There's a driver and another security guy in the front. The hostess and passengers are belted onto bench seats. Refreshments and 'services' are provided."

"Can they make a U-turn in here?"

"They pull in just like we are," he said. He drove down the ramp and stopped at about a forty-five-degree angle to the front door. "Once the garage door is closed, they let the passengers out. Depending on schedules, the hostess may or may not exit. Once everyone has entered the club, the driver reverses, driving back and forth until the limo is able to head back up the ramp. I think they can accomplish that in three or four maneuvers, going back and forth. They either leave to pick up more members, or they lock the limo and go inside."

I shook my head and said, "I'm not sure I'd ever want to drive one of those things."

"It's a learned skill," he said, then backed the SUV up, so it was facing the ramp leading up to the garage door. He turned off his SUV, locked the vehicle once we were out, and headed into the club.

Just like the place we were at yesterday, there were two steel doors, only here, both steel doors were painted in a woodgrain pattern. He punched in a six-digit code that turned off the alarm and then unlocked the second door.

"Is this the only entrance?" I asked.

He nodded as we stepped into a large, elegantly paneled room with plush carpet on the floor. A bar was in the far corner with a half-dozen stools in front of it. There were six tables throughout the room. A craps table and a roulette table were closest to the door. Behind them were three blackjack tables, and off to the corner, another large round table with eight chairs for Texas Hold'em.

"Did I hear correctly that this is only open Thursday, Friday, and Saturday?"

He nodded and said, "Mr. Gustafson found that we make just as much profit over the three days as we did when we were open for all seven. I mentioned before that anyone who is at one of these facilities is a very serious gambler. The individuals who come here have already paid twenty thousand dollars just for the privilege of entering. The members are super serious and obviously very wealthy."

"Amazing, and by the looks of the place, you have a pretty nice bar as opposed to bottles lined up on a table."

"Yeah, drinks are free, and they're served by our lovely hostesses, but I'm unaware of anyone ever being over-served. There's too much at stake financially for someone to throw caution to the wind like that."

"Does anyone ever win?"

"Mr. Gustafson earns his profit by providing the opportunity to gamble. He's adamant that there is never, ever any cheating by staff. Note the security cameras over each gaming table. Same thing you'd see in any lawful casino, except that these are the latest with HD resolution from twenty feet away."

He was right. Every table was centered beneath an 'eye in the sky' camera.

I looked around but didn't see any security screen monitors. "Where do they watch the games?"

"The security room is behind the bar. Let me show you," he said, and we walked toward the bar. The bar was U-shaped, looked to be mahogany, and had a total of eight stools arranged around it. The walls on either side of the bar were paneled. He walked up to one of the panels, pushed it, and it sprung open about four inches. He pushed it open, and we stepped into a small room. He flicked a switch on the wall, and a ceiling light flashed on. Three of the walls had counters attached to them, and a series of security screens and laptops were lined up on the counters. Five chairs were pushed in against the counters.

"Every table is monitored," he said.

"So, you've got five people in here, four or five hostesses, four or five security people, the drivers. There must be a staff of close to thirty working here. Can that even be profitable?"

"Oh yeah, very profitable. Remember, everyone who sets foot in here has already paid twenty grand just for the privilege. They're going to try to make that back and more. It's how they think. It's also why we're as successful as we are."

"I guess. Are there bathrooms somewhere?"

"Let me show you," he said. We left the monitor room and headed to the opposite side behind the roulette table.

There were two doors for two bathrooms. Just like yesterday, they were clean, but aside from the toilet, sink, and mirror, that's all that was in there. I knocked on the walls and ceilings. They were all solid.

"Anything else I can show you?"

I shook my head and said, "No. Thanks for the tour and for letting me interrupt your day. You seem to know more about this place than the facility we looked at yesterday."

He nodded, smiled, and didn't say anything. He dropped me off at my car a few minutes later. On my way back to the office, I pulled over to the curb as two squad cars raced past me with sirens blaring and lights flashing. In another mile, I took a right and headed down Randolph Avenue to the office. I made some more notes about Tubby's gambling locations, read them over, and didn't come up with any new ideas. Eventually, I headed home.

Twenty-seven

I parked out on the street in front of my house. There was no telling if my guest ministers were here or not. I opened the door, and Morton was right there, wagging his tail and hitting his head against my knee for a head scratch. I gave him a good scratch as I called Maddie's name.

"Back in the kitchen, Dev."

Morton and I walked back. Once again, the room smelled delicious.

"Hey, I could get very used to this. What are you cooking?"

"I just put a lasagna in the oven. We can have a glass of wine if you'd like. It will be a bit before the lasagna is ready."

"Anything with the Hoovers?" She gave me a funny look. "Our Airbnb guests."

"Oh, yeah, sorry. They hurried in the house just before three. Ran upstairs, and I haven't heard anything since."

"Must be involved in some long prayers. Hopefully, they'll mention us."

"How was your day?"

"Okay. I had to interview a crabby guy who was robbed and then actually toured an illegal gambling site. Man, I'll tell you. You want a red or a white wine?" She seemed to be staring off into the distance. "Maddie? Earth to Maddie. Maddie?"

"Hmm, what? Oh sorry I was just thinking of something, and I, I should put this away, I guess," she said and quickly gathered up a pile of papers scattered across the counter.

"What's all that stuff?"

"Oh, nothing, just some notes and things I was going over. I should probably put them away and get the counter set for dinner." She tapped the stack of papers on the counter a couple of times and tried to hurry past me.

I took hold of her arm and said, "Maddie, hold on for a minute, sit down, and let's talk."

"There's really nothing to talk about, Dev, and none of this concerns you."

"I think I'm respectfully going to disagree with you. Take a seat and let's talk. Two heads are better than one. Even if one of them is me."

Fortunately, she smiled, waited a moment, and then sat down.

"Now, answer my important question. Would you like a red or a white wine?"

She seemed to relax a little and said, "A red would be nice."

I pulled a bottle from the rack, a Sean Minor Pinot Noir. I twisted the cap off and said, "I suppose we should let it breathe." I took two glasses from the kitchen cabinet, set them on the counter. "There, it should have breathed long enough by now." I filled a glass and slid it in front of her and then filled my glass and raised it in a toast, "To your safe return."

She smiled as a tear ran down her cheek and said, "Thank you for not yelling, calling me a stupid bitch, and for not hitting me."

"I would never do that, Maddie. You're safe here. Now, can we be honest with one another and you tell me about those papers? If we're going to figure a way out from the Ferrals, I really do need to know what's involved. You want to tell me what you've got there?"

She wiped the tear from her cheek and pushed the papers toward me. "I've spent the past year putting these lists together. It's the people who work with, or for, Colton and his mother, along with some of their plans. I've got addresses of some business locations, drug houses, two or three drug labs. When you mentioned that illegal gambling place, that sounded like something they would be interested in. Desdemona had a line on some big wheel in town who was making a lot of money, and they knew someone who was working for him. They were planning to take over the guy's business. I just don't have any idea what the business was."

"Did you ever hear any names mentioned?"

"You mean like who was running that business? No, usually they were talking about the people in their organization. Any time I heard someone's name, I wrote it down." She rifled through the stack of papers and pulled out three sheets of notebook paper with handwritten names.

"I met or at least saw a number of these people, but usually they would just nod at me and go into the office. For maybe the last six months, when someone came to the house, Colton would tell me to go watch TV up in my bedroom and not come out. None of them trusted me, and it became pretty obvious he was beginning to make other plans for me. Not good plans either."

I did a quick run through the list. There were a few names I recognized. But there were a lot of nicknames like Penguin, Quack, Knockers, Owl, and Baldy. The list went on, and truth be told, it wasn't much help. "You said they were going to take over a business. Do you know where this business was?"

She shook her head, "No, I really have no idea, but when you mentioned the illegal gambling place, that sounded like it might be something they'd do."

"Does the name Tubby Gustafson ring any bells?"

"Yeah, maybe. I think I wrote that one down," she said and pulled the list back in front of her. She ran a finger down the list, checking the names, then turned the sheet over and ran her finger down the second page.

"Yeah, here it is. I knew I heard that name," she said, pointing to the next to the last name at the bottom of the second page. Tubby.

"You remember what they said about him?"

She shook her head.

The name just below Tubby's was Kitten. None of the names on the third page rang any bells. I suddenly wondered if Colton Ferral might be the guy behind the robberies of Tubby's clubs.

"How involved was Colton in the day-to-day operations?"

"Oh, definitely involved. But that said, he was always following his mother's direction. She's the real power, the person in charge. It's interesting, she's done it in such a way that he really thinks he's the boss, but he's not. Desdemona rules the roost, and I don't see that changing."

"Would you mind if I made a copy of all of this?"

"No, be my guest. But please, don't tell anyone where they came from."

I glanced through the other pages. Nothing really caught my eye. The kitchen timer suddenly rang, and Maddie slipped on an oven mitt, opened the oven, grabbed the lasagna pan, and set it on a cast iron trivet. While she was doing that, I turned on my printer, opened the lid, and copied her lists. We had a second glass of wine with dinner and talked about how we were eventually going to approach her family.

At one point, I heard someone come down from upstairs and head out the front door. I saw the black Toyota back out of the garage a moment later. It was back fifteen minutes after that, and Ethan walked in carrying a large McDonalds bag.

Maddie made it clear in our conversation that she wasn't going to contact her family until Colton Ferral and his mother were behind bars. "I'm simply not going to take the chance, Dev. If he knew I was staying here, we both would be dead within the hour, and then he'd go after my family."

After dinner, Maddie went into the den and turned on the TV. I joined her after I cleaned up the kitchen. We never heard a sound from our guests upstairs. We watched two more episodes of Maddie's romantic series and then clicked on the news. Between nothing getting done in Washington and a bank robbery in a western suburb, I was ready for bed. I let Morton out, and when he came back inside, I headed upstairs. Maddie clicked on another episode of her romantic series. I fell asleep almost immediately and dreamt about Tubby's gambling club. I never did hear Maddie come upstairs to bed, but Morton was curled up in front of her bedroom door the following morning.

Twenty-eight

I was online Googling the various names I'd copied from Maddie's list last night when I heard her enter the bathroom. Morton arrived in the kitchen a couple minutes later. He stretched once he entered and then came over for his head scratch. I let him outside and filled his food and water dishes. He was scratching at the backdoor a minute later.

My Googling effort was a complete waste of time. I went through all three pages of names in about fifteen minutes and came up with nothing specific. The names Oliver and Jake were on the list but not anywhere close to Tubby's at the bottom of the second page. The names Louie and Mike were also listed, but I highly doubted that meant my officemate, Louie Laufen, or Mike, the bartender at The Spot.

I mixed up a bowl of pancake batter and was just finished when I heard Maddie coming down the stairs. I filled a Nina's mug with coffee for her and handed it over when she entered the kitchen.

"Oh, perfect, thank you," she said, taking the mug from me.

"Grab a seat. I mixed up some pancake batter, and I'll make us breakfast whenever you're ready. No rush."

She sat down on a kitchen stool and took a sip of coffee. "Mmm-mmm, perfect."

"Do you need to go anywhere today?"

"Why do you ask?" she said and sipped more coffee.

"Just mentally planning my day. Unless something changes, I'll be down at my office all day." I didn't mention I was going to go over her notes again and see if something, somewhere, might click regarding Colton Ferral and his mother.

"No, I don't have to be anywhere. I plan on being the most boring woman in town."

"Yeah, and the safest. We don't need the wrong person seeing you or running into someone who's a friend of your folks or your sisters."

"True. You ready to cook up those pancakes?" she asked, changing the subject.

I didn't press her. We ate breakfast, and Maddie insisted on cleaning the kitchen since I did the cooking. I left Morton at home, got a peck on the cheek, and headed to the office.

Louie wasn't there, but the coffee was on. I filled my mug and spread out the copies of Maddie's notes. There were six pages, three of which were the laundry list of names. I pushed those off to the side and worked through the notes. I deciphered abbreviations, guessed at various symbols, and at no surprise came up empty-handed. I left a note for Louie telling him I would be back later and drove over to the Ferral's mansion on Summit Avenue. I parked on the side street at the corner of the alley and waited, hoping I would see a car back out of the triple garage.

I nearly froze to death before Ferral's garage door eventually went up, and a burgundy-colored SUV backed out of the garage and headed toward me. I picked up on the Mercedes logo centered on the grill. I could make out two individuals in the front seats but couldn't tell if anyone was in the backseat. As the SUV drew closer, I ducked down beneath the dashboard so they wouldn't see me. They pulled out of the alley, waited at the corner for a couple of cars to pass, and made a right turn. I started my car and followed three cars behind.

The Mercedes headed west on Grand Avenue for two and a half miles until it ran into Cretin Avenue. The word cretin is, or maybe was, a general term meaning a stupid person. This street was named after the first Catholic bishop in St. Paul. The guy died back in 1857. Anyway, Ferral's SUV took a right at the corner and a left at the next corner. They drove another block and took a left onto the River Boulevard. The boulevard is a curving street with elegant mansions on one side and the Mississippi River Valley on the other side.

Interestingly enough, it also happens to be the street where Tubby Gustafson lives. I'd say the traffic on the River Boulevard was light, but that would suggest there was some traffic. Ferral's SUV was the only vehicle on the road. I held back a good distance as they drove along the curving road at about twenty miles an hour.

Tubby's house is on the corner behind an eight-foot-high brick wall. Ferral's SUV took a left turn at the next corner past Tubby's. I slowed down to a crawl, and just as I approached Tubby's walled property, Ferral's SUV appeared alongside Tubby's mansion. They seemed to be checking the place out.

I watched in my rearview mirror as they turned the corner and drove past Tubby's in the opposite direction from me. Apparently, I drifted into the opposite lane. The blare of a horn from an oncoming car brought my attention back to my driving. The guy leaned on the horn as he passed and gave me the finger while screaming a colorful expletive.

I circled around the next block but never saw Ferral's SUV again, so I drove back to my office. Ferral's SUV checking out Tubby Gustafson's place convinced me he was the person referred to when Maddie wrote down the name Tubby. That got me thinking about the Ferrals wanting to take over someone's profitable business and the two robberies. Ferral was going to go after Tubby, which suggested the guy really was as dumb as he looked.

Louie wasn't in the office when I returned. I emptied the coffee pot and turned it off then phoned Ollie Woods. He answered on the third ring with a not-so-charming, "Yeah."

I could hear conversational noise in the background and guessed he was probably at Tin Cups. "Hi Ollie, this is Dev Haskell."

"Yeah, I know."

"Calling to see how Karaoke was the other night."

He seemed to lighten up. "Good, I did both my songs, got a nice round of applause, but some other pain in the ass won the contest."

"Oh, sorry to hear that," I said, trying not to envision all four-hundred pounds of Ollie Woods singing some song. "Hey, let me ask you a question. You ever have any dealings with a guy named Colton Ferral? Or do you know anything about the guy?"

"Yeah, I'm aware of him. Can't tell you anything good about him. The old man ain't a fan."

"You mean Mr. Gustafson?"

"Yeah, who else? He tried to get on board with us a couple, maybe three years back. Not sure of the particulars other than we all know in no uncertain terms to stay away from him. He'd screwed something up, not sure what it was. You do that, and you're done. In fact, he's probably lucky to even be alive. Why are you asking about him?"

"Oh, someone mentioned him to me and said he was with you guys, and that didn't seem to add up."

"Yeah, that's putting it mildly. Whoever that was, you can tell them to get their head out of their ass."

"I'll be sure to do that. Say hi to Ginger for me."

Click. Ollie hung up.

I phoned Jake Butler and ended up leaving a message to call me back. I figured he was probably passed out in his recliner. I watched out the window as Louie pulled up in his faded orange Ford Fiesta. He climbed out, carrying his briefcase and a brown paper bag from some fast food place. The stairs groaned as he made his way up to the office.

I watched him enter, red-faced. He gave me his little wave, set the briefcase on the picnic table, and settled into his desk chair. I got up and made a four-cup pot of coffee. I dumped the remnants from his mug into the sink and filled it with fresh coffee.

"Thanks," he managed to say and took a sip. He dumped the contents of the bag onto the picnic table. I counted what looked like a half-dozen soft shell tacos and some kind of dessert thing with whipped cream and a red cherry smashed up against the plastic lid.

"How'd things go?" I asked.

He took a large bite of the taco, cramming literally half the thing into his mouth, and gave me a thumbs-up. I didn't know if he was referring to his meal or whatever he'd been involved in.

I poured myself a coffee and waited maybe five minutes until he had finished eating. He had taco sauce on his shirt and a drop of whipped cream on his tie. He let go with a loud belch and said, "Oh, man, that was good. You been here all morning?"

I decided not to mention the taco sauce or the whipped cream on his tie. "No, working on something for Tubby Gustafson. I followed some guys, and they drove past his house and then went around the block and drove past it again. They seemed to be casing the place."

"Is someone thinking of taking on Tubby Gustafson? They can't be too smart."

"Two of his private places were robbed. In each case, they shot one of his guys and stole a good chunk of change. I'm thinking, based on the way things went down, the guys who pulled off the robberies probably had inside information."

"Is that what Tubby thinks?"

"I don't know. I'm hesitant to tell him that because he is liable to line everyone up, shoot 'em all, and build a new crew."

"You really think he'd do that?"

I shook my head. "No, but I don't want to point to anyone. He's not a happy camper. He'd want to eliminate the problem and send a message."

"Neither of which sounds very good," Louie said and belched once more. "You hear about that bank robbery last night?"

"I caught the headline on the news last night, but that's all."

"Well, speaking of inside information, apparently they hit this bank out in the western suburbs that had just received a large influx of cash. The news was kind of sketchy on the particulars, but they mentioned six figures in cash."

"Six figures? You mean like a hundred grand?"

"They weren't specific, but the FBI is involved. I'm guessing it could be half a million."

"Man, once again, I'm in the wrong business."

"Yeah, well, you don't want the feds on your ass."

"True." I spent the rest of the afternoon staring at Maddie's list and debating whether or not to phone Tubby Gustafson.

I was home a little before 5:00. I parked in front again and stepped into the house, looking forward to the smell of whatever she was cooking for dinner.

Morton met me at the door. After giving him a head scratch, I headed to the kitchen. Maddie was actually in the den. She was curled up on the couch watching the TV. She had tears rolling down her face, and her arms were tightly wrapped around a couch pillow.

"You're watching another episode of this dreadful series?" I said, recognizing the creep who played the leading lady's heartthrob.

"Shhh-shhh, be quiet. You're wrecking this."

"It's just a—"

"Dev, stop," she half-shouted. "I'm not kidding."

The creep on the TV was in a hospital bed, and the hot-looking leading lady was saying, "I'm sorry. I didn't mean for this to happen. I didn't. I didn't."

The creep groaned and said, "It's okay. I'll, I'll always love you." Suddenly, the hospital monitors set off an alarm, and about eight doctors and nurses rushed into the room. The hot-looking woman stood in a corner, and everyone pretended to do something as the camera slowly focused in on the guy's face.

"Oh no," Maddie cried and started to sob.

Morton and I headed into the kitchen. I set two wine glasses on the counter and filled them with the last of the wine from the night before. I took a glass to Maddie and handed it to her.

"Come on into the kitchen when you're able," I said and glanced at the TV. The guy was in the hospital bed with his eyes closed, and the copy on the screen said, *'Don't miss season four!'* with a date below that. I hurried back to the kitchen.

We had reheated lasagna for dinner that was just as good as the night before. After asking three or four general questions and getting one-word answers, I cut a second piece of lasagna from the pan, placed it in the microwave, and ate it in silence.

I heard one of the guys come down the stairs and go out the front door. I watched, waiting for the garage door to open, but it never did. I walked out to the front room and saw Wilmer stepping out of the restaurant across the street with a bag of takeout food.

"How's it going, Wilmer?" I said as he stepped into the entry room.

He jumped at the sound of my voice and then flashed a quick smile and hurried up the steps, saying, "Fine, just fine. Thanks for asking." He hurried down the hall, and I heard the door close behind him.

I thought about telling them they could have their dinner in the kitchen, but based on the way he hurried upstairs, I figured I'd just let it go. Maybe they were into some special prayer service or reading scripture or something.

Maddie seemed to recover from the season-ending episode as the night wore on. We watched a funny movie about a couple renting a beach house and went up to bed. I was already in bed when I heard her step into the bathroom. About fifteen minutes later, the door to my bedroom opened, and she whispered, "Dev?"

"Maddie? Is everything all right?"

"It will be in a little bit," she said, climbing into my bed and snuggling under the covers next to me.

Thirty

It turned out to be the best night I'd had in a long time. I woke the next morning just before the alarm went off. I turned it off and rolled over to look at Maddie. She was still sound asleep, but there was a smile on her face. I attempted to go back to sleep, and after the better part of an hour, I slipped out of bed, gathered up my clothes, and went into the bathroom.

I was on my laptop when Morton wandered into the kitchen. I let him outside and heard Maddie upstairs as I let him back in. She came downstairs a half-hour later, and I poured her a coffee. I got a kiss for my effort. We chatted for a few minutes, and I cooked up a pan of scrambled eggs and sausage for breakfast. Maddie ate two helpings.

I left Morton with Maddie and got another kiss as I headed out the door. Louie was in the office, and a fresh pot of coffee was on. I poured a cup, chatted with Louie for a bit, and then gathered up Maddie's three pages of names and headed out the door. I stopped at home for a minute and checked on Maddie. She was fine, the ministers had left for a prayer service, and Morton was curled up on his pillow in the kitchen.

I drove to Tubby Gustafson's mansion. I took a roundabout way, checking in the rearview mirror for any signs of Ferral's burgundy SUV but didn't see anything. I pulled up to the front gate, climbed out of my car, and pressed the intercom button.

A voice answered with a gruff sounding, "What is it?"

"Dev Haskell to see Mr. Gustafson."

"Do you have an appointment?"

"No, but I've been working on something for him, and I'd like to talk with him."

"One moment," the voice said. I stood at the gate for a good five minutes. The weather had warmed up a little, but it was still fifteen degrees below freezing. With the breeze coming off the river valley, I was shivering. The voice never said anything but the gate suddenly began to open slowly.

I hurried into my car and drove up the circular drive to the parking area. By the time I got out of my car, a guy was there to search me. He patted me down and escorted me to the front door. His partner repeated the procedure and then opened the front door for me.

I stepped into Tubby's mansion, and a guy I didn't recognize was seated in a chair just inside and next to a radiator.

"Where's Squiggy?" I asked.

He ignored my question and said, "Unbutton your jacket and stretch your arms out." He held a black and yellow wand that he ran over my body twice, then patted me down just to make sure I wasn't carrying. "Follow me. Mr. Gustafson is in his office."

We walked across the marble floor in the entry, passing the painting on the staircase of Tubby holding a bunch of rolled-up papers looking official, and headed down the hallway. Tubby's office was the third door on the left at the end of the hall. The guy opened the door and said, "Hassle to see you, sir." He closed the door behind me once I stepped into the office.

A fire was crackling and burning in the fireplace. Tubby was seated at his desk for a change. Usually, when I was here, he was oozing over the sides of a massage table as two attractive women rubbed his back. Amazingly, he actually appeared to be working today.

"What do you want, Haskell?" he asked without bothering to look up at me.

"I spoke to Ollie Woods and Jake Butler and examined both sites where the robberies have occurred. Your locations and the security have been so tight I can't understand how anyone could have pulled off either robbery."

Tubby set his pen down, sat back in his chair, and studied me for a long moment. "So what you're telling me is you've failed, once again."

"What I'm telling you is, I don't see how either one of those robberies could have been pulled off without inside information and assistance."

He placed his hands, one on top of the other, on his fat stomach and slowly tapped the index finger on his right-hand. "Exactly what are you suggesting?"

"Are you aware of a man by the name of Colton Ferral? Or his mother, Desdemona Ferral?"

"And what if I was?"

"I don't have solid proof, but I've picked up rumors that they were looking to take over someone's business. I don't know what kind of business. I don't know if they've proceeded beyond simply talking about doing so."

"So why waste my time?"

"I do know that someone kept a list of names they heard the Ferrals mention over the past year. Your name was on that list. This individual suspected that Ferral is running three gambling parlors."

Tubby scoffed. "Yeah, great business if you want to bet on a dog race. He's been shut down by the police twice and Federal authorities once. The Feds decided the other two locations simply weren't worth the effort."

"Wouldn't it make sense that your operation would appeal to him? The setup, your members, the fees?"

"Talk about being in over your head. I let the Ferrals continue to operate because it keeps the powers that be focused on them and not me. Besides, they're dealing in a nickel and dime customer base that can only dream about being allowed into one of my operations. No, nice try Haskell, but wrong again."

"What if I told you they checked out your home twice, as recently as yesterday?"

"What do you mean, checked it out?"

I told Tubby about seeing Ferral's Burgundy SUV driving past his mansion yesterday.

"Humf," Tubby said and shook his head. "So all they learned is what every kid on this end of town already knows. There's a wall around the property."

"Maybe, I don't know, sir. My sense is they're up to something, but I'm not sure what. Suppose the robberies were just a probing operation? If there's someone on the inside who's working with them, they've proven something. I'm not sure what, but they shot two of your staff, stole the money, and thus far have gotten away with it."

Tubby pulled open a drawer in his desk and took out a small box. "Haskell, let me warn you just in case you haven't caught on. The Ferrals are giving the business a bad name."

Amazing someone would do that to criminal enterprise.

Tubby opened the box and tossed what looked like a sole pad for a shoe across the desk to me. "Slip that into your shoe."

"Thank you, sir but my feet feel just fine. I take my dog for a walk every day and—"

"Silencio, you dimwitted moron. It's a tracking device. Ferral and his crowd take you, we'll know where to gather up the pieces. You might as well get used to it. It's for finding lost souls with dementia."

"That's very kind of you, sir. But I don't think—"

"Stop right there. You don't think. Now, slip it into your shoe."

I pulled my shoe off, slipped the pad into my right shoe, and pulled the shoe back on.

"There, was that so hard? God save me." He drummed his fingers on his desk for a long moment. "It pains me to say this, Haskell, but good work. No one is more surprised than me. See what else you can find out and keep me posted."

"You think it might be a good idea to get the police involved?"

Tubby shook his head. "Thank God you said that, Haskell. I was beginning to think you might finally be catching on. Fortunately, you've redeemed yourself, and once again, you aren't making any sense. Go forth and come back with some information I can act on."

"I just think—"

"No Haskell, you don't. Now go!" Tubby shouted.

Thirty-one

I drove out through the gate and headed back to my office. Just for the hell of it, I drove past the Ferral mansion on Summit Avenue. I pulled around the corner and parked next to the alley, where I waited for five minutes. Almost immediately, I began thinking there might be a chance to interact with Maddie over the noon hour. I pulled in front of my house just as the Hoover brothers were coming out of the front door.

Ethan had a black canvas duffle bag strapped to his back. They were both dressed in black, looking just like the ministers they were. "Hello, Mr. Haskell. How are you today?"

"Things are going okay. How's the trip working out for you guys? Sorry we haven't had the opportunity to chat."

"Not a problem, sir," Wilmer replied. "We like to remain focused on the word of our Lord. What better way to spend an evening than eliminating any interaction and simply reading the bible? Not that we wouldn't enjoy talking to you."

"God bless your day," Ethan said, and they headed up the driveway toward the garage.

Morton met me at the front door. I gave him a good scratch and then called, "Maddie?"

"Be down in just a minute, Dev," she called from upstairs. I walked back to the kitchen and opened the refrigerator. There was a pan on the middle shelf covered in tin foil. I was tempted to see what was inside when Maddie came around the corner.

"What are you doing home? Is everything all right?"

"Yeah, I just finished a meeting and wanted to make sure you were okay. I chatted with our guests out front for all of sixty seconds. They seem nice enough, but I don't know. I feel like there's something there I can't quite put my finger on."

"Yeah, awfully private. I saw them walking down the hall. They saw me making the bed but didn't say so much as a 'Good morning' or a 'Hello'."

"Well, their money is just as green. Hey, you want to grab something over the noon hour?"

"I can make up something in the kitchen. How does a chicken sandwich sound? We've got some chicken leftover from the other night."

"I umm, wasn't exactly thinking lunch. I—"

"Oh my God. You really haven't changed since we were in high school," she laughed.

"Maddie, I'm a guy. We never change."

She shook her head. "Sit down, and I'll make us some lunch."

"And for dessert, maybe…"

"Sit down, Dev."

I sat at the kitchen counter, and Maddie made chicken sandwiches. I didn't tell her about going to see Tubby Gustafson. I didn't mention Colton Ferral or his mother. I didn't mention her climbing into my bed last night, although I wanted to thank her profusely. We just chatted about general stuff. After lunch, I stole a kiss and went back to the office.

I sat at my desk thinking about Maddie, the Ferrals, and Tubby Gustafson. The only way I was going to get Maddie safe and reunited with her family was to get the Ferrals behind bars. Or get enough information for Tubby Gustafson that he could deal with the problem. I went through my copy of Maddie's list again and Googled the three addresses she had written down. One was a warehouse building in an old industrial park a couple of blocks behind the state capitol. Another was a one-story stucco house over on the east side of town. The third one looked like an old empty store.

I drove over to the warehouse building and parked on a side street. I could watch the building from where I sat. The parking lot was big enough for maybe thirty cars. Just now, there were three cars, all parked next to the entrance. I took out my binoculars and focused on the license plates. I wrote down the numbers in my pocket notebook. I focused the binoculars on the windows of the building, but there was nothing to see. Maybe if I came back at night, a couple of the windows would have a light on, and that might be where Ferral's operation was located. I waited another twenty minutes and drove over to the east side of town.

The stucco house was in the middle of the block. It stood out for two reasons. First, as a green stucco house with pealing dark green trim, it was, without a doubt, the ugliest house on the block. Second, it was the middle of winter, and the sidewalks hadn't been shoveled. The steps leading up to the house were buried under the snow, and there weren't any footprints in the snow, suggesting no one had approached the front door. I turned at the corner and headed down the alley. No sign of anyone even making an attempt to enter the place.

I drove to the third address and parked across the street. It was a two-story brick building that was probably a hundred years old. The area was in the midst of a stalled neighborhood renewal, and there was a vacant lot on either side of the building.

The first floor had six-foot-tall windows facing the street. The large room was vacant except for a bunch of empty shelves. Apparently, the place had been a retail store at some point, maybe a little neighborhood grocery or a hardware store. There was a small 'For Rent' sign, easy to miss, in one of the end windows. I wrote down the phone number on the sign. The second-floor windows all had shades drawn.

I wouldn't have given the place another thought except that there were three blue porta-potties along the side of the building. Even if there was construction going on in the place, and clearly there wasn't, there would normally just be one. Why three? Whoever owned the place had to be charged a daily rate on all three, and clearly, nothing was being done today.

A beaten path in the snow led to the last one. The first two apparently hadn't been used. I scanned them with my binoculars. All three doors were padlocked, strange, very strange. I made a mental note to come back and check it out later tonight.

I headed back to the office. Louie was asleep in his desk chair. I filled my coffee mug and turned off the burner. I went online and looked up the addresses of all three locations in the county tax records. All three were owned by the same LLC, a place called D.F. Properties. I wondered if that could refer to Desdemona Ferral.

I called the phone number I got off the 'For Rent' sign in the window of the place with the three porta-potties. I got a strange tone, and then a recorded voice said, "You have reached a number that is no longer in service. Please check the number and dial again."

Who would have a number that wasn't working on a rental sign? I Googled D.F. Properties, and the only thing even close was a company out in Washington, DC. I phoned a guy I know at the state Department of Motor Vehicles. The phone rang four times before he answered.

"Arthur Webster."

"Yes, I'm with the New York Times, and I'm calling regarding a report that you snuck into the girls' locker room at Central High School back in—"

"Is this you, Dev?"

"How's it going, Artie?"

"Pretty well up until a moment ago. How are things on your end?"

"Still here to tell the story."

"What's up?"

"I wanted to see if I could buy you a dinner, and we could catch up on old times."

"First of all, you know Carol laid down the law about meeting you for an evening. It wasn't the best idea last time."

"Yeah, sorry about that. Did you ever get the car repaired?"

"I did, thanks to you and your cop pal, who was nice enough to drive me home instead of arresting me."

"Happy to help," I said.

"So what can I do for you? Wait, don't tell me. Let me guess. You want me to violate department procedure and look up the owner of some vehicle."

"Actually, no. I want you to look up the owners of three different vehicles."

"Once again, I'm putting myself at risk for making the mistake of having you as a friend. Hang on. Okay, give me those plate numbers."

"All Minnesota plates," I said and read off the three plate numbers to Artie.

"Just a minute. Yeah, okay, here we go. You got a color crayon and a clean spot on the wall to write these down?"

"I do."

Artie proceeded to give me the names and addresses of the owners. I wrote them down and then reread them. None of them rang a bell.

"Anything else?" Artie said.

"Yeah, I wasn't kidding about getting together. We could just meet for dinner and not go bar-hopping afterward."

"That might work. Let me get back to you."

"Okay. You still at the same address?"

"Yeah, but I don't think it would be a very good idea if you stopped by. We got three kids. Carol's kind of particular about who they meet."

"This from the guy in the girls' locker room."

"I know, I know. Hey, it was worth it."

"Okay, thanks, Artie. Look, I'm going to send Carol some flowers. I'll put your name on them. That way, we'll fool her into thinking she married a nice guy."

"That's nice, Dev, but you don't have to—"

"And you didn't have to help me out, but you did. Thanks, Artie. Stay safe."

"Yeah, you do the same, Dev," he said and hung up.

Louie blinked his eyes open and stretched. "Oh, man, I must have dozed off for a second or two. Have you been back long?"

"Maybe fifteen minutes. How are things going?"

"Good, good," he glanced at his watch. "Mmm-mmm, I'm thinking about heading over to The Spot. You up for one?"

"Oh, thanks, Louie. I'd love to, but I've got Morton at home keeping an eye on my Airbnb guests, and I better head home."

"Suit yourself," he said and shut his computer off. A moment later, he pulled on his coat, gave me a wave, and headed out the door. I watched out the window as he hurried across the street and into The Spot.

I shut things down, locked the door, and headed for my car.

Thirty-two

I drove home and parked in front. I saw Morton on the couch, staring out the window. He jumped off the couch as I inserted my key in the lock and met me with a wagging tail when I opened the door. "Hi, Maddie. Maddie?"

"I'm, I'm in the den, Dev," she called, not sounding all that happy.

I hurried down the hall. Maddie was sitting on the leather couch with her legs crossed and her laptop resting on her lap. Tears were running down her face.

"What's wrong? What happened?"

"Oh, Hannah posted a video, all of us at a birthday party. Oh gee, it's so sweet. I miss them, Dev. My mom, my dad, Hannah, and Amy. I want to go home, Dev. I need to see them. Even if it's just for one night."

"Maddie, I want you to be able to go home to see them. But it's not safe right now. You'd be putting your folks and your sisters in all sorts of danger if the Ferrals ever found out you are alive. We have to deal with them, the Ferrals, first and make sure it's safe for everyone."

"I know, I know, but I just miss them so much."

"Of course you do because you're a good daughter and the best sister. I'm doing my best to get something that will put Colton Ferral and his evil mother away for life, or longer if that's possible. Unfortunately, it takes time."

She smiled and brushed the tears away. "I know you are. I just wish it would happen now. What do the police say?"

"I'm not really dealing with the police."

"What?"

"I'm working an angle that involves Tubby Gustafson."

"That gangster?"

"Yeah, the gangster who's going to shut down the Ferrals and make them flee into the protective custody of the police, the court system, and prison."

"What?"

I went on to explain again the two robberies at Tubby's gambling places. I explained how I was pretty sure the Ferrals were behind the robberies. I told her I was going to go to Tubby and tell him about the Ferrals planning to take over a business in town, namely Tubby's clubs. "I just need a little more time to gather more facts that will prove my case. Can you promise to hang in there a little longer until I can get to Tubby Gustafson and convince him?"

"I can, Dev. I didn't mean to sound like I was blaming you. Please don't think I was. It's just that it's hard, very hard."

"Yeah, I know it is. Just bear with me a little longer. I'm going back tonight to check out a couple of places. If I can get in them, I might be able to come up with something. Your job is to remain patient and hang in there. Okay?"

She nodded and turned off her computer. "No sense in going out on an empty stomach. I made us a beer stew for tonight. Let me dish you up, and you can tell me about your day."

"That would be great. Did you have any interaction with our Airbnb guests?"

"No, nothing really since this morning when they couldn't be bothered to say 'hi.' They came in maybe a half-hour ago, hurried upstairs with a grocery bag and a bag from McDonalds. I haven't heard so much as a peep from them since then. Kind of strange if you ask me."

"They must be up there reading scriptures. This is their last night. They paid in advance, and to be honest, other than to say hello and me having to park out on the street, we haven't had to do anything."

"They're still strange if you ask me. How 'bout I dish us up some beer stew?"

"That sounds perfect."

Maddie climbed off the couch, and I stepped aside to let her go first. I sort of posed, suggesting we could kiss, but she didn't pick up on it and headed into the kitchen. The counter was already set for two, so I pulled out a stool while Maddie dished up the stew in two large bowls. She set the bowls on the counter and then put some bread on a plate and set it on the counter.

The stew smelled delicious, and I had to force myself not to dig in until Maddie was seated. She seemed to be doing everything but sitting down so I could begin to eat. She took the butter dish out of a kitchen cabinet. Then grabbed two wine glasses, studied them for a moment, put them back in the cabinet, and opened the dishwasher. She pulled two wine glasses from the dishwasher and proceeded to wash them in the sink. She took the dishtowel from the rack, walked across the kitchen, and tossed the towel down the laundry chute. She pulled a new dishtowel out of the drawer, but since it had a Thanksgiving Turkey motif, she folded it, put it back in the drawer, and took out a different towel.

Finally, I said, "Maddie, sit down. I'll deal with the wine."

"No, Dev, I can—"

"You wait any longer, and your dinner is going to be cold. Come on, sit down. Let me pretend to be a gentleman."

She seemed to think about that for a moment and finally walked over to her stool and sat down.

I jumped off my stool, dried the wine glasses, tossed the towel onto the rack, poured the wine, and sat down. "Okay, ready, begin," I said, and we both had a spoonful of stew. It was delicious and worth the wait. I had a second helping and two pieces of bread. I poured Maddie a second glass of wine, and we gossiped. I cleared the dishes, cleaned the counter, and got Maddie settled in front of the TV. I took her computer into the kitchen just in case she was tempted to go online and try to watch the video that her sister had posted.

I gave her a kiss on the forehead, told her not to wait up for me, and went out the front door.

Thirty-three

I went to the bank and took some cash out from the ATM, then drove over to the warehouse building. The parking lot that had just three cars parked in it earlier in the day was almost completely full. All the windows were dark, with the exception of four up on the second floor. Three different cars were parked in the spaces by the front door. I drove into the parking lot then drove back and forth through the lot to the last lane. I backed into one of the half-dozen empty parking places and cut through the parked cars to get to the front door.

Two guys were seated just inside the front door. Both of them were larger than me. They were seated in lawn chairs and were watching a TV that sat on top of what I assumed was an empty half-barrel of beer. The TV was plugged into an orange extension cord about fifty feet long that led to an outlet on a distant wall. At the moment they were watching a basketball game.

Both guys wore leather jackets and gloves. Behind them was a space heater that looked like a little fireplace. It was plugged into a blue extension cord maybe twenty feet long. The extension cord was plugged into a socket on the opposite wall.

"Can we help you?" a guy with a crewcut asked but never looked up from the TV.

"Yeah, hope I got the right place. I'm here to win," I said.

Now they both looked up at me. "You on the list?" This from a guy with a ponytail.

"A list? I don't know. I might be. I've never been here before."

"How'd you hear about it?" Crewcut asked.

"A friend told me. She said I'd really like it."

"Your friend have a name?"

I remembered Ollie Woods telling me Ginger, the waitress at Tin Cups, liked to gamble at some dive place, so I took a chance and crossed my fingers. "Yeah, her name is Ginger."

They both smiled. "Oh, yeah, she's a piece of work. That'll be twenty bucks. What's your name? We'll put you on our list," Ponytail said and pulled out his phone.

"Haskell, Dev Haskell."

"Spell that for me," he said and then punched in the letters as I spelled my name.

"Don't forget the twenty bucks," Crewcut said.

I pulled out my wallet and handed him a twenty.

He handed me one red poker chip. "Thanks," I said and figured Tubby would never be this nice.

"Elevators ain't working. Go past 'em, take a right, and head up the stairs. When you get to the second floor, take another right and walk down the hall, second door on the left. Good luck, hope you win," Ponytail said, and they both chuckled like it was some sort of joke and settled back into watching the basketball game.

I walked past the elevator, took a right, and headed up the staircase. Just about the time I thought it was too dark to see, light from the second floor drifted onto the final section of stairs. Once in the hall, I could hear a little noise, nothing crazy, more like a steady hum of conversation. I walked down the hall to the second door on the left, opened it, and stepped inside.

The place wasn't as large as Tubby's clubs or as nice. To tell the truth, it was pretty rough looking. Holes in the walls and exposed sheetrock formed silhouettes of the shelves that had been removed. The threadbare beige carpet had stains from spilled drinks or maybe someone throwing up. It was hard to tell. I guessed there were at least forty people in the room. I counted eight women, two of whom were dealing cards at the blackjack tables. Looking around, I half-expected to see Ginger somewhere, but I came up empty-handed.

There were two craps tables and two blackjack tables. The players at the blackjack tables were sitting on metal folding chairs, the kind you'd see in a church basement or a school lunchroom. I wandered over to the craps table and checked out the crowd.

A heavyset guy was the stickman, and he was talking in the usual patter. I examined the table, and it dawned on me that it had originally been a bathtub. I stepped closer and softly knocked on the side. Yeah, it had definitely been a fiberglass bathtub. Two young guys, maybe eighteen or nineteen, were working as basemen. They stood on either side of the stickman, collecting chips and paying bets. Everyone seemed focused on the guy in the Green Bay Packers jersey who was currently throwing dice.

I stepped over to the other table, another repurposed fiberglass bathtub. Things were pretty much the same except that one guy was swearing with every toss of the dice and then watching the chips he'd just bet get swept up. He did not seem happy.

I walked to the back of the room and checked out the blackjack tables. Both tables were fold-down Formica topped tables. I think they ran about twenty-nine bucks at any home improvement store.

The top of the tables had been spray-painted green, and instead of the traditional half-circle, where the dealer in a casino would deal out cards, there was a straight white line, and the dealer tossed the cards to one of the six players seated on the opposite side of the table. Players were tossing chips and cards, and no one seemed to be really winning.

The entire place had a low rent sort of feel to it and was a far cry from the layouts I'd seen at both of Tubby's clubs. I walked over to the second blackjack table, more of the same, except that the green spray paint had worn off in some places, and the woodgrain Formica pattern could be seen. I noticed there weren't any security cameras, let alone high-definition ones in the ceiling above the gaming tables like at Tubby's.

I looked around for someone I recognized but didn't see anyone. I revisited the craps tables, then wandered back to the blackjack tables once more and decided I'd had enough. I headed out the door and down the stairs.

As I approached the door, the guy with the ponytail looked up from the basketball game and said, "That was quick. Leaving so soon?"

"Yeah, I only had a hundred bucks," I said. I climbed in my car and drove over to the vacant storefront with the three porta-potties.

Thirty-four

My first impression as I turned onto the street was something must be going on. Suddenly a light flashed on in my thick skull, and it dawned on me. All the parked cars belonged to people inside Ferral's place. As I drove past the building, the first floor was still dark and vacant, but there were lights on upstairs. Three guys were standing in front of the first porta-potty talking to some guy sitting inside. The door on the thing was open, and there was a light on inside it.

I had to park on the next block and walk back to the place. Along the way, I passed another vacant lot and two empty storefronts. So much for urban renewal. A woman walking in the opposite direction whistled, and when I looked over, she called, "Hi, looking for some fun?" and waved. I kept moving.

The path in the snow led to the third porta-potty, the one furthest back. As I approached, the door on the first unit suddenly swung open. A guy in a heavy jacket with a small heater blowing on him sat on a wooden chair. He had a beard and dark hair.

"Where do you think you're going?" he asked.

"Inside, a friend told me my luck might be a little better here. I got cleaned out in thirty minutes at the other place a couple of nights ago, and she said this place is a lot better."

"Oh, did she? Interesting. She happen to have a name?"

"Yeah, Ginger. She works over at Tin Cups. Is she here tonight?"

He shook his head and said, "Not yet. She usually shows up around eleven."

"That'll give me time to build up my bank," I said.

"It'll cost you twenty to get in."

I pulled out my wallet, handed him a twenty, and said, "You need to stamp my hand or anything?"

"No, go on in. Last shitter," he said and indicated the next two porta-potties with a nod of his head.

"Thanks," I said and stepped over to the third porta-potty. There was a thin shaft of light coming out from the second door. I wondered if that might be a security guy stationed in there just in case someone tried something stupid. I glanced up on the side of the building, and there were three cameras covering the immediate area, and I guessed most of the vacant lot as well.

I pulled open the plastic door on the third unit and stepped inside. The door automatically closed. Two steps ahead of me was a wooden staircase leading to the basement of the building. I counted eleven steps as I made my way down the stairs. The room at the bottom of the stairs was dark except for two lengths of soft blue lights along the floor. They led the way for maybe fifteen feet to a door. What looked like a doorbell was attached to the door frame. I pushed it.

A moment later, the door buzzed, and I opened it. I stepped into a room similar to Ferral's place that I'd just left. This one was a little more crowded. I counted maybe fifteen women. Two were seated next to one another at a blackjack table. I presumed they were a couple. The rest were standing either next to or behind a guy, but there was no question in their stance that they were with some-one.

Once again, there were two craps tables, two black-jack tables, and in a distant corner what looked like a Texas Hold'em table. Although there were only two guys seated at that table chatting away. No dealer was in sight.

Over the course of the next forty-five minutes, I walked through the place three different times. It was pretty much more of the same. The place looked like it was set up by a couple of college kids planning a week-end party. The craps tables were two more redone fiber-glass bathtubs. The blackjack tables were the same spray-painted folding tables. There were two areas on the table where 'Pays 2 to 1' was painted in white letters. On one of the tables the word 'Pays' was spelled 'Paz.' Not that anyone seemed to mind. Both tables were filled, and it looked like there were people waiting to take a seat should someone leave.

I glanced around for Ginger but didn't see her. A few guys looked familiar, and I thought I might have seen them at Ferral's house after the memorial service for Maddie. Back in a corner behind the mostly empty Texas Hold'em table was a staircase leading up to somewhere, I guessed the second floor. Two guys in black leather jackets were standing in front of the entry, chatting away. They looked like they were probably security, which suggested that whatever was up at the other end of the staircase was not open to everyone. I decided to give it a try.

I walked over to the guys and asked, "Are there more games upstairs?"

They studied me for a moment, and the guy closest to me said, "It's more of a private area. Probably better if you just stay down here and play."

"A private place? Does that mean I'd have to pay a fee?"

"It means if you're asking, you got no business going up there," the other guy said.

"How would I know if you won't tell me?"

"Go on back to one of the tables, pal. This is out of your league."

"Relax, Jimmy, he's just asking."

"Yeah, well, he can go ask somewhere's else. Go on, get your ass out of here while you still can."

"Not what I'd call very good customer service. You should probably—"

"I told you to get your worthless ass the hell away from here," he shouted and pushed me hard with both hands.

I had a natural reaction, well, plus the guy was a real jerk. I slapped him and, a nano-second later, kicked him hard between the legs. He dropped to the ground, curled up in a fetal position, and groaned.

His partner, the former nice guy, pulled a revolver and had it resting on the tip of my nose in a second. "Back the fuck up and get your ass out of here," he said. He didn't raise his voice, not that he needed to with the barrel on the end of my nose. His partner groaned from the floor again.

"Hey, sorry, man, take it easy. He just came at me, and that was my immediate response."

I heard the hammer click on the revolver as he pulled it back. "I told you to get your worthless ass out of here."

Sometimes it's best not to respond. I slowly raised my hands and stepped back. Two pairs of hands suddenly grabbed my arms and dragged me toward the door. It was dead quiet in the place as everyone sat and stared. As we approached the door, a guy opened it, and they dragged me down the path illuminated by the blue lights. I waited for a beating I was sure would happen, but instead, they pushed me toward the stairs and said, "It would probably be a good idea if you didn't show your face around here again."

"That sounds like some pretty good advice," I said, nodded, and hurried up the stairs. Amazingly, they didn't follow. I stepped into the porta-potty and then out into the snow. As I closed the door, I heard feet quickly stomping up the steps. I took off across the vacant lot and ran for my car a block away.

I was halfway to my car when someone yelled, "Hey." I heard footsteps running somewhere behind me. There was no point in wasting time looking to see who was after me. I stepped up my pace and saw the taillights flash on my car when I pressed the unlock button.

A figure suddenly stepped out from a building entrance, the same woman who'd called 'hi' to me on my way in.

"Change your mind?" she half-shouted as I ran past.

"Those two guys want you," I called over my shoulder. I slid across the corner of my trunk and pulled the driver's door open. I shoved the key in the ignition, fired up the engine, put the car in drive, and took off. I heard a thunk from the back of my car and looked in the rearview mirror. Two guys were standing where my car had been parked a second ago. One of them appeared to be shouting something in my direction and waving a baseball bat. The guy with him was bent over with his hands on his knees, breathing deeply.

So much for Ferral's clubs. Just to be safe, I pulled onto Interstate 94 and headed east past the next two exits until I was sure no one was following me. I drove home, pulled into the driveway, and parked more or less behind the house. I was looking left and right as I walked down the driveway, just in case.

I unlocked the front door and stepped inside. I quickly locked the door and peeked outside. I didn't see anyone.

"Dev?" Maddie called.

"Yeah, Maddie."

"I'm in the den," she said.

I walked down the hall and joined Maddie in the den. She was stretched out on the leather couch, watching the local news.

Just now, they were covering another bank robbery in town, the third one in as many days. The report went on to describe two masked men entering a bank. They showed a blurry security camera image of two guys holding automatic weapons and a number of people with their hands raised. The weapons looked like they might be AR15's. The report ended with the usual "Anyone with any information is asked to call…"

Once they moved on to sports, Maddie looked over at me and said, "You're home early. Everything go okay?"

"Yeah, everything went fine. In case I had any doubts, and I didn't, I reaffirmed the fact that there was nothing of any interest to me in Ferral's gambling places."

"You were able to get inside them?"

"They were the addresses you had written down. Pretty shabby places." I went on to tell her about the empty buildings. The spray-painted tables, the mis-spelled words on the blackjack table. I left out everything related to my hasty exit.

"Oh, God. I'll never understand how I put up with that creep and his mother for so long. Dreadful, absolutely dreadful. What was I thinking? Honest to God. I must have been nuts. Oh, and my poor parents having to watch from the sidelines. Dev, could I just call them? I wouldn't have to see them in person. But if I could just call them. I just need to tell them I'm alive, and I miss them." Tears started running down her cheeks, and suddenly she was sobbing.

I wrapped my arms around her. She leaned into my shoulder and then really began to cry. "I just need to tell them I love them, and I'm so sorry for marrying Colton Ferral. Please, Dev, Colton and his awful mother will never know I called my folks. Please, Dev, please."

"We can't take the risk, Maddie. If Ferral ever found out, he wouldn't go after you. He'd go after your parents and your sisters. We can't take the chance. We have to protect them. I promise it won't be long, and we'll get him. I promise, Maddie. I really promise you."

She cried for what seemed like another hour, letting it all out. Eventually, she regained control and headed upstairs to bed. I let Morton out, and once he was back inside, I hurried up to the bedroom, thinking I knew just the thing that would get Maddie's mind off her family. Unfortunately, she'd gone into the guest room. I noticed the key wasn't in the lock, which meant she'd most likely locked the door from the inside.

I was awake for the next twenty minutes hoping Maddie would join me. My luck being what it was, Morton climbed up on the bed, and I gradually drifted off to sleep.

Thirty-five

I got the coffee going the following morning and made myself breakfast. Morton wandered downstairs, and I let him out. I logged onto my computer and sent flowers to Artie's wife, Carol. I typed a note to be attached to the flowers that read, 'Just because you're so wonderful.' I figured that would be good for another license plate call or two. There was still no sound from Maddie or the Airbnb guys upstairs, so I tossed Morton a biscuit, climbed in my car, and drove down to the office.

Louie hadn't been in yet. I poured the remnants in the coffee pot down the sink and made a fresh pot. Louie wandered in fifteen minutes later.

"Hey, good morning. How are things?" I greeted him.

Louie tossed his briefcase on the picnic table and flashed me the 'OK' sign. As he settled into his chair, I got up, grabbed his coffee mug, and filled it. After a couple of sips and a few minutes to catch his breath, he said, "What's new on your end?"

"Not much." I went on to tell him about visiting two of Ferral's gambling establishments. "The joints were downright sleazy, even for the illegal side of things."

Louie shook his head. "Unfortunately, no surprise. You talk to Gustafson about it?"

"He knows I'm checking out the Ferral's. I spoke to him a couple of days ago. I still don't have anything concrete other than the addresses of the places I was at last night and the fact that they were so sleazy and run down he doesn't have to worry about them offering much competition. I'm sure he'd get a laugh out of the fact they've converted fiberglass bathtubs into craps tables."

Louie shook his head as he tossed a couple of files into his briefcase and said, "One more business I'm glad I'm not involved in."

"Are you in court this morning?"

"I've got two appearances a little later this morning, an initial appearance and a sentencing. It'll be interesting to see if my client shows up to be sentenced. I've got a feeling he's liable to skip town. It's his second offense in twelve months. He's going to get at least six months if he's lucky."

Twenty minutes later, Louie pulled on his overcoat, gave me a wave, and headed out the door. I watched as he waddled across the street and climbed into his Ford Fiesta. I sat for the next half-hour, attempting to figure out what my next move on Colton Ferral and his mother was going to be.

I happened to glance out the window just as a sporty-looking, dark-blue BMW pulled up behind my car. An attractive brown-haired woman got out of the car. She wore a double-breasted, long black winter coat that went down almost to her ankles. She flipped her hair back over her shoulders, waited for a car to pass, and strutted across the street. I figured she was going to the hairdressers across the way from my office.

A minute later, there was a soft knock on the office door as it opened. She looked even more stunning close-up, a radiant beauty. "Excuse me. Are you Dev Haskell, the famous private investigator?"

"Depends on who you talk to. Some people would probably say infamous."

That brought a smile to her face, and she flashed sparkling white teeth. "My boss thought I might be able to provide you with some information and suggested we should have a little conversation."

"Your boss? Who do you work for?"

"Why, Mr. Gustafson, of course. My name is Kait-lyn, but everyone calls me Kitten."

I felt like I knew her based on the comments I'd gotten from Ollie Woods, Jake Butler, and whatever the guy's name was who showed me around Tubby's gambling clubs. "Oh yeah, Kitten. I think your name has come up once or twice. You work as a hostess at Gustafson's clubs, don't you?"

"That's one of my duties," she said and flashed the sparkling white teeth again. "Mind if I sit down?"

"No, please, please, take a seat." She unbuttoned her long coat, exposing an extremely short black leather skirt that immediately grabbed my attention. Once she was seated, I asked, "Can I get you a coffee?"

"That would be nice, but I can only stay for a minute or two," she said. She crossed her legs and, in the process, exposed a strap from a black garter belt. I tried not to stare and hurried over to the coffee pot, grabbing Louie's mug along the way. Fortunately, he'd emptied his mug. I refilled it and handed it to Kitten.

"Thank you," she said and took a sip. "So, Mr. Gustafson suggested it might be a good idea if we had a chat. At least to start out." She took another sip of coffee. She didn't make a face, but she set the mug off to the side. "I'm honestly not sure where to begin."

"Maybe just explain to me what you do."

She nodded and said, "My job is to make every member's experience as pleasurable as possible. Within certain limits, of course."

"Of course," I said, and she smiled. "So you're a hostess in the van and the limo?"

"Yes, I'm actually in the limo more than the van. Once we've delivered the guests for the evening, we serve drinks in the clubs and, in general, just make sure everyone is enjoying themselves."

"How did you get the job?"

"Oh, I've worked for Mr. Gustafson for the past five years in a number of different capacities. He usually spends a good deal of the winter in the warmer climates.

He has gorgeous places in Costa Rica, Mexico, the Florida Keys. Sometimes it's just overnight, and sometimes it's a week. It's been, mmm-mmm, interesting."

I was tempted to ask if she'd ever had to give Tubby a massage, but why ruin the flow of the conversation? "Do you have any idea who could have committed these two robberies?"

She shook her head. "No, the security is very tight. To my knowledge, none of the members even know where the clubs are located. They're transported to and from the clubs in vehicles with no visibility to the outside. Both the van and the limo are monitored online to ensure they're not being followed. And, as a hostess, well, we like to make sure everyone is enjoying the trip."

"I'm sure they do," I said.

"Do you share this office with someone else?" she asked and glanced over at Louie's picnic table desk.

"Yeah, I have an officemate. He's an attorney. He's in court for the rest of the morning."

"I've got a busy next couple of hours running around town. I'm having some redecorating, painters actually, working on my condo. I'm staying at the St. Michael Boutique Hotel for a couple of days. Would you be interested in joining me for dinner this evening? We could chat and see where things go from there."

"Dinner? Tonight?"

"Yeah, if you can fit me in," she said and raised her eyebrows.

"Dinner. Hmm, yeah, I can probably do that. I'll have to make a few phone calls and cancel some appointments," I lied. "I can meet you somewhere."

"Oh, that would be wonderful. Why don't you meet me at my hotel? They've got a really great little restaurant. We could eat there."

"Your hotel? Yeah, okay. I guess we could meet there. What did you say the name of the place was?"

"St. Michael Boutique Hotel. It's down on the river."

"Oh, yeah, I know the place. A red-brick building, with towers on all four corners of the building?"

"Yes, that's the place."

"What time would you like to meet?"

"Would 5:00 be too early? We could have a glass of wine before dinner, and who knows where the night may go?" she said and shrugged her shoulders.

"Sounds good," I said. If this had been any other time, I would have jumped at the chance. But with Maddie staying at my place and all that was involved with that, I planned to remain on my best behavior, unfortunately.

Kitten stood and held out her hand to shake. As I extended my hand, she took hold with both hands and began to gently rub the back of my hand. "I look forward to getting to know you much better, Dev. Thanks for the coffee. See you tonight," she said and let go of my hand.

"Nice to meet you," I said as she strutted out of the office. As soon as she closed the door behind her, I stepped around my desk, grabbed Louie's coffee mug, and set it on his picnic table. I didn't want to sit in my chair and have her see me staring out the window. I busied myself rinsing out the coffee pot and straightening the client chairs in front of my desk. When I sat back down behind the desk, I glanced out the window. Fortunately, the blue BMW was gone.

I went out to my car and drove home. My Airbnb guests were due to check out of their room by noon, and I wanted to thank them and say goodbye. I figured I could grab some lunch with Maddie after they left.

Morton jumped off the couch in the front room as I pulled up in front. He met me at the front door, wagging his tail as I stepped in. Maddie stepped out of the kitchen as I was scratching Morton behind his ears.

"Oh, Dev, I was just about to call you. The ministers asked if they could stay an extra night and check out tomorrow. If that's okay, they'll pay you in cash when they leave."

"Yeah, that would be fine. Are they upstairs now?"

"No, they left about an hour ago. Said they'd be back later this afternoon. I don't get what they do. I'm having a hard time trying to think of two more boring people."

"Yeah, won't get any argument from me. But as I said before, their money is just as green. Are you up for some lunch?"

"Yeah, we've got a choice. You can have reheated lasagna or reheated beer stew."

"You decide," I said and followed her into the kitchen.

Thirty-six

Maddie was eating the last of the lasagna. I was finishing up the beer stew. We were maybe halfway through lunch when she said, "I'm sorry about being so morbid last night. I know you're absolutely right about not getting in touch with my family. I just wanted to say I appreciate you not giving in to my childish behavior."

"Don't worry about it, Maddie. In fact, I'm meeting with someone tonight who may be able to give me some more information. She actually works for Tubby Gustafson. In fact, her name was on that list of names you have. She's called Kitten. Anyway, I'm—"

"Kitten?" Maddie said and seemed to think for a moment. "Have you met her before?"

"Only briefly this morning. She stopped in the office to arrange a meeting and—"

"Longish brown hair? More than happy to prance around and have everyone stare?" Maddie said.

"Yeah, that sounds about right. I'm meeting her for dinner tonight," I said. I didn't see any point in mentioning we would be dining in the hotel she was staying in.

"Why are you meeting her?" There was a sudden edge to her question.

"She said Tubby Gustafson suggested we talk. I'm hoping she'll be able to point me in the direction of who-ever pulled off those two robberies at Tubby's gambling clubs. I still think it was an inside job, someone who works for Tubby. She was working at both places the night they were robbed."

"Maybe she did it."

"Mmm, I don't think so. One guy weighs about four hundred pounds, and the other guy is just plain mean. I can't see her doing it."

"Why? Because she's sexy?"

"Well, yeah, she is sexy. But that's not the reason. She strikes me as the type of person who wouldn't want to get her hands dirty. Based on the way I think these robberies were committed, crawling through a heating vent in one and probably hiding underneath a car in the other, I can't see her doing that. I think she'd be too con-cerned about breaking a fingernail or getting her hair dirty."

"You're sure about that?"

"At this point, yeah. It sounds like you're familiar with her. When did you meet her?"

"Oh, it was at least a year ago, and only once. In fact, I didn't actually meet her. I just saw her. She didn't do anything out of line, didn't make a pass at Colton, but then who would? No, I saw her for of all of five seconds, heard Desdemona mention her name as the three of them went into the office and closed the door. She just gave off a vibe. Her outfit, the hair, the walk. It was like she was on stage."

I thought about our ten-minute meeting this morning at the office. Maddie's comment definitely described the woman in my office. "And she met with the Ferral's?"

Maddie seemed to stare off in the distance. "Yeah, I was coming down the stairs. They weren't even aware I was there. Desdemona opened the office door, and idiot Colton pretended to be a gentleman. He extended his hand and said, 'After you, Kitten.' As she walked past, he grabbed her rear and growled this loud meow. I'll never forget it. It struck me for two reasons. First, just in case I needed a reminder that my husband was an absolute idiot, that served the purpose. But the other thing was when he grabbed her, she just turned, smiled, and ran her tongue across her upper lip. It was as if she was suggesting, 'You can get a lot more than that.' The whole thing was just weird."

"You must have been pretty mad."

"You know, no, I wasn't. By that time, I had a separate bedroom and figured it would serve her right if she let him anywhere near. It just convinced me, not that I needed convincing, but it convinced me I had to get out of there. He followed her into the office and closed the door behind him. Interesting that she's actually called Kitten. I just presumed that was Colton being his normal tactless self."

"What a jerk," I said.

"Yeah, but it's funny. I mean, it just took me about five times longer to tell you the story than the actual incident. But I remember her. In fact, I'll never forget her. Anyway, that's why I wrote her name on my list, and you told me it was right below Mr. Gustafson's name?"

"Well, the name on your list is just Tubby, and I'm assuming that means Tubby Gustafson. Kitten is right below Tubby."

"Right below Tubby on the list… That suggests I overheard either Colton, his mother, or the both of them talking about him, and the next person they're meeting with is this Kitten woman."

"Interesting. She told me this morning that her real name was Kaitlyn."

"How long was she in your office?"

I knew where this was going. "From the time she climbed out of her car until the time she drove away, it couldn't have been more than ten minutes, tops."

"Just watch out tonight. She's liable to try anything to get—"

"Maddie, all I'm going to do is try to get information from her. We're meeting in a restaurant. We'll be in a public place. I'll be safe. I do appreciate your story. I'm sure that's something Tubby doesn't know about, and I will pass the information on to him. Based on what you told me, I'm moving Kitten up to the top of the list of potential suspects who are working for Tubby. Maybe she's the brains in these robberies, and she got some other numbskull to do the dirty work."

"Just be careful, Dev."

"I always am," I lied. Thankfully, I was able to change the subject for the next few minutes before I headed back to the office.

Louie was at his picnic table eating the last piece of a pizza. The open pizza box was filled with crusts and resting on his keyboard. There was a sauce stain on the lapel of his wrinkled suit coat. I didn't see any point in mentioning it. I did note that the mug of coffee I'd poured for Kitten now had only a swallow left in it.

"How'd your cases go this morning?" I asked just as Louie crammed the rest of the pizza into his mouth. He nodded, tossed the crust in the box, and chewed for a long moment. "Mmm, pretty good. I, mmm, was afraid my client would get at least a year, maybe eighteen months. He got six months provided he attends meetings and there isn't another incident in the next two years."

"You think he can pull that off?"

"I think he figures he can fool everybody when, in fact, the only one he's really fooling is himself. We'll just have to wait and see."

I left the office a little after 4:00 and drove to both of Tubby's clubs that had been robbed. I walked around the sides of both buildings, looking for another way into the club that I hadn't considered before. I never found one.

It did occur to me that Kitten could have stood at the main entrance to the building where the club was in the former Chinese restaurant in the basement. Theoretically, she could have flashed her eyes at some guy to let her in, but then what? There wasn't any access to the club from there, and besides, she had been working here that night.

After poking around for the better part of a half-hour, I drove through downtown to Shephard Road, which ran along the Mississippi. The St. Michael Boutique Hotel was upriver about a mile.

Thirty-seven

The hotel was a five-story red-brick structure with a six-story rounded tower on all four corners of the building. It had been built back in the 1880s and was apparently quite the place up through the 1920s. It fell on hard times during the Great Depression, laid vacant for twenty or so years, and then served a variety of functions, one worse than the next, for the following fifty years. It was scheduled to be torn down and was saved from the wrecking ball by a series of protests. In 1997 the building was finally placed on the list of historical structures, protecting it from demolition.

Sold for a dollar in the year 2000, it underwent a massive renovation. Today, it's a prominent location for anniversaries, getaway weekends, weddings, or a simple escape for people who want to slip into another world for a night or two.

I pulled into the parking lot ten minutes early. As I walked toward the double oak entrance doors, I realized we had agreed to meet at 5:00, but I didn't know if we were going to meet in the restaurant, the hotel lobby, or Kitten's room.

I stepped inside and headed for the reception desk. I only knew her as Kitten or Kaitlyn, which meant whoever was at the desk probably wouldn't give me a room number or a phone extension.

Luckily, a voice called, "Dev? Oh, Mr. Haskell, over here."

I turned to see Kitten in the process of folding a newspaper and setting it on an end table. She'd obviously changed clothes from this morning. Still looking drop-dead gorgeous, now she was wearing a pair of black slacks and a low-cut white silk blouse. She had a gold chain around her neck with what looked like a diamond pendant resting just above her cleavage. She was seated in a wing-back chair in front of the fireplace and waved me over. Birch logs were burning in the fireplace. A rack with an iron poker, a small broom, and a dustpan stood off to the side of the fireplace. As I approached, she pointed to the chair opposite hers.

"Thanks for coming, Dev. Any problem finding the place?"

"No, I'm familiar with it. My father used to drive us past this place, and he'd tell us it was haunted."

"Did you believe him?"

"Absolutely," I said, and we both laughed.

A server suddenly appeared and said, "Good evening. May I interest you in a glass of wine or possibly an hors d'oeuvre?"

"Do you have a wine list?" Kitten asked.

He smiled and handed her a small booklet. "Sir?" he asked, looking at me.

"I'll let the lady decide," I said.

"Very good. I'll give you a couple of minutes."

"What do you feel like?" Kitten asked.

"I really don't care. Order two of whatever you're getting. I'll pay, by the way."

I expected her to say something like, 'No, I've got it.' Instead, she just nodded, suggesting everyone always bought her drinks. We discussed the weather and the warm spell. Twelve degrees above zero was forecast for the first half of next week.

The server returned. Kitten proceeded to order two glasses of something I couldn't pronounce. He set a bowl of salted peanuts on the small table next to her chair and left.

"So, Mr. Gustafson said you were investigating the robberies. What have you learned so far?"

"Based on what I've been told, the robberies were impossible to commit."

"Really?" she said and smiled. "If they were impossible to commit, then it must have been someone who was very smart. Any clues?"

"Oh, yeah. A few. We got a couple of fingerprints, and I'm taking them to a friend with the FBI who promised to run them through the system once he has a chance. It's just that they're so busy right now it's going to take a while. But sooner or later, he'll have an answer and get back to me," I said. It was a lie, of course, but just the way she was asking about clues made me more than a little suspicious.

"Do you think it was just one person?"

"Yes and no. I believe it was the same person who committed the actual robberies, but I don't believe that individual was acting alone. In fact, I think the robberies were committed, not so much to get the money, but rather as a test."

"What would someone be testing?" she asked just as the server appeared, carrying a silver tray with two glasses of red wine.

"Madame," he said, handing Kitten a glass with a white linen napkin. As she took the glass and napkin, he made a gracious bow. "And for you, sir," he said and handed me my glass.

I didn't get a bow, but I said, "Thank you," anyway.

"But of course," he said and placed the bill on the small table next to my chair.

I gave a quick glance, thirty-five bucks for two glasses of wine. You gotta be kidding me. I smiled and raised my glass to Kitten. "To you. Wishing you all success."

"Mmm," she said, taking a sip. "We'll see about that. Let's hope so."

I took a sip from my glass. It was just okay, but for thirty-five bucks, I expected a lot more.

Kitten spent the next twenty minutes describing her hotel room and the work being done in her condo. Finally, she drained her glass and said, "What do you think? Another wine, or should we head into the dining room?”

“I vote for the dining room. I’m looking forward to their menu. I’ve heard good things, but I’ve never actually eaten here.”

“Oh really? Interesting. Well then, let’s not wait any longer. I place their restaurant in my top ten.”

“Do you eat here often?”

“From time to time,” she replied and stood. I followed her into the dining room.

Thirty-eight

The maître d' smiled as we approached. "Good evening, madame. How are you tonight?"

"Just fine, Gerald, thank you for asking."

"I have the table you requested all set for you. If you'll follow me please," he said and led us to a table for two next to the fireplace. The tables in the place were covered with white linen tablecloths and place settings that included three different wine glasses. He pulled the chair out for Kitten and then snatched up her linen napkin, unfolded it with a flick of his wrist, and politely placed it on her lap. "Your server will be here in just a moment," he said and hurried back to the entrance to welcome another couple.

"Looks like a nice place," I said, attempting to unfold my napkin by flicking it. I hit two of the wine glasses and knocked them over. Fortunately, they weren't full, and they didn't break. "I guess practice makes perfect," I said, dropping the napkin on my lap and uprighting the glasses.

We chatted some more and ordered wine. I went for the eight-dollar glass. Kitten ordered something I couldn't pronounce. She ordered an hors d'oeuvre, something else I couldn't pronounce, and I took a pass. It turned out, she ordered snails in a shell. I wondered if there was maybe an aquarium in the kitchen but figured it would be best not to ask.

I ordered a steak for dinner, medium-rare. Kitten ordered something called Coq au Vin that turned out to just be a chicken stew. Actually, it looked pretty good. Against my better judgment, I let her order the bottle of wine for dinner. My steak was very good, and it came with a side order of fancy potatoes. Once again, I couldn't pronounce the name.

We talked about a number of things, but Kitten always, eventually, brought the conversation back to the robberies and Tubby Gustafson. She wanted to know how well I knew him. How long I'd dealt with him and what else, besides being his special security guy, I did for him.

I laid it on pretty thick. Told her I had a weekly meeting with Tubby, approved or disapproved any hires he was considering. I told her I'd done investigations on anyone Tubby considered doing business with.

She happened to mention casually that she'd heard I attended the memorial service for Colton Ferral's wife and that I was at Ferral's house. The only one place she would have gotten that information was either Colton Ferral or his mother.

"Yeah, I did stop in for just a moment. I really don't know Colton, but I went to high school with his wife, who fell through the ice. So I was just there for a moment. I saw Colton, but he was busy talking with his girlfriend, and I had to get to an appointment, so I never was able to give him my condolences."

"His girlfriend?" Kitten said. There was a definite edge to her voice, and if looks could kill…

"Some blonde woman. In fact, he has a painting of her in the room we were in. She's swinging on a brass pole."

"It's above the fireplace," Kitten said and pushed her dinner plate away.

"Yeah, that's the one. You've been to Colton's house?"

"Oh, umm, no, not really. I was just there once, running an errand for Mr. Gustafson. I was picking up an envelope, and they had me waiting in that room for a minute or two."

"What was in the envelope?" I asked, trying to sound innocent.

"I have no idea," she said, shaking her head. "You know, I think I'm ready for some dessert. But, if you'll excuse me, first I'm going to run to the ladies' room for a moment. Don't order anything until I get back." With that, she stood and hurried out of the restaurant. As she stepped out of the room, I saw her pull her cellphone from a pocket, tap the screen, and put the phone against her ear.

I had the sense I might have hit some sort of hot button mentioning the fact that Colton had a girlfriend who swung on a brass pole.

Our plates were cleared. The dessert menus were placed on the table. I was asked if we would like dessert, and I told the server, "The lady will be ordering." The 'moment' in the ladies' room was more like a good fifteen minutes. Maybe dinner didn't agree with her. Maybe it was the seventeen dollars and fifty cent glass of wine before dinner. Maybe, just maybe, she was working an angle with Colton Ferral, and the blonde on the brass pole was supposed to be a thing of the past.

She was all smiles when she stepped back into the dining room. Her cellphone was nowhere to be seen. She sat down and looked at the dessert menu. "What looks good to you?"

"I like everything on it, so I thought it might be best if you ordered for both of us."

She studied the menu for a minute or two, and the moment she put it down, our server stepped over and said, "Something for dessert?"

Kitten ordered, and once again, I couldn't understand what she was saying. "Oh," she added, "and a half-bottle of your best dessert wine."

"But of course, Madame," he smiled and hurried away.

The dessert was good, very good. Something I never would have ordered, pears with vanilla ice cream on top and everything covered with dollops of chocolate. She told me the name twice, but the only part I could remember was the name Helen. She promptly told me that I was mispronouncing the name.

Luckily, the dessert wine was in a small bottle. It was a chilled syrupy white wine. Kitten finished two glasses, and I had barely touched mine. I thought the stuff tasted more like cough syrup.

The bill arrived, and the server glanced back and forth, not sure which one of us was paying.

"Oh, I guess I'll take it," I finally said, hoping Kitten would say, 'No, Dev, it's my turn. It was my idea to meet over dinner.'

Instead, she flashed a quick smile and said, "Why thank you, Dev. I'll have to find a way to make it up to you."

Both the server and I smiled at that. At least I did until I saw the bill. Two hundred and seventy-five bucks. Ninety bucks for the bottle of wine with dinner, another thirty for the half-bottle of dessert wine. I signed the receipt and took a deep breath.

Kitten slid the receipt in front of her and said, "Dev, you forgot to add a tip." She proceeded to add a forty-dollar tip to the receipt. If I did the math, I probably would have had a heart attack.

"Well, that was a truly wonderful dinner, Kitten. Really, this was a great choice. I'll have to come back here again," I lied and pushed my chair back. I waited for a moment, but she didn't seem to be picking up on my not-so-subtle hint. So I said, "I should get going. I've got a busy day tomorrow."

"More work for Mr. Gustafson?" she asked.

"Never enough days in the week."

"Which reminds me. He gave me some papers I'm supposed to give to you. But I didn't want to bring them into the restaurant. You know, security and all."

"Yeah, do you know what they're about?"

"No, I don't. He handed me an envelope with the papers inside. I thought it best not to look."

Tubby giving me private papers in an envelope didn't sound right. He usually just yelled at me and either told me not to screw up or told me that I had already screwed up.

"Do you just want to give them back to him tomorrow? I'll be stopping in his office later in the day, and I could get them then."

"Oh, you know how he gets," she said.

"Yeah, I'm afraid I do. Okay, I'll follow you up, but then I'd better take off," I said, wanting to send the message I wasn't going to end up in bed.

"Of course," she said and wrinkled her nose as she shrugged. We took the elevator up to the fourth floor. The hallway had antique light fixtures hanging from the ceiling and walnut wainscoting on the walls. She was in the third room on the right. She stopped at the door, pulled out a keycard, and inserted it in the slot. A green light flashed on, and she opened the door. She held the door as I followed her into a very nice room with a fire-place and two couches facing one another in front of the fireplace. A small bar with two glasses was against the opposite wall.

"You sure I can't pour you a drink before you leave?"

"Oh, I'd love to, but I'd better head out. I've got a crazy day and an early morning."

"I think you're going to have a very crazy day," a male voice said from behind me. I turned to look as Colton Ferral oozed into the room, followed by two other threatening looking guys.

Thirty-nine

Ferral was dressed in a dark blue tracksuit with a red stripe on the pants and a yellow and red lightning bolt down the front of the top. The tracksuit was designed to be baggy and hide less attractive or even gross figures like Ferral's. That didn't seem to work in Ferral's three hundred pounds plus condition. Three rolls of fat could be counted along his sides, and a large belly hung over the waistband.

As Kitten pushed the door closed behind them, she said, "It took you long enough. You were supposed to be in here waiting."

"It might be best if you went into the bedroom," Colton said and took a bite of the Snickers bar in his hand.

"The bedroom? After I lined this up, you think you can just dismiss me and—"

Colton looked at one of the thugs behind him and said, "Get her out of my sight."

"Just wait a damn minute. Don't you touch me," Kitten said as the thug wrapped a muscular arm around her waist. He effortlessly lifted her off the floor and walked toward the bedroom door.

"Colton, I pulled off the robberies for you. I've got inside information on Gustafson. I got…"

I could see the corner of a four-poster, king-sized bed. The thug tossed Kitten halfway across the bed and said, "Might be best to shut up and just keep your ass on that bed."

"You can't tell me what to do," Kitten said but didn't make any effort to climb off the bed. As the thug stepped out of the bedroom, she gave him the finger. He closed the door behind him and stood in front of the door with his arms crossed.

"So, you're Dev Haskell, the douche bag everyone complains about," Ferral said.

"I don't know if they complain about me. I—"

"Where have I seen you before? Somewhere recently."

"I was at the memorial service for your wife, and then I stopped in at your home for a few minutes afterward."

He seemed to think about that for a second or two and said, "Okay… I can't really picture you, but there was a large crowd celebrating. You should have hung around. We partied until late in the night."

"I had things to do."

"So I hear. You're working for that piece of shit Gustafson? Looking into the robberies at his clubs." He smiled, actually grinned. He held his hands out to the sides and said, "Okay, you caught us. Guilty as charged. I did it. I lined them up. Kitten pulled them off. Everyone kept telling me fat ass Gustafson made his clubs impenetrable. Looks like I proved them all wrong, not once, but twice.

"Based on the little Kitten knows, it sounds like you do an awful lot of work for Gustafson. It would seem logical you know a lot of the ins and outs of his business. What works and what doesn't. Who the key people are, the names of his business contacts. I can use that information. I'll find it very helpful."

I shook my head. "Actually, Mr. Ferral, I don't know anything like that. All I know is he gets a massage every day from two women, and he has a guy drive him around. Beyond that, I'm in the dark. I'm sure you know way more than me."

Ferral shook his head, reached into his pocket, and pulled out his cellphone. "I have it on good authority you know a lot more than you're letting on." With that, he pushed a button on his cellphone and pointed it toward me. Unfortunately, I recognized my voice.

'I have a weekly meeting with Mr. Gustafson. Either in his office or, in the warmer months, quite often on his yacht. We discuss possible new hires. I investigate and vet them all. Same thing with any businesspeople he's interested in dealing with. He has me investigate them as well. He refers to me as his eyes and ears. He's always telling me I'm a major player in his operations and that he owes his success in no small part to me.'

'I heard you attended the memorial service,' Kitten said.

Ferral turned off his cellphone and said, "From what you were telling Kitten, it sounds to me like you're more than a little familiar with the Gustafson operation, Haskell."

"Oh, I may have been a little generous in my descriptions to her. To be honest, Gustafson really isn't a big fan of mine. As a matter of fact, he dislikes me intensely. You could call him, and I'm sure he'd confirm that. I'm constantly disappointing him. I've lost count of the times I've screwed things up for him or given him inaccurate information."

"And yet, he always seems to be coming back to you. Let me tell you what I think, Haskell. I think you and Gustafson are the best of pals. I think he probably doesn't make a decision without consulting you first. I think no one could possibly be as stupid as you pretend to be."

"Oh, I'm pretty stupid, sir."

"I think what we're going to do, Haskell, is you and I are going to have a long conversation. We're going to discuss Gustafson's businesses, in particular his gambling clubs. I plan on taking them over. I'm going to offer you the opportunity to benefit from that."

"Offer me the opportunity to benefit from that. Benefit how?"

"I always like to keep things simple, black and white, you know? So, we'll go back to my place and have a friendly chat. If, at the end of our discussion, you've answered my questions and provided the information I've requested, you will live to see another day. If, on the other hand, you choose not to provide the information I request, well then, things won't work out to your advantage. Any questions?"

"I, I don't mean to disagree, but I think you're making a big mistake. I really don't know anything about Gustafson's businesses. In fact, I can honestly say if I told him to go left, he'd take a right. If I told him something was black, he'd already know it was actually white. He, he doesn't respect or believe me, and for good reason, because I'm always, always, always wrong."

Ferral turned to the thug behind him. "Bring the van around to the kitchen door." The thug hurried out of the room, and Ferral turned back to me. "I hope we can make this a positive interaction, Mr. Haskell. We'll find out soon enough."

He shoved the remainder of his Snickers bar into his mouth and tossed the wrapper into the fireplace. "All right, let's go," he said to the thug standing in front of the bedroom door. "Haskell, for the next few minutes, you will have the undivided attention of Hammer. Let me warn you, try anything stupid, attempt to run, or call for help, and he has my permission to end it right then and there. Show him, Hammer."

Hammer looked around, then turned and put his fist through the wall. Kitten screamed from inside the bedroom.

"Any questions?" Ferral asked. "Good, let's go."

He opened the door, and I followed, thinking maybe we would pass someplace where I could take off running. If we went through the reception area, maybe I could grab that iron poker next to the fireplace. As soon as I stepped into the hallway, Hammer placed a huge hand on the back of my shirt collar and another on my belt. He half-lifted me off the floor as we hurried down the hall.

"Don't even think of trying something stupid, Haskell. Nothing would please me more than the chance to break your neck."

I hopped along the hall as Hammer lifted me off the floor about every third step. He pushed me onto the elevator, and Ferral pushed the button for the lower level. The elevator stopped on the third floor, and the door opened. A couple was about to step on but then stopped when they saw Hammer's paw holding my head against the wall. He glared at them and let out a low growl.

"Sorry, security, dealing with an obvious problem," Ferral said, pointing to me as the doors closed. When the doors opened again, we were on the lower level. We walked, actually, I was forced to hop, down a wide hallway, past double kitchen doors, a door labeled laundry, and another labeled maintenance. At the end of the hall was an overhead door. Ferral pushed a button, and the door rose with a clanking sound. Ferral stepped out onto a loading dock and took the stairs down to the burgundy

SUV waiting for us. He climbed into the front passenger seat.

The thug who was driving slid out from behind the wheel and opened the rear passenger door. Hammer suddenly lifted me up, tossed me off the loading dock and into the side of the SUV.

"Ooff," I said as I bounced off the SUV and saw stars. The thug that was driving picked me up off the ground and tossed me into the backseat. I attempted to sit up, but he grabbed me by the ankles and twisted them, causing me to roll onto the floor. A second later, muscle-bound Hammer hopped in and stomped both feet on top of me.

"Just lay there and don't do or say a thing, dumb shit," Hammer growled. I saw no point in arguing.

We drove for what felt like an hour. In reality, since we were going to Ferral's mansion, it couldn't have been more than ten minutes. No one spoke along the way. The only noise was what sounded like paper tearing which turned out to be Ferral opening another Snicker's bar.

We stopped, and I heard the sound of a garage door rising. A moment later, we drove into the garage, and Ferral climbed out of the front seat. The driver opened the rear passenger door, grabbed me by the ankles, and yanked me out of the backseat. I dropped about a foot and a half out of the SUV and onto the concrete floor. I broke the fall by putting my arms below me, which saved my head from bouncing off the concrete but really hurt both forearms.

My close personal friend, ass wipe Hammer, was right there to grab me by the shirt and lift me up. I heard my shirt rip as I landed on my feet. There was a set of stairs against the front wall of the garage. Ferral headed down the stairs, and we followed, taking a short tunnel into the basement of the mansion.

We passed a room with a pool table, a room with a workbench and tools, and then Ferral took a set of keys out, unlocked a door, and we all stepped inside. The lights came on slowly, flickering for a few moments and then gradually growing brighter. If I didn't know better, I would have thought it was a lantern or a series of candles. Actually, I wished they remained off. I wasn't too thrilled with the view.

Racks and chains and a machine with wrist and arm clamps that looked like it was designed to stretch someone. Whips, chains, riding crops, ropes, paddles, the place looked like a torture chamber.

"Hey, Mr. Ferral, I gotta tell you. I'm not really into the whole bondage thing. I much prefer a back rub or maybe… Uff," I groaned as Hammer suddenly punched me in the stomach. He literally lifted me off my feet, and I swallowed a couple of times to stop from throwing up, then thought, why not? But nothing came up.

"It all depends on how conversational you're feeling, Haskell. Your choice. Let me start by saying, welcome to the dungeon," Ferral said and laughed.

"Actually, I think a nap might be a better—"

Hammer took a step toward me and went to punch me in the stomach again. This time I was ready for him and slowed his fist using my hands. My stomach survived, but it felt like both my hands had been broken.

Forty

I was seated on a stool with my hands handcuffed behind my back. The handcuffs had fuzzy pink fur around them, not that it made any difference. I still couldn't get them off my wrists. Ferral was facing me, sitting backward on an antique spindle-back chair. There were five oak spindles on the back of the chair, and Ferral's massive blob of a stomach sagged between the spindles.

Ferral held onto a black leather riding crop. The end of the crop was in the shape of a red leather heart. Other than hitting me on the top of my head a couple of times, things had been relatively tame. I had a headache, and my stomach still hurt from Hammer punching me. My chest ached after being thrown off the loading dock. That said, given the current situation, I was still alive, so things seemed to be okay, at least for the moment. I didn't know how long I'd been stuck in the room with these idiots. It seemed like a day or two, but I knew that wasn't right.

"Let me get this straight, Haskell. You're suggesting to me that this guy that drives Gustafson around—"

"Yeah, Fat Freddy Zimmerman."

"You're telling me he's actually Gustafson's accountant?"

"Yeah, but that's not the term Gustafson uses. He calls him his chief financial officer. When you think about it, it makes sense. They drive around and discuss financial things in the car. They don't have to worry about eavesdropping, listening devices, or anything like that. They listen on little hearing aid devices and speak into microphones that are dialed into a special frequency so they can't be tracked."

Ferral looked at the two thugs leaning against a wooden bondage rack. Hammer shrugged his shoulders, and the other idiot shook his head.

"They've never seen anything like that, and they've followed Gustafson for miles."

"That's because you're not supposed to see anything. They have flesh-colored hearing aids in their ears. You can barely see the things even if you're right next to them. The microphones are clear, thin plastic, and even if you drove alongside, you'd think it was a wrinkle in their skin. That's why so much of their business remains a secret. Even the feds don't know about this."

"What frequency are they on?"

"I have no idea, and even if I did, Gustafson changes the frequency every day. Mr. Zimmerman, he's the chief financial guy, he's established pension accounts for all the employees. It's like a private social security fund. I think the accounts are set up in Panama or Costa Rica, someplace like that. It's one of the reasons Gustafson is so profitable. He puts a percentage of the profits into the guys' accounts."

"What?"

"Yeah, think about it. You work for him, and if you're loyal, you end up with a pension that is untraceable and won't be taxed. When guys get too old to work for him, they're not just left out there hanging and broke. It's a good incentive that keeps his team loyal."

Ferral shook his head and said, "That sounds absolutely crazy." I saw the two thugs glance at one another with a slightly different take on my tale.

"Why not just keep the money for himself?" Ferral said, making my line sound even better.

"Because Gustafson is looking at the long game. He's got guys on his team who have been with him for over twenty years. They remain loyal because they've got these accounts waiting for them. Anyone offers them money to come over, whatever the offer is, it can't compare with what they'd lose."

"I want to know about his gambling business," Ferral said, changing the subject.

"I'm guessing Kitten already told you a lot."

"Maybe, let's hear what you can add."

"Well, he runs an awfully tight ship, like all his businesses. The games are all above board, no cheating, no misbehaving. You walk through a metal detector to get into the clubs. Did Kitten tell you how the members are driven to the clubs?"

"You mean the limo?"

"Yeah, so you know about that. People have to pay a fee just to join the club. They have to make an appointment to be picked up. They can't just show up, but then how could they? None of the members know where the clubs are located. Inside, the places are nice, professional-looking, with real craps tables, blackjack tables, and Texas Hold'em tables. They're waited on and serviced by women like Kitten, meaning pretty, pleasant, and polite."

"So how does he make any money?"

"Well, first of all, he charges a hefty membership fee, members pay for each visit, and of course, he takes a percentage. People go there because they want to rub shoulders with the famous. Movie stars, sports figures, big businesspeople, they're all there and all just part of the crowd. Since everyone has paid a substantial amount just to join the club, they aren't going to screw it up by getting drunk, being obnoxious, or grabbing a hostess by the ass," I said, adding that last part, remembering Maddie's story of Ferral grabbing Kitten.

"It doesn't sound like much fun."

"It's a different kind of fun. You're there to win. You can party and be crazy, if that's your thing, when you leave. But when you're there, you're focused. Guys might have a drink or two, but they aren't going to be pounding them down. If they do, they're out."

Ferral yawned and looked at his watch. "Oh, shit, later than I thought. We'll talk in the morning. Nice of you to offer to spend the night." He turned to the thugs and said, "Put him to bed."

Once everyone was asleep, maybe that would be my chance to make a break. I could—

Hammer stepped behind me, undid the pink fur-lined handcuffs, and led me over to the wooden bondage rack. I was expecting another punch in the stomach or the heart-shaped riding crop bouncing off my head, but instead, he helped me onto the bondage rack, and I laid down. His pal watched as Ferral left the room, and then he clamped a shackle around both ankles.

"Not too tight," Hammer said to his pal as he clamped my wrists to a chain. He raised my arms over my head and attached the chain to the end of the rack.

"We're not making this too tight, so you'll be able to sleep. One of us will be right outside the door, so don't get any ideas."

"Okay, thanks."

"Your stomach okay?"

"Yeah, I'll live."

"Gustafson really do that, set up pensions for his people?"

"Yeah, that's why they're so loyal to him. That's why none of 'em end up on welfare. I think when they leave, they go somewhere else, you know, a place with nice weather, beaches, all that stuff."

"He ever hire guys?"

"He's always looking," I lied.

"Humf, you make it through this, maybe we should talk."

"I could put in a good word for you," I said. Hammer nodded, and the two of them left the room, turning the lights off on their way out.

Forty-one

I thought it would be impossible to sleep, but sometime in the middle of the night, I apparently dozed off, because the next thing I knew, I was opening my eyes as the door to the dungeon was unlocked. Ferral waddled in, still dressed in the tracksuit with the red stripes and the lightning bolt. He hadn't bothered to shave, and he was eating another Snicker's bar, apparently his breakfast. He was followed by Hammer and the other thug. Both of them wore different t-shirts from the ones they had on yesterday.

"All right, Haskell, time to rise and shine," Ferral called.

I blinked my eyes open and was immediately aware of a pounding headache and aches and pains all over my body from sleeping on the bondage rack.

"Unlock him and sit him up. I need some answers," Ferral said.

Hammer walked over and unhooked the chain that had kept my hands raised over my head. My arms immediately dropped to my side, and I could feel the blood rushing back into them. He unhooked the chain holding my ankles and then carefully sat me up and turned me, so my legs hung over the edge of the table.

"Give it to him," he said, and the other thug handed me a small glass of orange juice.

I sniffed it before I put the glass to my lips, playing it safe. I was so thirsty I emptied the glass in about three swallows, causing me to cough and drool.

"Honest to God, Haskell. You're an absolute disaster," Ferral said and laughed. "I'm going to need some specifics from you, starting with the names of Gustafson's gang. I know about his financial officer, Fat Freddy Zimmerman. Give me more names," he said. He set a yellow legal pad on the bondage table and pulled out a pen.

"Names of his gang? Well, let's see, there's Sneezy, Bashful, Sleepy, Happy, Grumpy, Doc—"

Ferral stopped writing and shook his head. "Always the wise guy. I don't think you understand. Let me make myself clear," he said and suddenly jammed his pen into my upper thigh. "Get the message?" he shouted as I screamed with the pain.

"Oh, God, that hurts. What did you do that for? Oh, son-of-a-bitch," I groaned as blood from my upper thigh began to soak into my trousers. "Are you nuts? That really hurt. God," I said and pressed my hand over the wound in an attempt to stop the bleeding.

"Apparently, you're still not getting the message, Haskell. You think I'm just another fool you can bullshit.

I'm wise to you. Now I want their full names," he said and wiped the blood from his pen on my shirt.

"I just gave you the names, Ferral. God, my leg hurts. Those are the names of the security team that guards his mansion. They're all armed and positioned all over the grounds. The place is covered by motion detector sensors, lights, and cameras that are monitored twenty-four seven."

"Tell me something I don't know."

"Your fly is undone."

His immediate reaction was to reach down and check before he remembered there wasn't a fly in his tracksuit.

I chuckled, and an evil look washed over his face. "Always the wise-ass, Haskell. Get me the torch, damn it."

"Are you sure, sir?" Hammer asked.

"Do I have to do everything? I said, get me the torch. Get me the damn torch. Now!"

"Be right back," Hammer said and hurried out of the room.

"You're about to learn the importance of paying attention, Hassle, you dumb shit."

"It's Haskell, Ferral, Dev Haskell," I shouted back.

Ferral smiled and said, "Along with paying attention, you're about to learn some basic manners." He wound up and took a swing at me.

I leaned back, and his fist flew past the tip of my nose.

He stared at me, with his chest heaving, just as Hammer hurried back in the room carrying a blue propane canister. Hammer was in the process of twisting on what looked like a brass flame tip.

"Hey, wait a minute, Ferral. Just hold on here a second. I'm a little nervous, but I can come up with those names. In fact, I'm thinking—"

There was a knock on the door, three loud raps.

"Now what?" Ferral groaned. "Who is it?"

"Your mother, let me in."

"The door's open, Mom," Ferral said. He picked up the flint ignitor and clicked it a couple of times. "Oh, you're going to love this, Haskell."

"Did you hear me, Colton? Get over here and open the door. I'm not going to tell you again. Get over here now."

"All right, all right. Calm down," Ferral said as he hurried over to the door. "I was just about to get the answers you wanted, and I—" He pulled the door open, and his wicked witch of a mother sailed into him, sending both of them onto the floor.

"Oof," was all Ferral said as his mother, dressed in a black terrycloth bathrobe with curlers in her hair, landed on top of him.

The thug next to Hammer reached for his gun, but one of the guys in the doorway shouted, "Don't!" and he slowly raised both hands. Hammer raised his hands as well. Three more guys stepped into the room, pistols drawn. I recognized one of them as Squiggy.

"You have any idea who you're screwing with?" Ferral shouted. He was now up on all fours, rocking back and forth in an effort to get to his feet.

"Colton, shut the hell up," his mother hissed just as Tubby Gustafson stepped into the room. Colton was halfway to his feet when Tubby kicked him in the rear, sending him on top of his mother.

"Get your fat ass off me. I can't breathe," Desdemona groaned as she rolled Colton off to the side.

Ferral rolled onto his back and grew wide-eyed as he focused on Tubby. "Oh, Mr. Gustafson, I was just talking with your head of security here. Telling him he was too loose with the information. He was giving me the names of your people, and I was warning him not to do that. He wouldn't listen. He—"

Tubby nodded at one of his thugs. The guy stepped over and slapped Colton three times across the back of his head.

"Ouch. Ooh. Stop," Colton shouted. "I even wrote down the names, sir. My list is on the rack next to Haskell."

Tubby nodded in my direction. Squiggy pushed his bifocals up on his nose and stepped over toward me. He picked up the list, glanced at it, smiled, and winked at me. "Got it. He's right, sir. Haskell did give him names." He handed the list to Tubby.

"See, I told you, sir. He's giving away all your secrets. He told me about your chief financial officer, Mr.

Zimmerman. I was going to take notes and come and warn you that your chief of security is—"

"Silencio! You idiot," Tubby shouted. He glanced over at Squiggy and said, "I want you to take lard ass and his mother to the place we discussed. I'm sure they'll enjoy themselves. You two," he said to Hammer and the other thug, "I'm going to come back for you. We're going to have a little conversation. Based on your response, it could be a new opportunity. Chain them up," he said to Squiggy.

Squiggy nodded at Hammer and the other thug, and while Tubby's guy kept his gun on them, Squiggy chained Hammer up on the bondage rack and handcuffed the other thug to a cast-iron plumbing pipe.

"Let's go, Haskell. Your chariot awaits," Tubby said and headed out the door. I limped behind Tubby, following him up the stairs to the main floor. Four of Tubby's guys were busy going through drawers and cabinets. He walked out the front door, and I followed. Surprisingly, it was sunny, and the temperature must have been above freezing for the first time in two weeks because the snow appeared to be melting.

Fat Freddy Zimmerman was sitting in the black Cadillac Escalade parked at the curb. As Tubby stepped out of the mansion, Fat Freddy hurried around to the passenger side and opened the door for Tubby.

"Get in back, Haskell," Tubby said. The Escalade rocked from side to side as he oozed onto the front seat.

Fat Freddy closed the door once Tubby was settled and hurried around to the driver's side. I hopped in back.

"Had an interesting visitor this morning," Tubby said as the car pulled away from the curb.

"A visitor, sir?"

"Yeah, a woman who's supposed to be dead," he said and just let that hang out there for a long moment. "She gave me a list of names, addresses, account numbers, canceled checks. Very interesting."

"I was going to tell you, sir. In fact, I met with Kitten last night to get some more information and—"

"How'd that work out?"

"Not so well."

"So she said." Tubby turned around and glared at me. "At no surprise, you've once again missed the boat, Haskell. Fortunately, Madeline McGuire came to me and asked me to help. I was only too happy to be of service. If you have any brains, you'd better think of a way to thank her. If it weren't for her, you'd probably be cut up in little pieces by now."

"Thank you for saving me, Mr. Gustafson. I really mean it. If you hadn't come along…"

"Haskell, thank you for not giving away any information on me. Once we drop you off, my Chief Financial Officer here is going to take me back to Ferral's house. We're bound to find something of interest. Thank you in advance for not mentioning this to anyone, ever. Now get out," Tubby shouted as Fat Freddy pulled to the curb in front of my house.

Forty-two

I slowly climbed out of the car. The moment I closed the door, Fat Freddy sped down the street. I wondered what was going to happen to Ferral and his mother, but to be honest, I really didn't care. A part of me hoped they'd be thrown through the river ice. I hobbled up to the front steps. Morton jumped off the couch as I approached and met me at the front door.

"Maddie? Maddie?" I called as I hugged Morton and got face licks in return. I heard footsteps running from the kitchen, and Maddie suddenly appeared with red puffy eyes.

"Oh, God. Oh, Dev. Thank goodness you're okay," she said. She wrapped her arms around me and began to sob. "God, I could just kill you. You had me so worried meeting with that Kitten person, and when you didn't come home last night, I didn't know what to do."

"Well, you sure did the right thing. Tubby Gustafson came and got me and dropped me off. He's a big fan of yours. Told me I'd better thank you."

"I'm just glad you're safe," she said, pulling away. "Come on, have you had anything to eat? Let me make you a late breakfast or an early lunch."

"Actually, if you don't mind, what I should probably do is grab a shower."

"Okay, I can make you scrambled eggs, French
toast, a sandwich, whatever you want when you come
back down."

"Give me twenty minutes, and I'll be back," I said
and hobbled toward the staircase.

"Oh, Dev, what happened? You're limping."

"I'll tell you all about it over French toast. I just
want to say thank you again. I really mean it. You saved
my life," I said as I slowly made my way up the stairs.

My shirt was torn. My trousers were bloodied and
had a hole in them from Ferral's pen, but I was home. I
left my clothes on the floor of the bedroom and stepped
into the shower. My thigh felt a lot worse than it looked.
The bleeding had stopped, and after a long shower, I
taped a gauze pad over my wound, and that seemed to do
the trick.

I pulled on jeans and a sweatshirt and headed down
to the kitchen. I could smell the French toast as I entered.
Maddie poured me a mug of coffee and gave me another
kiss. I settled onto a stool and said, "Tubby Gustafson
spoke very highly of you. How did you even know how
to find him?"

"Ferral drove me past his mansion last summer. I
remember him telling me someday people were going to
talk about him the way they spoke of Mr. Gustafson. I
called Uber and gave the driver directions. I brought all

my notes and gave them to Mr. Gustafson. He could not have been nicer."

"That's something rarely said about him."

"He was just very pleasant and told me not to worry."

"Ferral was about to turn a propane torch on me. They got there just in time."

"How did they find you?"

"It just dawned on me. The other day Tubby gave me a sole pad for my shoe. It has a tracking device for people with dementia. That's how they knew I was at Ferral's."

"What do you think they'll do to him? Will they call the police?" Maddie asked as she slid a plate of French toast in front of me.

"I don't think there's going to be any police involvement. Whatever they do, it's not going to be nice. If Ferral and his mother know any prayers, they'd better say them."

"Do you think I could call my folks?"

"You could, but I think it might be a better idea to go over to their house so they can see you in person."

"You mean it?"

"After last night and this morning, you bet I do. If you want to call Uber, we can go get my car, and we'll drive over. Maybe on the way, you might call your sisters, and they can meet us at your folks'. Be nice to have all of you together."

"Oh, Dev," Maddie said and started to cry.

The Uber driver arrived ten minutes later. Maddie hurried out to the car and called, "Come on, Dev, hurry up."

Once I climbed into the backseat, we headed to the St. Michael Boutique Hotel. My car was just where I'd left it, and amazingly, it started on the first try. Maddie gave me directions to her folks' place, a two-story frame house on a quiet street. Along the way, she had tearful conversations with both sisters. We arrived at her folks before her sisters got there. I hadn't completely stopped the car when Maddie opened the door, jumped out, and ran to the front door. She rang the doorbell and pounded on the door.

I was halfway up the front sidewalk when her father opened the door and stood wide-eyed, shaking his head. He wrapped his arms around her and started crying. "Oh my God. Oh my God. Oh my God." He shouted for his wife, "Helen. Helen. Oh my God." He held Maddie and wasn't about to let go. Her mother suddenly appeared and wrapped her arms around the two of them. "Maddie. Maddie," she cried, stroking Maddie's hair and kissing her.

I had just stepped onto the front stoop when a car screeched to a stop, and Maddie's sister Hannah came running up the sidewalk calling, "Maddie. Maddie."

She'd left her car running and the driver's door open. She ran past me and into the house. I walked back to her car, turned the engine off, closed the door, and pressed the fob to lock it.

Amy came around the corner, drove over the curb, and stopped. At least she turned the car off and closed the driver's door. I don't think she even saw me as she ran into the house and her sobbing family.

We'd been seated in the living room for a good two hours. I was in a wing-back chair next to the fireplace. It was gas-fueled and burning. The entire McGuire family was crammed onto the couch. Maddie in the middle, her folks on either side and her sisters at either end of the couch. Her parents each held one of her hands, and her sisters had an arm wrapped around their folks. There was a coffee table in front of the couch with two boxes of Kleenex resting on it.

Things had calmed down a little, although there was still someone crying at all times. Thus far, nothing had been said about Maddie faking her death, her meeting with Tubby Gustafson, or the Ferrals. I wasn't sure any of them had accepted the current situation as reality yet.

"I'm going to run out and get some sandwiches for lunch. I'll be back in maybe forty-five minutes."

"Oh, you don't have to do that. I think I've got—"

I held up my hand and cut Maddie's mother off. "Mrs. McGuire, you stay right on that couch with Maddie. All of you have been through a terrible ordeal, and you've more than earned the right. I'll be back in a bit. Oh, and welcome home, Maddie."

That last bit brought another round of tears. I pulled on my jacket and went out the door. I drove down to Rooster's and ordered six pulled pork shoulder BBQ sandwiches. I stopped at the liquor store and got four bottles of champagne, and then drove back to Maddie's folks.

They sipped champagne and ate the BBQ sandwiches, and no one made a move to leave the couch. I couldn't blame them. It was close to 4:00 when I stood and excused myself. Everyone stood. Maddie's folks were still holding her hands and touching her face or running their free hand through her hair.

"Thank you for watching over Maddie," her father said. "I don't know how we can ever thank you."

"You already have. You've got a lovely daughter."

"Dev, I'm going to stay here tonight," Maddie said.

"I think we all should," Hannah said, which brought another round of hugs and tears.

"I think that's a good idea. Besides, Maddie, you have to reclaim all your clothes." The girls all laughed at that.

"Oh, Dev, I forgot to tell you. Your Airbnb guests extended for another night. So, they'll be staying there tonight, too."

"Okay, great. One more night I'll be paid. Give me a call tomorrow when you have time. I can run things over if you need anything, and I want to check with Mr. Gustafson. I'll let myself out. I'm sure you have a lot of catching up to do."

They all said thanks and settled back onto the couch.

I listened to Public Radio News on the way home. They mentioned another bank robbery in town and that the robbers were in a standoff somewhere with police. Crime in the city was definitely on the rise.

Forty-three

I still had a lump in my throat as I drove home. Maddie's family, especially her parents, joined a club no one wanted to belong to, parents who lost a child. Maddie revoked their membership today. I thought for a brief moment about the Ferrals and Kitten then slowed for the stop sign and switched on my turn signal to turn onto my street.

Two squad cars with flashing lights were pulled perpendicularly across the street, blocking my turn. Given the temperature, the cops were sitting in their cars. I pulled alongside one of the squad cars and lowered my window. The cop did the same.

"I'm trying to get home. I just live up the street."

He shook his head. "I'm afraid you're not going to be able to go up there. There's a hostage situation, a pair of bank robbers."

"Bank robbers? Is that the standoff with police I heard about on the radio a few minutes ago?"

"Sounds like it," he said. "I wish I had more information, but everything is up in the air at this point, and it's too dangerous to go up there. We've got the house surrounded. We've evacuated the neighbors."

"I can't believe it. One of my neighbors is a bank robber?"

"Afraid it might look that way. What's your address?"

I told him, and he gave me a strange look, then said, "Let me just check on something for a moment." He raised his window and talked into his radio. It was a good five minutes before two squad cars came down the street. One pulled in behind me. The other pulled in front of me at an angle, effectively boxing me in. The cop I'd been talking to lowered his window, pointed a pistol at me, and said, "If you would please step out of your car, sir. Let me see your hands."

The two cops who just boxed me in were out of their cars, kneeling behind an open car door with weapons pointed at me. I decided this was not the time to argue. I turned off my car, opened the door, and slowly stepped out. I kept my hands at about shoulder height.

"Turn around and assume the position," one of the cops said.

I turned, placed my hands on the roof of my car, spread my legs, and leaned forward. A pair of hands patted me down.

"Clean," he shouted and said, "Turn around, please, sir. I'd like to see some identification."

I slowly pulled my wallet out, opened it, and handed it to him.

He read my driver's license, looked at me, back at the license, and at me again.

"Okay, sir, if you wouldn't mind stepping into my car, the heater's on." He handed my wallet back and opened the rear door. I settled into the backseat, and he got in behind the wheel. Another cop joined him in the front seat.

"You're Devlin Haskell?"

"Yes. Do you want to see my license again?"

"No, and that's your current address?"

"Yeah, just up on the next block. Right across from the La Grolla restaurant. Are these bank robbers near my house?"

"Actually, they're in it. You got someone living with you?"

"Well, yes, I mean sort of, but I just dropped her off at her folks' house and— Wait a minute. Is this two guys?"

"It is."

"I just started renting a bedroom out through Airbnb. There are two guys staying in there. They've been here, well, this is their fourth or fifth day. They extended another night, and as far as I know, they were planning to leave tomorrow."

"They have names?" the cop in the passenger seat asked.

"Yeah, umm, Ethan and Wilmer Hoover. They said they were brothers and told me they were ministers. Said they came to town to do the Lord's work. They've been quiet. No problems. I hardly ever saw them. At night, they stayed in the room reading the bible. At least that's what I thought they were doing."

"Anyone in the house with them?"

"Yeah, Morton, he's my golden retriever. He didn't seem too interested in them."

"Can you give us a layout of the floor plan?"

"Yeah, sure, you want me to draw it out for you?"

"Maybe bring him to the van," the other cop said.

The cop behind the driver's wheel nodded and said, "If it's okay, we'll run you over to the man in charge. He's set up in the alley behind us."

"Yeah, sure, anything I can do to help," I said. I couldn't believe the two ministers were involved in robbing banks.

The squad car backed up, made a U-turn, drove a half block, and turned into the alley. Three white paneled vans and four squad cars were parked in the lot behind the La Grolla restaurant. I thought I might be able to sneak something from the restaurant kitchen, but instead of the restaurant, we headed into one of the vans. Three cops were in there talking on headphones. One of them held up his index finger, signaling to wait a moment. Maybe a minute later, he raised the mouthpiece on his headphone and said, "What is it?"

"This gentleman owns the house the suspects are in."

I noted the rank on his collar. "Hi, Captain. I'm Dev Haskell. I'm a private investigator. I was renting an

Airbnb room to two guys. They told me they were minister. They've been here for three or four days and, actually, just today asked if they could extend one more
day."

"What are their names?"

"Ethan and Wilmer Hoover. At least that was what
they told me."

"Hoover, like the former director of the FBI?"

"Yeah. I never looked at an ID. They paid, and actually, they were nice guests. I never heard anything
from them. They remained in their room when they were
in the house. I figured they were just reading the bible.
No noise, and they usually got their meals at fast food
places like McDonalds."

"Who else is in the house?"

"Other than my dog, Morton, no one I know of. A
friend was staying there, but I dropped her off at her
folks' house this morning. She was still at her folks thirty
minutes ago."

"Step over here," he said, and we moved to a counter attached to the side of the van. Three laptops sat on
the counter. He pressed the shift button on one of the
keyboards, and a screen illuminated. The image looked
like it came from a security camera. Three women and a
man were lying on the floor with their hands over their
heads. A guy dressed in black and wearing a black balaclava stood over them. He had what looked like a black

canvas bag strapped over his shoulders, and he was holding an automatic weapon, maybe an AR15, but I couldn't be sure.

"That could be one of them. They were always dressed in black. Like I said, they told me they were ministers and were 'doing the Lord's work.' That's a quote. That bag on the guy's back looks an awful lot like the one they carried. They drove a black Toyota. I gave them access to my garage, so their car is probably parked in there. I don't have a license number on the car."

"There were just the two of them?"

"As far as I know."

He pulled a yellow legal pad from a rack attached to the wall. "Can you draw a floor plan for me?"

"Be happy to. I have house keys on my key ring." I sketched out the first floor on one sheet, labeled the rooms, the staircase, the front and backdoors, and windows. I did the same for the second floor, adding closets and the tub and shower stall in the bathroom.

"You said you've got a dog in there?"

"Yeah, a Golden Retriever named Morton. He's probably hiding under my bed. I've got their cell phone number here," I said, pulling out my phone.

"Oh, thanks, this will help. Owen, have them do a trace on this. See if we can't confirm a name and make sure they're located in the house." He read off the phone number, and one of the other guys wrote it down and a moment later talked to someone on his headphone.

"I'd like to get my dog out of there if I could."

"Yeah, I'm sure you would, but I can't let you risk it."

"Has anyone been injured in the bank robberies?"

"Not as of yet, and I intend to keep it that way."

"What if you try calling that number and tell them I'm coming to get my dog?"

"Are you crazy?"

"Probably. Look, I can just open the front door and call him. I won't even step inside."

"No, sorry, but we can't do that. We can't take the chance. Under the circumstances, the pressure level is extremely high for them as well as us. I'd much prefer to move slowly, and hopefully, we'll be able to talk them into surrendering. First things first, let's see if we can't contact them."

Forty-four

Ten minutes later, the information came back that the cellphone number was indeed registered to the name Ethan Hoover. The captain spoke into his headphone, and a moment later, a guy in civilian clothes stepped into the van.

"Jackson, this gentleman owns the house. Our suspects were Airbnb guests. We've got their phone number. I'd like you to try to make a call. There's a dog in there named Morton. As far as we know, no hostages."

Jackson nodded and sat down at one of the computers. "I'm going to be on speaker. No one is to speak. Only me. Is that clear?"

Everyone, including me, nodded.

"Here's the number and the names, Ethan and Wilmer Hoover. You said they told you they were brothers and ministers?" Jackson said.

"Yeah, told me they were here doing the Lord's work."

Jackson scanned the list for a long moment then said, "Okay, I'm going to place the call. No one says anything." He clicked in the phone number on the keyboard. After the third ring, a voice answered.

"Yeah?"

Jackson glanced at me, and I mouthed the word, Ethan.

"Hi, is this Ethan?"

"Who wants to know?"

"My name is Jackson. My friends call me Jack."

"Are we friends?"

"Well, I don't want to see you, or Wilmer, get hurt. That's not going to do any of us any good. What I'd like you to do is calmly step out of the house. I could meet you on the front porch so you'll feel safe, and we can put this whole unfortunate episode to rest."

"What if you just give us a five-minute head start?"

"Come on, Ethan. You know we can't do that. After four bank robberies in as many days, it just can't work like that. I can make sure that no one gets hurt. Everyone just takes it easy. All you have to do is meet me on the front porch."

"What do we do with the woman?"

"The woman?" Jackson said and looked at me.

I held out my hands and shook my head.

"Yeah, yeah, her name is Karen," Ethan said. "She lives here, and if you want to keep her safe, you'd better pull everyone back for your own good. Well, and for hers too."

Jackson looked at me.

I shook my head then stepped over and quickly wrote on the legal pad, 'She's at parent's house. Spending night. Not with them. I drove her.'

"I have to tell you, Ethan. We have it on pretty good authority, she's not there." Jackson mouthed the words 'Call Her.'

I pulled my cell out and called Maddie. It seemed to take forever. She finally answered on the fourth ring. "Maddie," I whispered.

"Dev? Is everything okay? Why are you whispering?"

"You're at your folks?"

"Have you been drinking?"

"Are you at your folks'?"

"Of course, I am. What's going on?"

I nodded at Jackson and hung up.

"Ethan, you should probably stop screwing around. We know Karen isn't there. We know the owner isn't there. It's just you and Wilmer in the house. Now, we can sit this out and wait for a few hours or even days, but it's going to end, hopefully with you guys stepping outside. I'd like to make that as safe as possible for you, for both of you."

"You got the owner there with you?"

"The owner, you mean Mr. Haskell? The owner of that house?"

"Yeah, Dev Haskell, you got him there?"

"No. We haven't seen him."

"Well, when you do see him, call me back. Until then, we got nothing to talk about," Ethan said and hung up.

"What the hell does he want with you?" Jackson said, looking at me.

"I have no idea. I barely know the guy. I've seen him for maybe a total of ten minutes over the last four days. Other than saying hi and letting him park in my garage, we haven't talked."

My phone rang. I pulled it out, thinking it might be Ethan. It was Maddie. "Hi Maddie, sorry about that call. I'm kind of in the middle of something. Let me call you back in a while."

"You're okay?"

"Yeah, fine. Give my best to your folks and sisters. Enjoy," I said and disconnected. I explained to Jackson that we referred to Maddie as Karen, where the Hoovers were concerned. He seemed to think about that but didn't ask a question.

We sat around for a good half-hour, then Jackson said, "I'm going to call him back and tell him we couldn't find you."

"I'll go up on the front porch with you if you want. I'd just like to bring this to a close," I said.

"That's what we'd all like to do is bring this to a close, but I can't have you on the front porch with me. I'm going to call him back and tell him we can't find you. It will add some pressure to the situation and, sooner or later, hopefully, force them to step outside."

Jackson clicked on the number, and Ethan answered on the second ring. "Is this Jack?"

"It is, Ethan. Everything okay on your end?"

"Everything is just fine here. You find Haskell yet?"

"No, we didn't. I'm thinking he and Karen left town for a romantic couple of days. Maybe up north somewhere with no phone access. Could turn out to be a long wait, and we all need our beauty sleep. What do you say we just meet on the porch?"

"Told you before, no." Click.

"Damn it," Jackson said. "You have any discussion or disagreement with him?"

"No, I'm not kidding, nothing more than hello. I don't believe Karen, or umm, Maddie, hardly ever talked with either of them. They told her they were going to stay another night but that was it."

"He's stalling for time," Jackson said.

"I told you, I'll be happy to go with you."

"No way," Jackson said.

It was another two hours, and my stomach was growling. Jackson placed another call. After a half-dozen rings, Ethan answered. "Yeah, what now?" he said. It sounded like he was eating something.

"Ethan, just checking in to see if there's anything you need. It's going to be a long night. We're all hunkered down. Heaters are going. Can you believe it? They've got a couple of women serving us hot chocolate with marshmallows. I gotta tell you I haven't had that since I was a kid."

"Yeah, me either. Our mom used to make it for us when we'd come home after skating. All we found here was a piece of chicken in the fridge. We made some peanut butter on toast."

"We had a nice stew delivered, big chunks of meat, cooked onions, a slice of French bread. I could barely finish it. You know, I'm thinking you guys are going to be down to eating oatmeal pretty soon. Maybe it's about time you come in, and we'll head downtown, get you fed. I know I said it before, but we aren't going anywhere. We can't, Ethan. We gotta bring it to a close sooner or later. What do you say?"

"You talk to Haskell yet?"

"No, haven't heard from him."

"Call me back in ten minutes," Ethan said and hung up.

"What do you think?" the captain said.

"I think he's going to do two things. He's talking with his brother. They know there's no way out. They can either surrender or shoot themselves. The other thing is, be prepared to have them say they'll give themselves up if Haskell's here."

"Haskell, why him?" the captain said.

"I'll do it," I said.

"No way."

"It may be because you're the only guy they know here, even if you just said hello. They may trust you."

"No, we can't do that."

"Look, Captain, they're holed up in my house. I want this to be over. I go up on the porch with Jackson. You got guys all around. It's not like they're going to escape. How about this, Jackson tells them I'll go, but I want to see my dog, Morton. They can bring him outside. Have their hands up, unarmed. If you sneak some guys along the front hedge and the side of the porch, they can cover us. There aren't any first-floor windows along that section of the house."

"I don't like it, too dangerous."

"What if I sign something that says I release you, the city, and the entire department from any responsibility?"

"I'll probably be fired." He seemed to think for a moment, then said, "Okay, let me make a call," he said. He pulled the microphone on his headset down to his mouth and stepped over to a corner. I could hear him talking but couldn't understand a word.

He was back a couple of minutes later. "Okay, against my better judgment, they've agreed to it. I want you to put a vest on first."

Jackson placed his call as I pulled my jacket off and slipped on the black vest. I pulled the Velcro straps tight and then forced my arms back into the sleeves on my jacket and buttoned it up.

"Hi Ethan, I got some good news. Haskell just showed up. I guess he heard about this on the news and came back to town. He's going to join me on the front porch."

"Is he with you? I want to hear his voice."

"Hold on just a minute," Jackson said and motioned me forward. "Okay, here he is."

"Hi Ethan, sorry to hear you're in a bit of a mess. I want to get Morton out of there. He hasn't been out since this morning."

"Wilmer let him out earlier this afternoon."

"Oh, good, thanks. I still want to get him out of there. You guys, too. Let's shut it down and get everyone safe, especially you guys."

There was a long pause, and then Ethan said, "Okay, we'll see you at the front door. We pick up on anything happening, all deals are off."

"I got it. See you shortly. Remember to bring Morton and no weapons, okay?"

"Yeah," Click.

"Okay, I'm ready if you are," I said.

"Give us five minutes to position people," the captain said, then walked to the corner again and began talking.

After a couple of minutes, Jackson and I stepped out of the van. "Appreciate you offering to do this, Haskell. Keep your distance. Don't say anything. And something starts to go wrong, you drop to the ground. You carrying?"

"No. Are you?"

He shook his head, and we headed around the side of the building and stood on the sidewalk across the street from my house. All the lights were off in the house.

Forty-five

Two guys had crawled through the snow and were lying below my front porch. A man with a long gun, looking through the scope, was lying on the floor of the neighbors' porches on either side of my place. Two more guys were crouched down in my driveway and up against the house. That was six guys plus the ones we couldn't see who, no doubt, were around.

"You ready for this?" Jackson asked.

"Ready as I'll ever be."

"I want you to remain a step behind me. Anything happens, you drop to the ground and let us deal with it. Got it?"

"Yeah, I heard you the first time. Let's get going. I want to get Morton out of there."

We slowly crossed the street. I remained a step behind Jackson, who was walking very slowly. We stepped over the curb, walked across the public sidewalk, and up the two steps into my front yard. Jackson took four more steps and stopped.

"What are you doing? You told him we'd meet them on the porch."

"We will. I just want to give them a chance to scope us out. We'll head up in a second. We're going to go very slowly. Keep your hands out where they can see them," he said and slowly placed his hands off to the side. I did the same.

"Now, follow me, but off to the right so they can see you. I don't want them thinking you're hiding something," Jackson said and headed toward the front porch. When we got to the steps, he called, "Ethan. Ethan, you there? Ethan, Haskell and I are out here."

The front door opened a crack. "You two step up onto the porch."

We climbed the three steps and took another two steps on the porch, so we were halfway to the front door. The door opened wider, and Morton appeared. When he saw me, he lunged in my direction but was held back by his leash.

"Need to have you guys come out real slowly, Ethan. Let's get this part over so we can go somewhere nice and warm," Jackson said.

"You mean your damn jail?"

"That's better than the alternative," Jackson said.

Morton strained on the leash and barked.

"Come here and get your damn dog, Haskell."

"You need to step outside, Ethan. Both of you. You and Wilmer. Come on out. We're freezing our asses off standing here."

Ethan's head suddenly peeked out the door and looked around. "It's just you two?"

"That's what you said you wanted. It's just us."

"And I want Morton. Give him to me, please," I said. He gave Morton some more room on the leash but not enough to come to me. "What are you doing, Ethan? Let him loose. We've done everything you wanted us to—"

Morton suddenly bounded toward me and was up on his hind legs, licking me.

Ethan was out the door with a pistol pointed at me. Before I knew what was happening, he pushed Morton away and was wrapping an arm around my neck. Morton suddenly sprang with his teeth bared, clamping onto Ethan's wrist. He screamed, dropped his pistol, and took hold of Morton. I suddenly snapped when he went for Morton. I kicked his feet out from under him and chopped him in the throat. Wilmer stepped into the doorway, armed, and I charged. I slammed my shoulder into him full force, wrapped my arms around him, and we sailed through the air. I felt the wind get knocked out of him as I landed on top of him. His AR15 fired off three rounds.

I kneed him between the legs, took hold of the AR15, and rolled off to the side. Wilmer curled into a fetal position and threw up as I aimed the AR15 at him.

Jackson was holding Ethan's pistol and was in the process of pulling Morton off of Ethan's bloody face. Two officers rushed past me, rolled Wilmer onto his stomach, and cuffed his hands behind his back. Three officers were on top of Ethan, cuffing him. One of them was on his radio, calling in the paramedics and giving the all-clear.

I stepped outside and hugged Morton.

"He saved both of us, Haskell. I'm buying that dog a steak!" Jackson said and hugged Morton. Morton licked his hands and then went back to licking me.

The police began to search my house. I showed them the Airbnb room where Ethan and Wilmer had stayed. I thanked Jackson, the Captain, and as many cops as I could. I talked to two reporters from the newspaper for a couple of minutes, and finally, Morton and I headed down to my office. I stretched out in my desk chair, and Morton curled up on his pillow in front of the file cabinet. We were both asleep almost immediately.

Epilogue

My cellphone ringing woke me the following morning. "Hello," I said without looking to see who was calling. Morton snuggled further down on his pillow and placed a paw over his ear.

"Dev. Are you okay? I'm reading about you and Morton in the paper," Maddie said.

"Oh, the story made the morning paper? I talked to some reporters last night. I'm surprised they made their deadline. What does the article say?"

"Well, start with the headline 'Golden Retriever Saves the Day.' They almost suggest Morton made the arrest."

"Not far from the truth. How're your Mom and Dad doing?"

"We're all doing just fine. I slept in my old room, and my mom climbed into bed with me. It's better than I ever could have imagined."

"That's great, and no surprise, it's wonderful. You all deserve it. Your room is always open at my place whenever you're ready to return. I've decided not to do

Airbnb anymore. Once was enough for me." Maddie didn't say anything for a moment. "You still there?"

"You know, Dev, I'm not sure how to say this. Please don't take it personally, but I'm going to need some time. We all are. I think it would be better for everyone involved, including you, if I move back with my folks for the foreseeable future."

"You sure? I mean, if that's what you want, I'm okay with it. But I'd love to have you at my place and no pressure. We could just see how things work out. You set the pace, and I'll—"

"Oh, that's sweet of you, Dev. Really it is, and I appreciate your generous offer. But I took a big gamble after being married to Colton Ferral. I'm probably going to be in recovery mode for quite some time. I'm going to contact the police today. I'm sure they'll have lots of questions, and I'll tell them everything I know."

I took a deep breath and said, "Well, I get it. Just remember the door is always open."

"Thanks for not putting pressure on me, and thanks for being there when I didn't know who I could turn to."

"Yeah, that's me."

"Thanks, Dev. You stay safe," Maddie said and disconnected.

I put the coffee on, took Morton for a walk, and was just about to go back into the building when a faded orange Ford Fiesta parked across the street, and Louie climbed out. "Well, he has risen," Louie called as he crossed the street. "What have you two been up to?"

"I got the coffee on upstairs. Let's grab a cup, and I'll fill you in." We chatted for a couple of hours. I told Louie most of the story, leaving out any hints of a relationship with Maddie. He left for a court appearance, and maybe a half-hour later, there was a knock on the door, and Jackson stepped in. "Good morning, Dev. How'd you sleep, or should I ask where?"

"Hey, Jackson, good to see you. We camped out down here last night. Any idea when we can get back into my place?"

"I just got the word. They're finished. They recovered the money. So, you're free to go back home."

"Was there much damage?"

"From what I could see, no. Given your involvement last night, they were pretty good at returning things to their proper place. I did see three bullet holes in the staircase wall. The BCA team removed the slugs. I want to thank you again. Things were about to go the wrong way. If it weren't for you, well, and Morton. I told you I was going to buy him a steak. All right with you if I give this to him?" he said and held out a package wrapped in white butcher's paper.

Morton leaped off his pillow. His tail was wagging and beating against one of the client chairs.

"Yeah, give it to him. He more than earned it. I just can't believe those two were the bank robbers, and I had no idea."

"Hey, if they hadn't pulled that last robbery and just left town, I'm not sure we ever would have got them. The first three robberies went so well, they dropped their guard. They took three or four minutes longer on yesterday's robbery, and a squad car was in pursuit as they fled the scene."

Jackson unwrapped the steak and held it out to Morton. He snatched it and hurried back to his pillow so he wouldn't have to share.

"Oh, you just went to the very top of his friend list."

"Never enough of that. Well, I've got a follow-up interview in thirty minutes. They'd like you to stop down sometime this morning for one as well, strictly procedure, no problems."

"I'll be happy to do that. Thanks again for doing a great job," I said.

"I was just in a supporting role. You and Morton were the stars," he said and laughed. We shook hands, and I watched out the window as Jackson drove off.

I left a note for Louie, letting him know I was doing a follow-up interview, and headed down to the police station. The interview took maybe two hours, really just questions about how I knew Ethan and Wilmer. Did they interact with anyone else? How did they find me? The usual standard stuff. The police had recovered all the stolen funds from the trunk of the Toyota parked in my garage. Aaron LaZelle stopped in just as we were finishing up and gave me a hard time. We arranged to have dinner the following week. He promised to buy.

On the way back to the office, I got the urge to drive past the spot where this all started, the riverbank. I planned to just cruise past, but there were fresh tire tracks in the snow. My first thought was maybe Maddie had been down here, but that didn't seem right.

I turned off the road and followed the tracks for maybe twenty feet, then climbed out of the car. There were a number of boot prints in the snow and some blood. The trail led maybe ten feet out onto the river where there was a hole in the ice. The hole was a lot bigger than the one Maddie had made. It had frozen over, but the ice on the hole was nowhere as thick as the area around it. I couldn't figure out what the deal was, so I decided the best plan was to get off the ice, and I headed back to my car. As I opened the driver's door, my question was answered. There it was, resting in the snow beneath my car, the wrapper for a Snickers bar.

I picked up Morton at the office. We went for a quick walk and headed home. Jackson was right. Pretty much everything was just the way I left it. I tore the sheets off the bed in the Airbnb room. Anything belonging to Ethan and Wilmer, luggage, clothes, and of course, the stolen money, had been taken by the police. I took the bed linens down to the laundry room and tossed them in the washing machine.

Apparently, Maddie had been here sometime this morning after the police were finished because a bottle of Jameson and a card from her rested on the kitchen counter next to the house key I'd given her. I opened the card:

'Darling Dev, where to begin? I can't thank you enough for all that you've done, protecting me, my sisters, and my parents. Not to mention eliminating Colton and his mother from any future dealings. Thank you so much. Because of you my gamble paid off. Now I'm going to be working on getting my act together, and that's going to take some time. I grabbed my clothes, and I'll send someone over to haul all the boxes out of your front entry. I think it best if we don't contact one another. You've been so kind, thank you. I ask only one more thing, that you understand and not take this personally.

God bless. Stay safe.
Maddie'

For some reason, I wasn't surprised. I wasn't even mad. I guess I half-expected it. I was going to miss her, but unfortunately, it seemed like the logical move, and Maddie had always been logical, not to mention smart, sexy, gorgeous, and a number of other things, all good.

The load in the washer would be finished in thirty minutes, so I went up to the guest room. The key was in the lock, and I opened the door. Everything looked neat, and it wouldn't surprise me if Maddie had dusted and vacuumed before she left. I checked the dresser, and what few items had been in there were gone. All the drawers were empty.

As I removed the pillowcase from the pillow, I caught just a hint of her perfume, and I got a lump in my throat. I pulled back the spread and blankets on the bed and tossed the sheet onto the floor. I lifted the far corner of the fitted sheet and the mattress pad, pulled them back, and stopped. There was a packet of $20 bills wrapped with a violet-colored paper strap labeled $2000. I pulled the sheet and pad back a little further, and another, and another packet appeared. All in all, I counted ten packets. I flipped the mattress but didn't find any more. I hurried into the Airbnb room, pulled off the mattress pad, but that bed was empty. I went into my room and stripped the bed, nothing.

I went back to Maddie's bed in the guest room. Ten packets added up to a total of twenty grand. Maybe my gamble had paid off, too…

The End

Thank you for taking the time to read **The Big Gamble.** If you enjoyed the read, please consider taking a moment to leave a review. Even if it's just a short line it really helps.

Don't miss the sample of **Bad to the Bone,** the next book in the Dev Haskell series.

Sneak Peek

Bad To The Bone

Second Edition

MIKE FARICY

Prologue

The server asked, "Can I get you a glass of wine?" "Actually, I think I'll order a bottle of…" It was my third date with Sandie, which meant this was the one where we finally got down to business. On the first date, we learned a little about one another. On the second date, she had to prove she wasn't a slut, so I got a lingering kiss on the cheek. Now tonight, our third date, with all that out of the way, well, let's just say tonight would be memorable.

Of course, she was stylishly late, but that had been the case on our previous two dates, so no big deal. The server returned with the bottle of wine and showed me the label. It didn't make any difference to me, so I just nodded. She poured a small amount into my glass, which I was supposed to sniff, sip, savor, and hopefully give approval. Instead, I just said, "Go ahead and fill my glass."

Sandie entered about five minutes later. She was an attractive blonde with a great figure. She glanced around the restaurant and caught sight of me just as I raised my wine glass toward her. As she headed over, I noticed two guys at different tables giving her the once-over. Ever the gentleman, I stood and pulled out the chair for her.

"Thanks," she said but didn't follow up with a peck on the cheek. "What a day. I gotta tell ya."

"Crazy?" I asked and took hold of the wine bottle to fill her glass.

"Oh, thanks, no wine for me tonight. Excuse me, ma'am?" she said to our server who was stepping away from another table. "If I could get something from the bar?"

"Certainly. What would you like?"

I was hoping she'd order a triple martini or a double manhattan.

"I think just a glass of sparkling water with a twist of lemon."

I felt a cloud suddenly descending on my hopes for the night. "You feeling okay?"

"Me, yeah, not a problem. Why? Are you upset just because I'm not drinking?"

"No, no, not upset. I wanted to make sure you were feeling okay, is all." I thought her tone came across as a little aggressive, but I let it go. Maybe this was her way of getting me to have a little too much to drink and lower my moral standards, not that I really had any.

"I feel fine."

"So, how was your day?" I asked and followed up with a smile.

"Could we just talk about something else?"

"Yeah, sure. Not a problem. I had an interesting thing happen today. My office mate is an attorney and—"

"Yeah, I know, you told me that the last time we met."

Things more or less went downhill from there. We ordered dinner, and it could not have been on the table for more than five minutes when Sandie signaled our server.

The woman plastered a smile on her face and hurried over to the table. "Is everything all right?"

"Actually, would you mind placing this in a takeout container? I'm going to have to leave."

"No, not a problem. Back in just a moment," the server said. She picked up the plates with Sandie's main course and her salad and hurried off to the kitchen.

"You're leaving? What's the problem? Something I said?"

"I shouldn't have to tell you, Dev."

"I thought we were just having a nice conversation. You were telling me about the lake place your folks have and—"

"Yes, and you said you'd like to see it sometime, basically inserting yourself into my personal life. Turns out you're just like every other guy I've dated. You want to line up my family against me, isolate me, and—"

"Sandie, what are you talking about? It sounded like a nice place. What lake did you say it was on?"

"See, there you go. Next thing I know, you'll be up there knocking on the door, introducing yourself, and I'll—"

"Here you are, ma'am," the server said, placing two boxes on the table in front of Sandie. She glanced at me for half a second.

"Thank you," Sandie said. Once the server left, she stood, picked up the boxes, and said, "Call me if you want to get together this weekend." With that, she turned and headed out the door. I poured myself another glass of wine and shoved a forkful of ravioli into my mouth. I paid the bill, ninety bucks, by the way, plus a tip, and headed home. Morton, my golden retriever, met me at the door. We watched a movie we'd seen before and then went up to bed.

One

I was up before my alarm went off. Morton wandered downstairs an hour later. I let him outside, filled his food and water dishes, and let him back in.

I was on my computer going through emails. I deleted just about all of them until I reached the email from Heidi Bauer, my on-again, off-again friend with benefits. I hadn't heard from her in over a year. There were actually two emails. One was sent last night, about the time I was listening to Sandie as she went off the deep end. I clicked on the first one.

Hi Dev. Long time no see. Interested in coming over for dinner tomorrow night?

Coming from Heidi, I knew or used to know, that was big. The second email was sent this morning, just after 5:00 am.

Please tell me you can make it tonight and you're not going to the meat raffle at The Spot bar or leering in some poor woman's bedroom window.

I dialed her number. She answered on the second ring. "Dev?"

"Hi, Heidi. Long time since I heard from you."

"I know, I know. Of course, that works both ways. I've missed you," she said, ignoring the fact that the last time we spoke, she told me not to call her and then followed up with telling me she never, ever wanted to see me again.

"Yeah, I've missed you too, Heidi," I said and meant it, not that I hadn't been enjoying myself, well, with the exception of last night and maybe a half-dozen other dates that had gone that way over the last year.

"Can you come over tonight?"

"You bet I can. You name a time and tell me what I can bring."

"Is 6:00 too early?"

"No, I think I can do that. Let me just cancel a meeting I've got and—"

"Oh, you don't have to do that, Dev."

"It's not a problem," I said since the meeting was a lie. "I didn't want to go anyway. It's a meeting with city staff. You know how boring they can be."

"Oh, good. I can't wait to see you, Dev."

"What can I bring?"

"Just yourself and make sure you're well rested."

"You sure? I could—"

"No, Dev. I *need* to see you." She emphasized the word *need,* suggesting all sorts of wonderful options.

I was whistling "Walk on By," an ancient hit by Dionne Warwick from back in the 1960s, when we arrived in the office. Morton waited patiently until I tossed him a biscuit then hurried over to his bed so he wouldn't have to share with me. I put the coffee on, and my officemate, Louie Laufen, wandered in about twenty minutes later. I heard the stairs creaking as he made his way up to our office and had a coffee mug waiting on his picnic table desk when he entered. True to form, he was red-faced and gasping for breath. He gave me a little wave and settled into his desk chair. It took a couple of minutes and a half-dozen slurps of coffee before he had recovered enough to talk.

"Sounds like your dinner date was a success," he eventually said.

I'd switched from whistling to humming and suddenly couldn't remember the song I'd been destroying. "Oh, actually, it was a complete and utter disaster. A ninety-dollar dinner bill, and she left five minutes into the meal."

"You're kidding. She left? What did you do to cause that?"

"Nothing I can think of." I went on to give him the details.

"Holy cow, Dev. It almost sounds like she set you up right from the get-go and had planned all along to run off with a meal. I'd say you dodged a bullet."

"Gee, I never thought of it like that, but maybe you're right. Anyway, what's the old adage, 'when a door closes, you can climb out a window'?"

"I think it's 'when one door closes a window opens.' Alexander Graham Bell. Actually, his original quote was—"

"Something I don't need to hear. Right now, I'm more in the mindset of having dodged a bullet. Good riddance to gorgeous, crazy, Sandie. Guess who sent me an email last night?"

"I give up. Who? The IRS?"

"Not even funny, Louie. No, Heidi sent an email last night and another one this morning."

"Heidi? When was the last time you heard from her? She's not asking to be repaid for the time she had to post bail for you, is she?"

"No, and I don't see any point in even going in that direction. If you must know, she invited me over for dinner tonight. Told me I should probably rest up."

"That sounds rather promising," Louie said and slurped some more coffee.

"You think? Perfect timing. I only wish I could let Sandie know I already have a hot date for tonight."

"Call her and tell her."

I shook my head. "No, at best, she was just scamming dinner. I'm thinking she was really going crazy, and I intend to stay away, as far away as possible."

"You can sure pick 'em, Dev," Louie said just as my phone rang.

"Haskell Investigations."

"Hi, Dev, a voice from the past, Augie Douglas." We'd played hockey together in high school. He was a lot better than me, and we thought he'd go pro. A broken leg from a car accident put an end to that dream.

"Hey Augie, great to hear from you. It's been what, ten years?"

"More like twenty, dude."

"What's up?" I asked, figuring he wasn't calling just to catch up.

"A problem in the family I'm hoping you might be able to help with."

"What kind of problem?"

"You read in the newspaper where they arrested this kid for murdering the girl on the front porch?"

"Was that a week or two ago? She was a teenager, a college kid if I remember correctly. Was she going to the U?"

"Yeah, that's it. The boy's mother is a cousin of Mary Beth's. He swears he's innocent. Doesn't know anything about it."

"He was dating this girl, wasn't he?"

"I think that's what led the cops to him. Apparently, she broke up with him a few weeks earlier."

"I'm vaguely aware of the situation. I don't know anything other than what I heard on a couple of news reports," I said.

"You think you could maybe check some things out? See if you think he's getting screwed on this deal. From what I know of the kid, he's a nice guy, smart, just treading water after high school while he figures out what he wants to do."

"Yeah, I suppose I could check it out. You remember Aaron LaZelle? He works in homicide now."

"LaZelle? He's a cop?"

"Yeah, and a good one."

"Humf, I had no idea. Obviously, this doesn't sound good. To my knowledge, the kid doesn't have a record. At least, I don't think he does. I know he had a job bussing dishes at Tracy's bar."

"That place down on Robert Street?"

"Yeah, that's it. He'd been working there for almost a year. Unfortunately, he didn't show up for work the night the girl was murdered."

"Where was he?"

"He maintains he was out running."

"Does he have an attorney?"

"I believe someone has been appointed. Kid lives with his mother in a small apartment. There's no money."

"What's his name?"

"Cornell Thomas, his mom is Christine. She's a single mom, works in the school system, food service at a grade school. She lives—"

"Before we get to that, let me check out a couple of things. If he's got a court-appointed attorney, I'd like to see who it is. Let me touch base with the cops and find out what they have, and I'll get back to you."

"What's this gonna cost me?"

"Well, for starters, I'm thinking at least a lunch or dinner. Let me see what I find out, and we can take it from there."

"You mean that?"

"Yeah, at least to begin with. Let me check things out and we'll see what we're dealing with."

"Oh, thanks, Dev. That's really kind of you."

"I'll check things out and get back to you, Augie. Great to hear from you. Sorry it's under these circumstances."

"Thanks, Dev. Let me know when you have something, and I'll buy lunch or dinner."

"I'll hold you to that, Augie," I said, and we disconnected.

"New business?" Louie asked.

"Maybe, a freebie unfortunately," I said, turning on my computer. "You going to be here for a while?"

"I'm here all morning," Louie said.

"You mind if I leave Morton in your trusted care? I should be back before noon. You got plans for lunch?"

Louie shook his head and said, "I was thinking a barbecue from Rooster's might be just the thing."

"Consider it done, Louie."

I googled the Pioneer Press, our local newspaper, and searched for any articles on the murder. There were two, one the day following the shooting mentioning the victim, Penny Larson. A picture was attached of a pretty blonde girl. It may have been a high school yearbook photo.

The second article was two days after the shooting and was two paragraphs long. Cornell Thomas had been arrested the day before. The article mentioned that he had a prior relationship with Penny Larson. No specifics were given as to the reason he was linked to the murder.

TWO

I drove down to the courthouse. I had to park a block away in front of the public library. I could probably get the information by making a phone call, but I wanted to be there in person just in case someone gave me access to the files. I walked over to the courthouse, went through the security check, and then took the elevator up to the fourth floor. I stepped into the clerk's office and walked up to the counter.

"Hi, how can I help you?" a young man asked and smiled. He looked to be in his late twenties. I wasn't sure, but I pegged him for a law student.

"Hi, I'd like information on a murder case that has yet to go to trial. The defendant is a young man by the name of Cornell Thomas. I'd like the name of the attorney for the defense."

He ran his fingers across the keyboard, looked up after a moment, and said, "The court-appointed defense attorney in that matter is Martin Meyer."

"Would you happen to have an office address?"

He stared at me for a few seconds and then gave me the address. The office was over on University Avenue. I wrote it down in my notebook.

"Anything else I can help you with?" he asked, suggesting no other information was forthcoming.

"No, appreciate the help. Thank you."

He flashed a one-second smile, and I headed out the door.

Martin Meyer's building was a two-story structure on University Avenue. His office was a small storefront with his name on the door. My first thought was that it looked more like the office for someone who was handling evictions and speeding tickets, not a murder defense. The unit to the right was vacant and had a dusty 'For Rent' sign leaning against the front window. The unit to the left was a Cambodian restaurant. I pulled on the door to open it, but it was locked. Given the neighborhood, I wasn't surprised. There was a woman inside seated at a desk, and I knocked on the door. A lock buzzed. I opened the door and stepped inside.

The floor was concrete. There were four folding metal chairs arranged against a wall that looked like they'd been stolen from a church basement. The ceiling was open. There weren't any ceiling tiles, just steel beams, dangling light bulbs, and concrete slabs that made up the second floor. The woman at the desk looked up from her computer screen. "May I help you?"

"I hope so. I'd like to see Mr. Meyer."

"Do you have an appointment?"

"No, I'm afraid I don't. I'm here on behalf of an individual he's representing, Cornell Thomas."

That seemed to get her attention. "And you are?"

"My name is Devlin Haskell. I'm a private investigator."

"Let me check with him. Wait just a minute," she said as she pushed her chair back and stood. She knocked on the door in the corner and stepped inside, closing the door behind her.

I looked around the office. Not so much as a picture frame hanging on the walls. Other than the four metal folding chairs and the desk, chair, and computer, the only other item was a black plastic wastebasket. There was a pleasant scent that must have come from the Cambodian restaurant next door because my stomach suddenly growled.

The office door opened. The woman stepped out and said, "He can see you for a minute." She held the door for me.

As I stepped into the office, she closed the door behind me. Martin Meyer was seated behind his desk. He smiled at me, extended his hand, and didn't stand. "Hi, Martin Meyer," he said.

"Dev Haskell," I replied as I stepped over and shook hands with him. He had an iron grip, and it felt like I was squeezing a brick. It was then that I noticed he was seated in a wheelchair.

"Take a seat. Mind if I call you Dev?"

"God, no. I'm called a lot worse by this time on any day."

"Please call me Martin. Edith said you're working for Cornell Thomas?"

"Not exactly." I went on to explain my phone call from Augie Douglas. "So I'm just taking a perfunctory look at things. I'll visit the police next. At this point, all I know about the case is what I heard on the news. I couldn't pick Cornell Thomas out of a crowd of two."

He nodded a couple of times as I spoke, then seemed to think for a moment. "Here's the deal. I was appointed to represent Cornell. I've met with him three times over the last seven days. Right from the start, I believed he was innocent. Let me be clear here. Because of my physical condition, I could just as easily back out of representing him. On the other hand, my physical condition has a tendency to make me rather stubborn at times, and this is one of those times. The boy is innocent. I have no doubt. It's my opinion that, in an effort to close this case quickly, he was arrested without any real evidence and locked up."

"Do you know who the arresting officer was?"

He nodded and said, "A detective by the name of Norris Manning." The expression on my face apparently gave me away. "You know him?"

"Oh yeah. I'm lucky he didn't arrest me. Any crime that occurs in this city, Manning has me at the top of his suspect list. We are not what you would call friends. That said, I would have to admit that he is otherwise very good at what he does."

"Arresting the innocent?"

I smiled. "Current case not included. My understanding is your client claims he was out running at the time."

Meyer nodded. "He runs five to ten miles every other day. On the evening in question, he ran the length of Summit Avenue from the Cathedral down to the River Boulevard and back."

"That's nearly ten miles," I said.

"You're familiar with it? Are you a runner?"

"No, I live about three blocks from the Cathedral. I'm familiar with the streets. Lots of runners up and down Summit. Is there any proof of his running? Did anyone see him?" I was replaying the length of Summit Avenue in my head, wondering if any businesses or homes may have had security footage.

"You seem to be thinking of something."

"Wondering about security cameras that may have caught Cornell running past. Unfortunately, that was over a week ago. We could check, but it's a pretty thin chance there'd be a digital file."

As he wrote something down on a yellow legal pad, he asked, "Are you planning to go to the police today?"

"Yes, but informally. I have a friend down there I can talk to, provided he's in the office."

"You're not going to talk with Detective Manning?"

"Not at this point. I'm just trying to get some general information. Over the years, I've found it seems to work out best for all involved if I can avoid Manning."

"Would it make sense for me to list you as an associate in this investigation?"

"Maybe hold off on that and let me see what I can pick up in a friendly conversation. Once things become official, everyone tends to act as if they're on thin ice. One thing that would help, Cornell lives with his mother?"

"Yes."

"Would you happen to have an address? I'd like to get a sense of the home life."

Meyer nodded and ran his fingers over his keyboard. "Yeah, here we go. Christine Thomas, age thirty-seven. Her address is 422 Ravoux Street"

"Is that Capitol Plaza?"

"It is. You're familiar with it?"

"Somewhat, it's been a couple of years since I've been in the place. My memory is the units were awfully small."

"Well, nothing's changed. Christine has a two-bedroom unit. I think it's just seven-hundred and fifty square feet. Pretty tough to get any privacy unless you want to lock yourself in a bedroom. Might be one of the reasons Cornell ran so much."

"Does he own a car?"

Meyer shook his head. "No. He's been saving his money to pay for classes this fall at a community college. Unfortunately, now that's been put on hold."

"Let me see what I can learn this afternoon, and I'll get back to you," I said and stood.

Meyer held out his hand, we shook, and he handed me a business card. I pulled one of my cards from my wallet and gave it to him.

"I look forward to hearing from you, Dev."

Three

I stopped at Rooster's on the way back to the office and purchased three barbecue pork shoulder sandwiches. I parked in front of my building and took two of the sandwiches up to the office. Louie and Morton were both asleep when I stepped inside. Louie blinked awake as I set a Styrofoam tray on his picnic table desk. Morton remained asleep.

"Mmm-mmm, perfect timing," Louie said and stretched.

"Busy morning?"

"I got a lot accomplished. But all of a sudden, I found myself nodding off while on the computer, and experience has taught me that, in that situation, whenever possible, close my eyes for twenty minutes and then get back to work. One of the benefits of being self-employed. How was your morning? Did you learn anything?"

"Yeah, I did. You know an attorney named Martin Meyer?"

Louie shook his head.

"He's the court-appointed attorney representing Cornell Thomas. The guy has an office over on University Ave. Not the best part of town. The place is pretty much bare bones." I went on to describe Meyer and his office. "Anyway, he believes the kid is innocent and decided he wanted to represent him. Oh, and then he just happened to mention that the arresting officer in the case was Detective Norris Manning."

"Oh, really. Your favorite person. Gee, small world."

"Yeah, I'll be down there after lunch. Hopefully, just chatting up Aaron. The less Manning knows about me looking into things, the better it will be for everyone involved, me especially."

"He'll find out sooner or later."

"Yeah, I know that. But the longer he doesn't know, the better it'll be for me, well, and this kid, Cornell Thomas."

"Sounds like you're already on board," Louie said and took a large bite of his sandwich. A chunk of barbecue pork bounced off the cuff of his formerly clean white shirt and landed on a document resting on his desk. He frowned and then picked up the piece of pork, crammed it into his mouth, and licked his fingertips.

"Yeah, from the little I know, it looks like they could use some help. The arrest, at least initially, appears to be based on some awfully thin ground, but you know how that works. You get the wrong prosecutor on the case, and you've suddenly got a real uphill battle on your hands," I said.

We talked as we worked our way through the sand-wiches. Just as I was finishing up, Morton stretched and groaned but remained on his pillow. He looked at Louie and me for a couple of minutes. Eventually, he got to his feet, stretched once more, walked over, and stood at the door.

"Oh, I guess that's my sign to get up and take him for a walk." At the word, 'walk,' Morton's tail began to wag back and forth. I clipped the leash onto his collar, and we headed out the door. Morton visited his favorite fire hydrant and then sniffed every front gate and every other boulevard tree. We were back in the office twenty minutes later. I tossed him a biscuit which he inhaled in three quick bites.

"Hey, I was thinking about this kid you're going to be checking out," Louie said.

"Cornell Thomas."

"Yeah. Be interesting to find out how they landed on him. Did a friend of the victim friend him? The girl's parents?"

"Yeah, I'll keep that in the back of my mind. To tell you the truth, I'm not expecting much."

"Well, good luck. I'm here for another hour at least, and then I've got a 2:00 at the courthouse. Morton should be okay," Louie said.

"Thanks. I'll be back as soon as I can." I headed out the door. I climbed in my car, which now smelled like barbecue pork since the sandwich I was taking to Aaron had been resting on the passenger seat for the better part of the past half-hour.

Ten minutes later, I pulled into the gravel parking lot across the street from the police station. I managed to avoid the two large potholes and found an empty parking spot. I grabbed the barbecue sandwich and headed into the station.

Four

I recognized the desk sergeant and read his name tag. "Hi, Sergeant Cody, Dev Haskell to see Aaron LaZelle in Homicide."

"Is he expecting you?"

"No, I just wanted to drop this off for him," I said and lifted the Styrofoam container up toward him.

"Mmm-mmm, that wouldn't happen to be from Rooster's, would it?"

"As a matter of fact, it is."

"Lucky, LaZelle. Take a seat, and I'll see if he has time. You may just have to leave that meal with me," he said, then laughed at his joke.

I sat down on an orange plastic chair and waited for just a couple of minutes. A door suddenly opened, and a guy yelled, "Haskell?"

"Yeah, right here," I said as I hurried over. The guy was dressed in a blue shirt with the sleeves rolled up to his elbows. His pistol and badge were attached to his belt. As I approached, I looked at Cody behind the front desk and said, "Sorry, Sarge."

We took the elevator up a couple of floors. "Thanks for coming to get me," I said and got a nod in return. I followed the guy down the hall. He input his code into the keypad next to the Homicide door. The door buzzed, and he pulled it open. We stepped inside the squad room. Just like always, there was a bunch of activity. People talking on phones and typing away on computers.

"The LT is in his office," the guy said and headed over to a desk buried under stacks of files.

Aaron's office door was open, and I knocked on the doorframe. He was on the phone, and he waved me in and pointed to the two chairs positioned in front of his desk. "Yeah, I get it, but that still doesn't change the fact that he used a crowbar to make his point. The medical examiner is saying five blows to the head. I think at that stage, we're beyond this being an unfortunate mistake."

I set the Styrofoam container on his desk, and he raised his eyebrows, pulled it in front of him, and opened it up.

"Yeah, I guess that will be for the jury to decide. No, I can't comment on that at this time. Yes. Thank you," he said and hung up.

"That sounded lovely," I said.

"Someone's lawyer fishing for an excuse."

"And let me guess, he didn't find one."

"She actually," Aaron said and picked up the sandwich. "Mmm-mmm, perfect. I'm guessing from Rooster's?"

"Yeah, where else? Only the best for you, Aaron."

"So, to what do I owe the pleasure, a driving while intoxicated charge? Indecent exposure? Sex with a minor?"

"What? All of a sudden, I can't come down here and just be nice without getting accused. And besides, that girl said she was almost eighteen."

Aaron stared for a second.

"Okay, bad joke. No, actually, guess who I heard from this morning?"

Aaron had just taken a large bite and pointed to his bulging cheeks.

"I got a call from Augie Douglas. Haven't talked to him, let alone seen him, in twenty years."

Aaron chewed for a long moment then swallowed and said, "What's he up to? God, I thought he'd really go places. He was skating for the U and getting calls from all sorts of agents when he was in that car accident. Who was the girl that was driving that night?"

"Mary Beth Angelo. Guess what? He married her."

Aaron stopped in mid-bite. "Really?"

"Yeah."

"Mmm-mmm, I never would have guessed. What's he doing now?"

"We never really got into that."

"Why'd he call you?" Aaron asked and took another bite.

"Well, he wanted me to look into something. In fact, I'm hoping you might be able to help me."

Aaron set his sandwich back in the Styrofoam tray. "I knew this was too good to be true. You get nailed on something?"

"No, honest, Aaron, this isn't about me. It turns out Augie's wife, Mary Beth, has a cousin. She's the mother of a kid named Cornell Thomas, and he's been arrested for the murder of—"

"The Larson girl. Penny Larson. Did Augie happen to mention that Penny and Cornell had a fight, broke up, and a week later, he shot her?"

"No, he didn't say anything about that."

"That would suggest that he failed to mention the kid was in possession of the murder weapon."

"In possession of the murder weapon?" I asked.

"Yeah, a Glock 17. The serial numbers had been filed off the weapon. We've run a ballistics test, and at no surprise, it's a match to the round that killed the Larson girl. She was shot at about twenty-five feet. Murdered on the front porch of her home, one round to the head, just above her left eye."

"He had the weapon?"

"Yeah, of course, he denies having it. The only problem is, it was found in his bedroom. Right under his pillow as a matter of fact. He said he'd never seen it before."

"Fingerprints?"

Aaron shook his head. "Wiped clean, but DNA was—"

"That could have come from the bed. If someone had put it there to—"

"Really, Dev. The kid's room is searched, and the pistol is found. Now either he put it there, or his mother did. My money is on him."

"But under his pillow, why not at least stuff it beneath the mattress or tape it to the bottom of a chest of drawers?"

"Yeah, or better yet, drop it off a bridge and into the Mississippi. But he didn't do that, Dev. He was probably going to toss it in a dumpster the next day but was just too busy to do it that night. Or maybe, he just thought he'd never be caught, and now, after taking a life, he's a big bad gangster, and who wouldn't want to have him in their gang?"

"He's into gangs?"

"Not that we know of, yet. But we're checking it out."

"He's being represented by an attorney named Martin Meyer," I said.

Aaron took another bite of his sandwich and nodded. "Yeah, he's pro bono, and from what I know, this is his first time in the big leagues. Look, Dev, at this point, the case is out of our hands and is on the district attorney's desk. I basically told you everything we got. I'm not trying to be a wise-ass, but it has all the looks of an open and shut affair. As for his attorney, I'm sure Martin Meyer is a hard-working guy who just wants to see justice served. But if I found out he was one of those happy thoughts guys where everyone deserves a second chance, and they didn't mean to do something bad, well, tell that to the Larson family. Tell it to the girl's folks."

"The kid didn't have a record, did he?"

"No, he didn't, but he jumped right into the big time, and now he's about to get thirty years to think about the decision he made. It's an open and shut case, Dev. Mmm-mmm, thanks for the sandwich, by the way."

To be Continued . . .

Better grab your copy of **Bad to the Bone**, and see what happens. Things are about to get crazy…

Books by Mike Faricy
Crime Fiction Firsts

A boxset of the first four books in four crime fiction series:

Russian Roulette; Dev Haskell series
Welcome; Jack Dillon Dublin Tales series
Corridor Man; Corridor Man series
Reduced Ransom! Hot Shot series

The following titles comprise the Dev Haskell series:

Russian Roulette: Case 1
Mr. Swirlee: Case 2
Bite Me: Case 3
Bombshell: Case 4
Tutti Frutti: Case 5
Last Shot: Case 6
Ting-A-Ling: Case 7
Crickett: Case 8
Bulldog: Case 9
Double Trouble: Case 10
Yellow Ribbon: Case 11
Dog Gone: Case 12
Scam Man: Case 13
Foiled: Case 14
What Happens in Vegas… Case 15
Art Hound: Case 16
The Office: Case 17

Star Struck: Case 18
International Incident: Case 19
Guest From Hell: Case 20
Art Attack: Case 21
Mystery Man: Case 22
Bow-Wow Rescue: Case 23
Cold Case: Case 24
Cash Up Front: Case 25
Dream House: Case 26
Alley Katz: Case 27
The Big Gamble: Case 28
Bad to the Bone: Case 29
Silencio!: Case 30
Surprise, Surprise: Case 31
Hit & Run: Case 32
Suspect Santa: Case 33
P.I. Apprentice: Case 34
Rebel Without a Clue: Case 35
Puppy Love: Case 36

The following titles are Dev Haskell novellas:
Dollhouse
The Dance
Pixie
Fore!
Twinkle Toes
(*a Dev Haskell short story*)

The following are Dev Haskell Boxsets:
Dev Haskell Boxset 1-3
Dev Haskell Boxset 4-6
Dev Haskell Boxset 7-9
Dev Haskell Boxset 10-12
Dev Haskell Boxset 13-15
Dev Haskell Boxset 16-18
Dev Haskell Boxset 19-21
Dev Haskell Boxset 22-24
Dev Haskell Boxset 25-27
Dev Haskell Boxset 28-30
Dev Haskell Boxset 1-7
Dev Haskell Boxset 8-14
Dev Haskell Boxset 15-19
Dev Haskell Boxset 20-24
Dev Haskell Boxset 25-29

The following titles comprise the Jack Dillon Dublin Tales series:
Welcome
Jack Dillon Dublin Tale 1
Sweet Dreams
Jack Dillon Dublin Tale 2
Mirror Mirror
Jack Dillon Dublin Tale 3
Silver Bullet
Jack Dillon Dublin Tale 4
Fair City Blues

Jack Dillon Dublin Tale 5
Spade Work
Jack Dillon Dublin Tale 6
Madeline Missing
Jack Dillon Dublin Tale 7
Mistaken Identity
Jack Dillon Dublin Tale 8
Picture Perfect
Jack Dillon Dublin Tale 9
Dublin Moon
Jack Dillon Dublin Tale 10
Mystery Woman
Jack Dillon Dublin Tale 11
Second Chance
Jack Dillon Dublin Tale 12
Payback Brother
Jack Dillon Dublin Tale 13
The Heist
Jack Dillon Dublin Tale 14
Jewels To Kill For
Jack Dillon Dublin Tale 15
Retirement Scheme
Jack Dillon Dublin Tale 16
The Collector
Jack Dillon Dublin Tale 17

Jack Dillon Dublin Tales Boxsets:
Jack Dillon Dublin Tales 1-3
Jack Dillon Dublin Tales 4-6

Jack Dillon Dublin Tales 1-5
Jack Dillon Dublin Tales 1-7
Jack Dillon Dublin Tales 6-10

The following titles comprise the Hotshot series;
Reduced Ransom! Second Edition
Finders Keepers! Second Edition
Bankers Hours Second Edition
Chow Down Second Edition
Moonlight Dance Academy Second Edition
Irish Dukes (Fight Card Series)
written under the pseudonym Jack Tunney

The following titles comprise the Corridor Man series:
Corridor Man
Corridor Man 2: Opportunity knocks
Corridor Man 3: The Dungeon
Corridor Man 4: Dead End
Corridor Man 5: Finger
Corridor Man 6: Exit Strategy
Corridor Man 7: Trunk Music
Corridor Man 8: Birthday Boy
Corridor Man 9: Boss Man
Corridor Man 10: Bye Bye Bobby

Corridor Man novellas:
Corridor Man: Valentine
Corridor Man: Auditor

Corridor Man: Howling
Corridor Man: Spa Day

The following are Corridor Man Boxsets:
Corridor Man Boxset 1-3
Corridor Man Boxset 1-5
Corridor Man Boxset 6-9

All books are available on Amazon.com

Thank you!

Contact the author:
- Email: mikefaricyauthor@gmail.com
- Twitter: @Mikefaricybooks
- Facebook: Mike Faricy Author
- Website: http://www.mikefaricybooks.com

Published by

MJF Publishing

Mike Faricy • 348

www.ingramcontent.com/pod-product-compliance
Lightning Source LLC
Chambersburg PA
CBHW051310300726
48976CB00002B/347